A WREATH
FOR UDOMO

A WREATH FOR UDOMO

by

PETER

ABRAHAMS

FABER AND FABER

London

First published in 1956
by Faber and Faber Limited
3 Queen Square London W.C.1
First published in this edition 1965
Reprinted 1971 and 1977
Printed in Great Britain by
Jarrold and Sons Ltd, Norwich
All rights reserved

ISBN 0 571 06346 2 (Faber Paperbacks)

Did we think victory great?
So it is—But now it seems to me, when it
cannot be helped, that defeat is great,
And that death and dismay are great.

WALT WHITMAN

PART ONE

THE DREAM

Lois would not have noticed him if it had not been for his eyes. She did not want to notice anybody. That was why she had come to the pub. She wanted a drink and to be alone with her thoughts and the quiet loneliness that took hold of her at ever-decreasing intervals these days.

You'll end up a desperately lonely old woman, Lois. She was not afraid of the thought, did not try to stifle it. Instead, she examined it calmly, with cold clarity. Yes, she would end up like that. She would have to prepare herself for that. She would have to begin now to find the things that would make supportable that ultimate reality of being alone. Better fix that shack up in the mountains and fill it with all the books you'd always wanted to read. There would be time later. Lots of time. That damned war made sure of it. John would still have been with her but for that damned war. . . . You're lying, Lois. You're indulging in sloppy thinking. . . . She smiled at having caught herself out. And then she knew those eyes had seen her smile, had probably misread it. Damn him with his sullen, haunted eyes!

She raised her glass, touched it to her lips, then looked across the length of the bar counter. All right, haunted eyes! She stared at him. She'd outstared brassy men before now. But there was nothing brassy about the eyes that looked at her. It was not the look of someone trying to make a pass. Just haunted and lonely.

They stared at each other for a few seconds, then he turned his eyes back to his companion, a tubby little Englishman who seemed vaguely familiar to Lois. The tubby little man talked earnestly. The man with the haunted eyes only half listened though he nodded often. At regular intervals he looked across the bar counter briefly to assure himself that she was still there.

I'll wait, Lois told herself. I'll wait and see. She ordered another drink and waited, freed of thinking about loneliness and John for the present, watching the man whose eyes she thought of as "haunted" though she knew the word was inadequate for the smouldering, caged restlessness she sensed rather than saw.

At last the tubby man stopped talking and turned to the door. The other shook his head and his lips said words that might have been "No, I'll stay on for a while longer". Then the tubby man left.

The man looked at Lois, then away, quickly. He seemed to shrink now, to grow into a lost little boy in a frightening, hostile world. Lois sighed, straightened her back and got off the bar stool. Probably the first time he's in a pub on his own, and he wouldn't have the guts to come to her. She walked round the people clustered at the bar and stopped beside him. She sensed some of the people watching, especially those at the table by the fire. Smutty-minded fools. She turned her head quickly and looked at the table. Of course they would pretend not to be looking. She grinned, and there was wicked malice in her eyes. Fools! Then she looked at the man again.

"Good evening."

"Good evening," he said.

His voice was deep and soft. It had that special rusty richness they all had. And he was handsome in a sulkily sullen, brooding way. Height about five-seven or -eight, she decided, and strappingly made. He'd probably look godlike in his native cloth. Instead, he wore a suit he had outgrown and which made him look stocky. Mouth without laughter-lines. turned down at the corners.

"My name's Lois Barlow," she said; then, as she saw the misunderstanding in his eyes, "You're wrong. This isn't a pick-up. I'm not in search of a man."

The hint of a shame-faced, caught-out smile touched his lips and was gone.

"I did not think that."

What now, Lois thought.

"I told you I'm Lois Barlow."

"Sorry . . . I'm Michael Udomo."

"You're new here. . . ." It was a statement.

"How do you know?"

"Oh, I don't mean in this pub, though I expect it's your first time here too. I mean in Hampstead . . . I know most of the Africans here and I haven't seen you before."

"I've only just arrived."

"Africa?"

"No. The Continent. Canada before that."

"And your home?"

"Panafrica. . . . You interested in Africa?"

"More in people and the sun, really. A countryman of yours is a great friend of mine. Know Tom Lanwood . . . ?"

"Lanwood! Mr. Thomas Lanwood?"

He had come out of his shell now. His excitement was tangible. He gripped her arm.

"Did you say Thomas Lanwood?" he said again.

"Yes, I did say Thomas Lanwood," she said quietly.

He pulled his hand away quickly.

"Sorry. . . . Please, when can I meet him? I must meet him!"

Lois laughed. He was out of his cage now. The haunted loneliness was gone from his eyes. But even as she watched, it came back.

"Any time you like," she said.

"Tonight? Now?"

"As desperate as that!"

"You don't understand. . . ."

"Never mind. Let's have a drink and then go and find Tom."

13

"I don't really drink. I only came here because . . ."

"Mind if I have one before we go?"

"No——" The boyish, shame-faced smile flitted across his face again. "Sorry I can't pay. I'm broke."

"I'm not. Have one with me, unless you object to women paying."

"I don't. But I really don't drink."

"Not at all?"

"A little when I have to."

"Like with your tubby friend?"

"Yes. But he's not a friend. He lectures at the university. My tutor on the Continent said he might help and gave me an introduction."

Lois caught the barmaid's eye and ordered her drink.

"And did he?"

"I'm sorry?"

He wasn't really interested in this. His mind was on Lanwood.

"Did he help?"

"Oh yes. Yes. He helped me to find a room."

Lois felt the force of the man's impatience as she paid the barmaid and sipped her drink. Strange man, this Michael Udomo, strange and enclosed. And breath-taking when he burst out as he did over Lanwood. Odd, too.

Michael Udomo watched the woman sip her drink. He'd looked across at her because she was alone and because he was bored with that fellow. Not young but not bad to look at. She must be well over thirty, probably over forty. Hard to tell with these Englishwomen. Maybe he had looked at her hopefully—hell, what of it! A man's lonely sometimes in a strange land. But he hadn't thought about it. You've got to get to know these people before you can do things like that. Anyway, you never know where the enemy is. God, Lanwood! He'd see him tonight. Lanwood! The greatest political writer and fighter Panafrica had produced. Nearly ten years now since

14

Lanwood wrote him that letter. *In order to be free we must marshal our forces and husband our resources for the coming struggle. Our young men must ceaselessly prepare themselves for the fight. All their strength, all their energy, all their talents must be devoted to preparing themselves for the fight that will result in the liberation of their country and the freedom of their continent. There is no nobler task on earth.* Those were the key words of that letter Lanwood had written him nearly ten years ago. And now this Lois Barlow would bring them together. It was a sign, this, a great sign.

"Still thinking of Tom?" Lois said.

"Lanwood—yes. You know him well?"

"For fifteen years. Met him when I was twenty-one. That should tell you my age."

"That's a long time. And you two are . . ."

"Just friends, Michael Udomo."

"He's a great man. Is he very old?"

"Heavens, no! . . . But I suppose he must be getting on. He hasn't changed in all the time I've known him. He must be between fifty and sixty though. . . . Come, let's go."

"I'm very glad I met you," Udomo said.

"Because it's leading you to Tom?"

"Yes."

"Quite a hero of yours, isn't he?"

"He's a great patriot."

Lois felt impatient suddenly.

"You men and your patriotism!"

He smiled. There was a hint of superiority to it.

"You don't understand . . ." he murmured.

"Of course not. How could I? I'm the primitive backward woman. Let's go."

She turned her back on him. She pushed past people to the door, sensing him behind her. Really, it was stupid to be angry with him. It's old age creeping up on you. Watch out, woman. She waited for him at the door and smiled sweetly to make up for the rush of impatience.

The cold night air struck them as they went through the door. The sky was clear. The moon was in the first quarter. The stars were coldly bright. A sharp wind travelled across the earth. They turned up their collars and lowered their heads against the bite of the wind. The wind sang softly about their ears.

"This way," Lois said.

They crossed the broad road, walked some distance up, then turned into a narrow street leading up a steep hill. The cold air rushed at them more fiercely.

"God, it's cold!" Udomo gasped.

"We'll soon be there," Lois said with a tenderness wrung from her by the desperation of his voice. "Soon now."

They climbed the hill in silence after that, heads down, bodies braced against the force of the hissing wind. At last they reached the top and turned left into the wide drive of a big house. Lois led the way to a side door and let them in. Udomo sighed as the cold was shut out.

Lois turned on the hall light and saw how thin his overcoat was. There were tears in his eyes. His lips had turned purple and his dark face ashen. He was fumbling in his pocket for a handkerchief. She turned away quickly and went into her sitting-room.

"It's warm in here," she called.

He came in and made straight for the gasfire. She stood with her back to him, pouring brandy into two tiny glasses.

"Nice place you've got," he said, his voice normal again.

His hands scraped like corn husks against each other as he rubbed them. She thought: I can look at him now. She turned as though it were an effort. His face was less drawn and ashen. But the bright purple was still on his lips. He had wiped his eyes. She tried to shut her mind to the scraping

16

of his hands. He was almost on top of the fire. She walked across and gave him the glass of brandy.

"No, thanks."

"You will drink that," she said firmly.

He looked up and smiled. The smile, this time, kindled his eyes. It brought a glowing sunniness to his face. He took the brandy from her, gulped it down, pulled a face and shivered.

She wondered whether she would see the purple leaving his lips or whether it would just disappear.

"You ought to smile more often," she said. "I mean really smile, not just with your lips."

Yes, she could actually see the purple leaving his lips, growing thin and misty and fading away, like a cloud of cigarette smoke.

"Yes?" He was interested.

"Yes."

She took out a packet of cigarettes and offered him one. "I don't smoke."

"You don't drink, you don't smoke. What do you do?"

She knew she'd made a mistake the moment she'd said that. His eyes grew bold suddenly and he started to strip her mentally.

"I have other pleasures," he murmured.

"Such as patriotism and Tom Lanwood?"

"Please, will you get him now."

"Yes. Have you eaten?"

"No, but that's not important."

She left him by the fire and went out, first to the kitchen where she put a light under the stew, then into her bedroom where the phone was.

Udomo, warmed now, got up and walked about the room. It was a very large room, with french windows leading out to the back garden. One entire wall, to the level of a man's height, had shelves filled with books. He took out one book after another, glanced at it, then put it back again. He listened for the woman. But there was no sound.

Must be a big place, he decided. Hope Lanwood doesn't take too long. He moved to the little desk in the corner near the french windows. There were open letters on it. He began to read the top one, then he turned away quickly. A very comfortable room. It took money to have a room like this; money to pay for these deep armchairs and large heavy curtains and the carved mahogany lampstands on the little corner tables. Perhaps she was rich. Her talking about eating had made him hungry. A nuisance. It never bothered him unless he thought about it. Come on, woman!

The room was getting very hot. He took off his coat and flung it on a chair. He eased his trousers down. They were becoming uncomfortably tight between his legs; so was the jacket across his shoulders and under his arms. He'd have to do something about it soon. This was his best suit and he was fast growing out of it.

He heard the door open and turned. Lois Barlow pushed a trolley in front of her. She had taken off her coat. She was well-shaped, not flat-chested. She looked younger without the coat.

"Is he coming?"

"He can't make it tonight," she said. She watched him shrink into himself; his eyes went dull and lifeless, his face became a dark mask.

"I see," he said, and reached for his coat.

"I caught him just as he was going out," she said quickly. "He was on his way to a meeting. He said it was an important one. It was too late for him to put the people off. He's to be the main speaker." She thought: Why am I lying? Why not tell him Tom doesn't want to come out in this cold? "He asked me to ask you to meet him here tomorrow afternoon if you can. If not, he would fit in with any other time you suggest. He would have spoken to you himself if he hadn't been rushed to get to his meeting in time."

He relaxed.

"Yes, I see. . . . Tomorrow will be fine. I hope he has a good meeting. Wish I could be there. What time tomorrow?"

"I get back from school a little before four. He'll be here by four. . . . Sit down—I've hotted up some food."

He sank into a chair. She sat opposite him. They ate. When he had finished he said:

"I was really hungry."

"I know," she said.

They sat in silence for a while, watching the row of upright flames in the gasfire.

Lois Barlow felt tired suddenly. This Michael Udomo had made heavy emotional demands on her. She got up.

"Forgive me but I'm terribly tired. I have a hard day's teaching ahead tomorrow."

"Yes, I must go." He got up and put on his coat. "I'll be here at four tomorrow. Thank you for the food."

She led him out to the hallway and opened the door. Then, on an impulse, she shut it again and hurried into her bedroom. She returned carrying a dufflecoat.

"Put this on. That thing of yours is useless."

"But it's yours," he said.

"No. It's a man's," she said harshly.

She held the coat for him. He slipped it on over his own.

"Thank you very much," he said.

She opened the door for him. "Good night."

He looked at her face, then went out into the cold, more protected than before.

2

Lois Barlow was making tea when Udomo arrived.

"Tom will be here soon," she said. "He rang to say he's bringing David Mhendi and Richard Adebhoy with him."

She led him into the sitting-room. A young woman knelt

19

on a pillow in front of the fire, drying her long corn-coloured hair. It reached almost to her waist.

"This is Jo Furse," Lois said. "She shares the flat with me."

The young woman flung back the mass of hair and jumped up. She wore a tight-fitting bright-blue sweater and wine-coloured cord slacks. Her eyes, a light green, were slightly slanted and seemed to go round the corners of her face, following the curve between cheekbone and temple. Her mouth curled upward at the corners.

Beautiful, Udomo thought as he took her slender hand. The mass of corn-coloured hair excited him.

"She's vain about her hair," Lois said.

The doorbell rang.

"I'll let him in," Jo Furse said. She went out with catlike grace.

"I can see Jo's made an impression," Lois said.

Udomo did not answer. He was waiting for Lanwood now, his excitement so great that he felt unnaturally limp and calm. He had seen a picture of Lanwood once, a long time ago. A fine stern face it was; the face of a leader of men.

Lanwood came in and filled the room. Udomo saw only him. Those behind him were like shadows. Lanwood was big and burly, going to fat round the middle; but he was tall, so the fat did not show. His face was small for his great size. It was slender and tapering; a smooth near-black face tinged with the slightest hint of red. Nose and lips were boldly chiselled on broad aristocratic lines. He wore thick-rimmed glasses that enhanced his air of intellectuality. His dress was impeccably correct and English: just the right amount of shirt-cuff showed at his wrists; tie harmonised with shirt, and both with the immaculately cut suit. He moved, too, with the easy, self-assured grace of a prosperous West End clubman.

The picture Udomo had carried in his mind was of a younger, thinner man without glasses, and not so well-dressed and polished. But this was Lanwood all right.

Lanwood's face cracked into a broad smile. He gripped Udomo's hand.

"Welcome! Sorry I couldn't make it last night."

"I told him you had a meeting," Lois said hurriedly.

"Yes," Lanwood murmured. "Yes, the meeting."

"I've wanted to meet you ever since I got your letter," Udomo said.

"Letter?"

"Yes. You wrote to me nearly ten years ago. Remember?"

"Oh yes. . . ." Lanwood turned quickly to those behind him. "Meet some of our comrades."

Lois stifled a smile and moved to the door. Jo followed her.

"We'll get the tea," Lois said.

"David Mhendi's from Pluralia," Lanwood said.

"Hello, man," Mhendi said.

Mhendi's name sounded familiar to Udomo. He'd seen or heard it somewhere. They shook hands. He tried to remember where he'd heard or seen the name but Lanwood's voice interfered.

"And Adebhoy's a fellow countryman of ours."

The fat and very black little man grabbed Udomo's hand.

"Hi-ya, country!" He had a fixed, happy smile on his lips. He spoke in little rushes of words. "Heard of you from one of those fellows who call themselves Frenchmen. Told me about the student strike you tried to lead." The laughter-lines near his eyes deepened. "Said you didn't understand they were not oppressed colonials but Frenchmen enjoying all the rights of Frenchmen! Ha, ha, ha."

Udomo smiled weakly.

"Those fellows let me down badly."

"French imperialism's more cunning than the British brand," Lanwood said. "They buy off the leadership by giving them seats in their Assembly and marrying them off to their daughters. . . . Let's sit down."

Lanwood led the way to the divan. He adjusted the creases

of his trousers, then took out his pipe and began to stuff it.
Udomo sat on one side of him, Adebhoy on the other. Mhendi
hesitated for a while, then left the room and went in search
of the women in the kitchen.

A faint smile played on Lanwood's lips. He could almost
feel the enthusiasm of this young chap, Udomo. He liked it.
It was rewarding. He had spent his life in the fight and he
knew his influence was at work all over Africa, but it was
good to meet this young man who was the living proof of it.
One grew a little tired sometimes, got caught up in occasional
doubt and uncertainty sometimes. It was good for morale to
meet a chap like this.

"Tell me about yourself," he said.

Udomo leaned towards Lanwood and talked quietly about
himself. Lanwood knew the story he listened to. It was made
up of the common experience of most colonial students. The
missionaries had picked out the brightest boy in a little village
in Africa and set about educating him. Education had brought
awareness. The boy had then examined the world in which
he lived and found it wanting by the very standards the
missionaries had given him. He had turned against them then
and struck out on his own. And he had luck—he had got to
Europe and Canada and got a higher education. Of course
he'd had to work and go short on food and clothes. But then,
only the lucky few whose people had money or who had the
blessing of the colonial government did it the easy way. The
majority got it as Udomo had done: working their way, going
hungry often. . . . What was all this about a letter he had
written being this boy's inspiration?

Pride grew in Lanwood as he listened. Yes, it was good to
see the results of one's efforts. Just as well he kept copies of
all the letters he wrote. Ten years back. He'd go through his
files when he got back tonight.

Udomo stopped talking.

"And your plans?" Lanwood said.

"To get my doctorate and go back. You know how our people worship a man called 'doctor'."

"How long?"

"I've done most of the work for it. It's just a question of fulfilling the conditions for submitting my thesis."

"Good. You'd better join our group while you're here. We're a sort of brains trust behind the various colonial organisations in this country."

"That's why I was so anxious to see you," Udomo said.

"I'll fix it with the boys for a discussion at my place."

Mhendi moved restlessly about the kitchen while the two women buttered bread and made sandwiches. A wind had whipped up outside. It whistled about the house, shaking the kitchen windows occasionally. Mhendi picked up a knife and felt its edge, then he flung it back on the table and went to the window. He pushed his hands deep into his pockets and stared up at the visible piece of the sky. It looked dark and heavy, as though the clouds sagged under the weight of snow anxious to come down.

Lois kept looking up at Mhendi. He'd been with them now for nearly twenty minutes without saying a word. Jo raised her head and opened her mouth to speak to him. Lois shook her head.

"Take that in, Jo."

She waited till Jo had left the kitchen, then she got up and went and stood beside Mhendi.

"What's the matter, David?" She began to touch him, then changed her mind and pulled back her hand. "Anything I can do?"

"Nothing short of getting me drunk," he said bitterly.

Lois waited for him to look at her; he kept staring out at the patch of sky. She waited a while, then said:

"Tea's ready. We'd better go in."

Lois went out, pushing the trolley in front of her. Mhendi

stood alone in the kitchen for a while, staring up at the sky. Then, suddenly, his eyes filled with tears. His shoulders drooped. He closed his eyes but the tears kept coming through the closed lids. Then he jerked himself erect, almost violently. He took his handkerchief out of his pocket but it was too dirty, so he used his sleeve to wipe his face.

He turned and walked quickly to the bathroom. He turned on the cold tap in the wash-basin. He bathed his face in the running water, stung by the bite of the icy water. He dried his face and looked in the mirror. Really, he needed a haircut badly. He touched the grey hair at his temples. At this rate I'll be completely grey in a year, he thought—if I'm not dead. He felt faintly disgusted as he looked at the reflection of his stained and dirty jacket. Never mind, it hid the rents in his shirt. He tried to flatten and straighten his crumpled tie. But it kept curling any old how.

Watching his face in the mirror, he recalled what he had looked like five years earlier. Then he closed his eyes quickly and turned from the mirror. He squared his shoulders and went slowly to the sitting-room.

"David," Lois called.

Udomo looked up and memory flowed back to him. Of course! David Mhendi! The man who had led that unsuccessful Pluralian rising five years ago. He'd been in Canada at the time. Udomo watched him with new interest. Nothing striking about him, nothing to show that he was a man who had led a revolt. Ordinary-looking. Copper-brown and on the smallish side; drably dressed. Even more drably than I, Udomo decided. A sad-looking man.

"I've got your drink," Lois called.

Mhendi went to the corner near the french windows. Lois gave him a tumbler half-filled with whisky. Mhendi took a huge swig, then sat down.

"That's Mhendi's one trouble," Lanwood snapped. "He takes too much."

24

"He led that Pluralian rising. I've just remembered. I read all about it in Canada. God! It nearly came off!"

"It would have if he'd done what I told him," Lanwood said.

"Anybody else want a drink?" Lois called.

"Me," Adebhoy said and went over to Jo.

"But why's he here now?" Udomo said.

"He slipped through their lines the night they slaughtered the Liberation Army and got smuggled out on a boat."

Udomo recalled the sensational newspaper headlines about the Pluralian rising five years earlier. The people had held out for a year. Thousands had been slaughtered. He turned back to Lanwood.

"Why don't these people send him back?"

"And have a trial! It might start a new rising. And don't forget there are many who would ask awkward questions at the Council of Nations. No. They like it better to have him here in exile where they can watch him drink himself to death."

"God! We must do something!" Udomo exclaimed.

"We will. World forces are moving in our direction. Our friends and allies are getting stronger. Time is with us—meantime, tell me about your own set-up. Have you a place and how are you fixed?"

Udomo watched Lois talking to Mhendi and said:

"I've got a room but it's expensive."

He looked across the room. Lois had pulled up a low stool and sat facing Mhendi. They were close to each other. As he watched, she took one of Mhendi's hands. Are they lovers? he wondered.

Lois said:

"Tell me, David. It might help a little."

Jo and Adebhoy switched on the radio, turned it low and lay side by side on the floor listening to it. Lanwood kept on talking. Udomo divided his attention between listening to Lanwood and watching Lois and Mhendi. Lanwood was giving him examples of imperialist immoralities in their dealings with colonial peoples.

Mhendi emptied his third glass. He said:

"I've just heard from home that they shot my wife."

"Oh God," Lois whispered.

"She and the other shot women were the first victims of 'Squatter A'. They've been trying to move my people from their old lands to a near-desert strip of land. The settlers don't like to see us on fertile land. Anyway, my house was on fertile land at the foot of a hill. The earth was rich and red there, too good for inferior wogs. . . ."

"Oh David."

"Am I too bitter for you, Lois? . . . Anyway, they decided that really that was European Land and told the people they had to move to Squatter A. No doubt they will, in time, mark out enough desert strips to run from A to Z. Well, my people didn't want to move. The women didn't want to give up the homes and lands that had been theirs as far back as our history goes. So they turned on the whites who came to supervise their removal. My wife led the stoning party. A Native Commissioner and his assistant were killed. . . ."

"Oh God." She touched his hand.

"Give me another drink," he said.

She filled his glass again. He gulped it down. From across the room, watching, Udomo thought: He does drink and she feeds him all he wants. He found it hard to believe that that man was the Mhendi who had led the Pluralian rising.

"How many?" Lois murmured.

"How many were killed?"

"Yes."

"Eleven."

Lois poured herself a drink and swallowed it down. She too, Udomo thought.

"It could have been more," Mhendi said. "They could have decided on twenty, or thirty, or a hundred. . . ."

Lois poured more whisky into his glass. His eyes were turning blood-shot. She sensed him relaxing.

They'll soon be drunk, Udomo thought, and listened to what Lanwood said.

Mhendi touched his cheeks.

"I need a shave," he said absently.

"Tell me about her," Lois said.

Mhendi sighed.

"She was illiterate. She couldn't sit at table with me. She wouldn't. A woman's place is in the kitchen or in the fields, working for her lord. People here think that's the way we men want it. I didn't. It's lonely out there and I wanted to talk to her. I tried to teach her. Perhaps I didn't try hard enough. . . ."

"What did she look like, David? Have you a picture?"

"No. I sometimes looked at her and felt old and fatherly. She had a small round face and big eyes. She used to come into my room sometimes in the evening when I was alone and her children were asleep. She liked to sit on the floor then, near me, not saying a word. I felt the quiet of her presence then. At first, when she did this, I used to open a book and read aloud. But then the quietness left her, and she left the room. I tried music. But this also drove her away. In the end I just sat when she came in. That seemed to make her happy. Strange, she was my wife but I never really knew her or what she thought. . . ."

"But you loved her."

"I wasn't even sure of that till now. You see, she was chosen for me. I found my father had arranged it all when I got back. Don't forget there are two Pluralias: that of the cities and the white men and that of the countryside and the old tribal ways. And though I had been to school in the cities and had come to Europe, I was still a son of the tribe. They couldn't think of me as anything but a son of the tribe. I couldn't outrage my old father's great dreams. . . ."

"And now. . . ."

"I know I loved her. And it's too late."

"And you must still go on?"

"Yes. There is the burden of all those lives now. Many people have died. And I've led them. So I must go on."

"Do you *want* to go on?"

Mhendi smiled.

"Fill my glass, Lois. . . . If you're saying it's no game, I agree. Suppose I once felt as bouncing about it as our new friend over there. I can see marching flags in his eyes. Tom's the luckiest, though. For him it's an impersonal game of chess. He doesn't really care about people. He hates imperialism impersonally and wants African power impersonally. I was the flag-waving type when I went home. Blood will flow, I thought then. God, how it's flowed. . . ."

Lois shivered, then said suddenly:

"Let's have a party tonight!"

"To comfort me?" A hint of laughter crept into Mhendi's eyes.

"Because I feel like it, damn you!"

On the other side of the room Adebhoy said:

"It's settled then. You come and stay with me. Move in any time."

Udomo began to thank him but Adebhoy silenced him with laughter.

"That's settled," Lanwood said and got up.

"Tom!" Lois called. "I'm throwing a party tonight. Staying?"

"I can't. Things to do."

"David is staying. Anybody else?"

"I have to look in at the hospital," Adebhoy said. "But I'll come back. What time?"

"Seven. Bring some liquor with you. What about you, Michael Udomo?"

Udomo glanced quickly at Lanwood.

"Relax and have fun," Lanwood said.

Lanwood turned to Lois at the door.

"You're feeding David too much drink."

"Don't play the political God with me, Tom. I've known you too long."

"You're sentimental," Lanwood said and went out.

She went back to the sitting-room. Jo and Adebhoy were dancing. Udomo had joined Mhendi. Udomo was talking freely now, using his hands. She watched them for a while. When Mhendi began to talk back, began to wave his arms, she smiled and relaxed a little. Michael Udomo certainly had something. Damn Tom with his smug narrowness. And yet he was the rallying point for all of them. Better open a new bottle of wine. She changed her mind and went quietly out of the room and into her bedroom. She sat on the bed and picked up the phone. She dialled. Was she doing this for David? Or for herself? Or for Michael Udomo? God, how mixed human motives can be. One thing was clear: there was a growing need to have people around her all the time these days. She spoke into the phone, made her first invitation, replaced the receiver, then dialled again. Faintly, the music from the other room came to her.

The traffic lights changed and the car shot forward. Udomo smiled at the white person scuttling out of the way. He felt relaxed, more at peace now than he had been for a long time. He was among people who saw things as he did. He'd been right about Lanwood. Great man, Tom Lanwood. He could relax and have a little fun now. He would do that tonight. Adebhoy was beside him, driving; Mhendi was in the back, and everything was fine. They had been to Adebhoy's flat and he had seen his room there. He and Mhendi had talked while Adebhoy had gone to his hospital. He now had a key to the flat in his pocket. And he now wore a pair of Adebhoy's slacks and a loose, comfortable sports jacket. Must find out if Lois Barlow wants the dufflecoat back. She may do. Comfortably warm. Hope she doesn't.

Adebhoy turned right out of Haverstock Hill, drove through some narrow streets and pulled up outside Mabi's house. Two huge blocks of wood were stacked beside the front-door steps.

"Oh my God!" Adebhoy said, and roared with laughter.

"Let's go on, we're late," Mhendi said quickly.

"Too late! Too late! Out you come."

"What's all this?" Udomo asked.

"Those blocks," Adebhoy said and roared again.

Mhendi led the way up the stairs and tried the door.

"It's locked."

"Better knock."

"You do it. Last time I knocked a dirty, long-haired composer chap threatened to break my neck!"

Adebhoy banged the knocker once. Mhendi moved down to the bottom of the steps. A thin woman wearing cords opened the door.

"Oh, it's you, Doctor. Paul's in but two people came this afternoon and he blew up because they were let in."

"D'you know the bearded man who threatened to break my neck?" Mhendi asked.

The woman smiled.

"That was my husband. He's a pacifist really."

"It's all right," Adebhoy said. "Paul's expecting us."

"All right." The woman went away.

"Better start with one of those blocks," Adebhoy said.

Mhendi and Adebhoy lifted one of the blocks and staggered up the stairs. They moved to a small door on the right of the landing.

"Open it, Mike," Adebhoy gasped.

Udomo tapped tentatively on the door.

"For Christ's sake . . ." Adebhoy groaned.

The block slipped from his fingers. It crashed to the floor and struck his big toe at an oblique angle. Mhendi jumped clear. Adebhoy yelled and sat on the block holding his foot.

"It's crushed!" His face contorted with pain.

The door near which Udomo stood opened quietly. A little black man, not much more than five feet tall, stood framed in it. The others didn't notice him for a while. His face was long and lean, tapering to a point at the chin. His long thin black fingers were strong and restless. His huge mop of kinky hair was a crown about his face. He had big pop-eyes. The lids drooped over them like an owl's, giving him a sleepy appearance.

He took in the scene and began to chuckle. He put his hands on his slender hips, flung back his head and roared with laughter. His voice was surprisingly deep. The others became aware of him.

From somewhere upstairs a voice yelled.

"Shut up down there! I'm working!" It was charged with rage.

"You're a fine one!" Mabi yelled back. Then, to the others: "Come on in." He turned his back on them and went in.

"That," Mhendi told Udomo, "is Paul Mabi, our artist. Now you know all the group. Come." He followed Mabi in.

"What about me?" Adebhoy wailed.

"Get up and walk," Mabi called.

"That's all the thanks we get for trying to bring in your wood!" But he got up and hobbled in.

"Never again!" Mhendi said bitterly, but his eyes twinkled. "Dick nearly kills himself and all you do is laugh! If you have a thousand blocks blocking up the road I'll not help you again!"

"You silly sausages!" Mabi said. "Come in!"

"That's all I get for crushing my foot," Adebhoy moaned.

"Come in and let's see."

31

The room was as large as a public hall and took up the whole ground floor of the house. It had a huge table in the centre. This was piled with papers, books, small pieces of sculpture, unwashed plates, newly laundered shirts, a nibbled-at loaf of French bread and a nearly-full bottle of wine. Larger pieces of sculpture were stacked all over the floor. The wall opposite the door was of glass nearly all the way and let in the light wonderfully. An easel with a nearly-completed drawing in charcoal stood in a corner. A tiny divan was tucked away in an alcove against the wall where the light was poorest. Innumerable drawings hung on the walls.

"Sit down," Mabi said.

He went on his knees, undid Adebhoy's shoe and eased it off his foot. He pulled off the sock. His examination was careful and quick.

"Your crushed foot is only a bruised big toe."

"I'm sure there's a broken bone!"

"Hypochondriac!"

"This is Mike Udomo," Mhendi said. "We came to fetch you to Lois' party. You and your blocks!"

Mabi turned and gazed up at Udomo: a cold, searching look that embarrassed Udomo, made him feel awkwardly cautious. Then Mabi jumped up and held out his hand. His grip was firm. Udomo turned away from his searching eyes. He saw a bust of Lanwood on the floor and went over to it, glad to get away from Mabi and startled by the inhibiting influence the little man had on him.

"Better change if you're coming," Mhendi said.

"Tom there?"

"No."

"Nobody cares about my foot," Adebhoy moaned.

"Put on your shoe," Mabi snapped. "Walk on it."

He stripped and changed quickly, washed his face and brushed his thick mop of hair, then he said:

"This darky's ready."

Udomo tensed and turned quickly. Mabi was looking at him, laughing at him with those eyes. Mhendi looked from one to the other and grinned.

"Come on," Adebhoy said and hobbled out.

The party was in full swing when they got to Lois'.

A young noble lord hailed Mhendi. They went into a huddle in a corner. Jo Furse, already slightly tight and with shining eyes, left the man she danced with and grabbed Adebhoy. He immediately forgot his crushed foot. Udomo turned to Mabi. He would have to talk to him now.

"I . . ." he began.

Then Lois saw them and came to them.

"Paul, darling! Haven't seen you for weeks!"

"Working, my dear," Mabi said.

"What are you on?"

Just then two women came in. One was a tiny, beautiful, black-haired woman. She saw Mabi and shrieked:

"Paul!"

Mabi groaned. The woman flung her arms about him, hugged him, and dragged him away to the drinks table. Lois laughed with a hint of malice in her voice. Udomo thought: This one doesn't really like other women.

"Come out of your cage, Michael Udomo!" Lois snapped. "This is a party. Relax!"

"I'm in no cage," he said.

"No?"

She's a little drunk, he thought.

"No."

"So you're in a cage but not in a cage. Know what I'm talking about?"

"No."

"Thought so. . . . Let's have a drink."

"Not for me. Shall I get you one?"

"Let's have a drink," she said again.

33

Her eyes challenged him. He smiled as one smiles humouring a child.

"All right."

"I'll get it," she said.

"Nothing strong, please."

He noticed her bare shoulders, round and curved and with a light sheen of tan over them. And the neck sat well on the shoulders; and the head on the neck. Then he noticed the lines of her body. Why hadn't he noticed before just how striking she was? Not young, not beautiful, but very striking with her erect carriage, the slight leftward tilt of her head.

A dancing couple came between her and his line of vision. He adjusted his shoulders more comfortably against the wall and recrossed his legs. He'd have to find somewhere to sit soon. Jo Furse and Adebhoy moved into his line of vision. They danced cheek to cheek. The girl's eyes were closed. A broad grin was fixed on Adebhoy's face. He winked. Then they passed out of sight.

Lois returned and gave him his drink. He tasted it and grimaced. It was smooth but strong.

"What is it?"

"The key to a cage," she said.

He looked her up and down quickly.

"Getting round to figures . . ." she jeered.

"I'm just noticing how good-looking you are."

"You're improving, Michael Udomo."

"One doesn't notice it quickly with you."

"It's because I creep up on people. I creep up on them while their backs are turned. Then, suddenly, without knowing how, they realise I'm there. And they want what's there. Only, they can't have it." She drained her glass, then watched him, a mocking smile on her lips.

He emptied his glass in one gulp and shuddered.

"Let's dance," she said.

"I can't dance."

34

"Now's the time to learn."

She took the glass from him, opened her arms and waited. He put his arm awkwardly about her waist, took a few uncertain steps, then he caught the rhythm of the music. It all became easy, familiar, something remembered from a long, long time ago.

"Thought you didn't dance."

"First time I'm doing it."

He adjusted his arm, held her more firmly, more confidently, felt the rounded softness of her body. Yes, she did creep up on people, this one. Just as she said.

"It is as you say," he said. "You creep up on people."

"I also said they can't have it."

They danced in silence after that till the record finished.

She left Udomo and went to help Jo select new records.

Udomo went over to the corner where Mhendi and the young peer argued. Each had a bottle of wine from which they kept refilling their glasses. Mhendi's eyes had gone bloodshot, the young peer's were slightly glazed. To the left of them, sitting on the floor, flanked by two young women, was Paul Mabi. He had a drawing pad on his lap and sketched rapidly. What he did sent the two women into hoots of laughter.

The peer stabbed an unsteady finger at Mhendi's chest.

"I agree. But you chaps aren't reasonable. You're always attacking those of us who are on your side."

"We don't want anyone on our side," Mhendi snapped. "We want justice and freedom."

"That's what we're on your side for."

Mhendi looked at Udomo and shook his head.

"You don't understand, my friend. Look, it's simple. I'm black; my friend, Mike, here, is black. We don't have to be on our side. We are our side. We don't have to understand the problem: we are it. When you say 'colour bar' they're words to you; to us they're an experience, a reality which you

35

never have and never will enter into. It's easy for you to say be reasonable. It's an abstraction, so you can afford the luxury of reasonableness."

"I understand all that," the peer said patiently. "I'm sure I'd feel the same in your position. But this is my point: to make people see that, to make them understand your position, you'd have to speak to them with diplomacy rather than anger. That's the way to win their friendship and support. D'you see?"

A wave of anger swept over Udomo.

"What do you mean by diplomacy?" Mhendi asked.

"Be constructive and responsible when you write or speak. Drop Tom Lanwood's violently irresponsible slogans. You people can help us work out a basis for co-operation. . . ."

Udomo could contain himself no longer.

"Co-operation!" He glared at the peer. "What kind of co-operation can there be between master and slave . . ."

"Now that's the old clap-trap . . ."

"It is our business to be irresponsible! A slave's business is to get rid of his chains; not to be reasonable! Only the free can afford to be diplomats!"

The young peer sighed.

"Too much violent passion, my friend. It won't do."

"But it's real," Mhendi said quietly.

"It will get you nowhere."

It's useless, Udomo decided. He fought back his mounting rage. The man's drunk and stupid. He felt himself trembling. Drunk and stupid. They understand only one thing. Well, they'll get it. They'll get it all right.

"We'll see if we get nowhere!"

He turned his back on Mhendi and the peer. A dancing couple bumped into him. He pushed them away, almost violently. The man began to protest. Udomo walked away, out of the room. He heard voices in the kitchen and went there. Lois and Adebhoy were there with Jo. They were per-

suading her to eat. She had reached the weepy-drunk stage.
Jo saw Udomo, got up, swayed, and stumbled into his arms.

"Nobody loves me," she moaned. "Nobody loves me. You
love me? Want you to love me, big strong Michael Udomo.
Want you to love me. D'you love me?"

She leaned heavily against him, sagging at the knees.

"She's drunk," Lois said. "Eat that food."

"Don't want to eat," Jo said.

"For Mike and me," Adebhoy urged.

"No! You don't love me."

"They do," Lois said.

"You lie. I'm young and beautiful but they love you—
everybody loves you, nobody loves me."

She began to weep.

Paul Mabi came in.

"What's going on? . . . Oh . . ."

"Can you do something, Paul?"

Mabi put his arms about the girl's shoulders.

"Come on, Jo. Let's go into the garden for a minute. I'm
hungry but I'd like some air first. Come on."

He helped her up. She went meekly with him.

"For which give thanks," Lois said.

"He'll make her eat," Adebhoy said, and went back to the
big room. Lois looked at Udomo.

"What's the matter with you?"

He smiled. The sombreness left his face.

"Only an argument," he said.

She gave him a quick, sidelong look. He was relaxed now,
almost completely relaxed.

"I'll make some coffee," she said. "Sit down."

He watched her move about the kitchen. The music from
the big room came faintly through doors and walls.

"I wanted to ask you about the coat," he said.

"I meant you to keep it."

"But . . ."

37

"You worried about my husband?"

"Yes. He might want it."

"He won't. He won't come back."

She knew he wanted to ask about her husband. She knew he would not do so.

"Then may I keep it?"

"If you want to."

"I do. I'm hard up and it will be useful."

"Then it's yours."

"Thanks a lot."

She poured the coffee.

Udomo thought: She makes one feel quiet, this one.

Mabi came back with Jo. The cold night air had cleared her head somewhat. She walked more steadily. Her face was in less of a mess.

"Now for something to eat." Mabi said.

Lois poured out coffee for them. Adebhoy came back.

"Ah! Coffee and then we go," he said.

Lois felt Udomo watching her. She looked quickly at him. Their eyes met. Then they both became aware of Mabi watching them. Mabi smiled suddenly, a lost little smile of infinite sadness. He gulped down his coffee and jumped up.

"Time to go, my friends!"

"I'm going to sleep," Jo Furse said thickly.

She got up, swayed, put one leg forward and sagged into Udomo's lap. Disgust showed on his face. He began to push her off his lap but Adebhoy grabbed her and led her to her room.

Mabi and Lois watched Udomo's face. Udomo withdrew. His face went blank.

"Anything helpless disgusts," Lois said softly.

"It's not that," Udomo said quickly.

"No," Mabi said, watching Lois' face. "It's not that."

Lois felt hemmed in suddenly. She fought it off.

"Then what?"

Udomo rose and turned to the door.

"It's just that I'm not used to women."

Adebhoy poked his head into the room.

"She's all right now, Lois. Tuck her in in a little while. Come on, boys. 'Bye, and thanks for the party, Lois."

"Good night," Udomo said. He went out without looking at her.

"Be with you in a minute," Mabi called. "Lois. . . ."

"Yes?" Must go and see to the others, she thought. She felt awfully weary suddenly.

"You've known us a long time, as a group and as individuals." He chewed his lower lip.

"Well?"

"Don't rush me."

"I've to see to the others."

"They can hold on for a minute."

"I'm tired."

"Yes. . . . You've known us and the thing that binds us together for many years now. Of our own free will, if there is such a thing, we've elected to live for a cause. We would liberate a continent. That is what we live for. Someone once told me we are the lost generation: we don't belong to the past of our own people and we have not found a place in your world. . . ."

"Why all this now?"

"Because you're a fine person. Because you've been a good friend to us. I know you, Lois dear. I don't want you to be paid back in pain."

"I see. . . ."

"Do you? As you saw just now with Jo, life is an act of will for us. The strands are pulled taut. There is no room for weakness. I think we've largely accepted the communist dictum of means and ends. To liberate Africa we must live by an act of will."

"You sound a little bitter—for a would-be liberator."

39

Mabi laughed without humour.

"Don't forget what I've told you, Lois. He frightens me a little too. But I'm a man and you're a woman who knows the terrors of loneliness. . . ."

"Oh Paul. . . ."

"And, of course, he has the kind of muted violence that appeals to your peaceful sophisticated mind. I must get to know him. He could be our spark."

"Go 'way, Paul!"

"God bless, my dear."

Lois leaned against the table after Mabi had gone. It was all nonsense, of course. But Paul saw things. Understood things. The Liberators of a continent. Men are such stupid creatures. Only the liberation of the heart and mind from fear are real. They all miss the greatest reality. And Paul too, for all his seeing, in spite of all his seeing. And this other, this Michael Udomo—— She pulled herself together and went to the other room. The party was still in full swing. Mhendi was dancing. He only danced when he was really drunk. Another liberator. Paul was wrong about that act-of-will business with its sinister coldness. Here was a liberator dancing, being drunk and human, an ordinary man with a burden of unhappiness on him. But could that other . . .

Someone put an arm about her waist. She turned to dance.

3

Lanwood lived in a three-roomed flat in a mews off Hampstead Heath. The flat was, in common with all the others, above a garage. In the dim distant days of imperial glory, when Victoria was Queen-Empress of the most powerful throne on earth, these garages had been stables. The flats above them had been the quarters of those who looked after the horses and carriages of the great families. There were still watering troughs in the mews. But now little boys sailed paper boats on them in the brief months of summer. And there were still cobble-stones underfoot.

The biting arctic wind that had swept across the land for days had died down. There was a softness about the air. April, at last, was behaving like April, hinting, shadowlike, at the coming of warm days.

Udomo stopped outside the mews and looked at the slip of paper. This must be it. Then he saw Adebhoy's car on the other side of the road. This was the place all right. He turned into the mews. His shoes clanked against the cobble-stones. He found walking on them awkward. Adebhoy had said it was the flat right at the end, in the left-hand corner of the mews. He pushed the bell that said "Press". He heard it ring faintly a long way away. He waited, turning his back on the door, watching a white man polishing a shining black car outside the garage opposite. These people seemed to love working for its own sake. The thing was shining already. Suppose I'm just another damn nigger or darky to you—hey, Mister? Mabi shouldn't joke about that word. It's insulting. I'll tell him. He became aware, suddenly, of someone behind him. He swung about.

A woman stood holding the door open. She was tall, as tall as himself and terribly thin. But she looked strong; big nose and sticking-out chin; heavily-lidded eyes; an old-looking face set on a long, graceful, young girl's body; only, the body was flat-chested enough to be that of a young boy. She looked coldly at him.

"I'm looking for Mr. Lanwood," he said.

"What name?"

Her aloofness put him off.

"I'm Michael Udomo."

She smiled then, held out her hand and changed into a friendly person giving off warmth. "People sometimes turn up at awkward times without appointment. Come in."

He followed her up a short flight of narrow stairs.

"It's Michael Udomo," she called.

Lanwood opened the first door on the landing.

"Hello, Mike. We've been waiting for you."

They were in a long narrow room, filled with books. Only the strip of wall immediately above a small divan was free of books. Udomo wondered if Lanwood had read all the books.

"Coffee, please, Mary," Lanwood called, then shut the door.

Udomo crossed the long room and sat on the divan between Mhendi and Adebhoy. Mhendi's face looked drawn. Mabi looked up from the paper-littered desk where he sat reading.

"Hello, Mike."

"Hello, man."

"Hear you had a good party," Lanwood said.

"Yes," Udomo said.

"Don't get caught up in these things, Mike." Lanwood's manner was fatherly. "We have work to do. That's what we're here for. Not for parties. Mhendi forgets that sometimes."

Udomo looked quickly at Mhendi, then back at Lanwood. Mhendi braced himself and squared his shoulders.

"I think we'd better start," Mabi said quickly.

Mhendi relaxed. He stared at Lanwood's highly-polished shoes; first without seeing them, then becoming aware of them. They were new shoes. He looked at his own: old and worn, down at the heels and toes, unpolished. His eyes shifted to Lanwood's clothes. They, too, looked new. He felt angry suddenly. He jerked his head up.

"I don't like your attitude, Tom!"

"Then pull yourself together and my attitude will change."

"It's easy enough for you to sit in London and be godlike."

"Easy, David," Adebhoy said.

The woman came in with a tray of steaming cups of coffee.

"He started it," Mhendi snapped. "He's good at sneering at other people. Well, has he tried to lead a movement? Not in London where he's safe, but in Africa? Movements are led

42

by more than godlike speeches and pontifical books from the safety of London. Go out to Africa! Fight there! And then come and lecture me about self-discipline."

"Oh my aunt!". the woman jeered. "At it again, David! That self-pity of yours is going to destroy you. That's what's leading you to drink. You're not the only one who's attempted a revolution that failed. Only, yours needn't have failed if you had followed the advice we sent you!"

"You'd better stay out of this, Mary," Mabi snapped.

The woman dumped the tray on a chair and swung round to Mabi.

"Why should I? Or is the fight for freedom the preserve of men only? Many women have died in the struggle without whining or self-pity." She was angry now, her face flushed.

"I suppose you fancy yourself as one of these heroic women!" Mabi got up. He ignored the woman and spoke to Lanwood. "I thought we were here for a meeting. If this is it I'm going."

The woman started to say something, then checked herself. She turned to Lanwood. They all watched him, waiting for him to speak. He worked at the bowl of his pipe with a long thin knife. At last he looked up.

"If you've all finished with your long subjective wrangle we can start."

"You make me sick, Tom," the woman snapped and flounced out.

Udomo stared at the door.

"You take her too seriously." Lanwood tried to smile. "All women are emotional."

Adebhoy jumped up and took the tray of coffee from person to person.

Lanwood went out of the room. Udomo leaned towards Mhendi.

"Who is she?"

Mhendi laughed bitterly.

"Read his latest book?"

43

"No."

"Pass it to him, Paul."

Mabi took a book from the desk and passed it to Udomo. *The End of Empire,* by Thomas Lanwood. He opened it and saw the dedication: "For my dear friend and comrade, Mary Feld, without whose sustained and sustaining support neither this nor any of my other works could have been completed." But she has no respect for him, Udomo thought.

Lanwood came back.

"You'll make your peace with her but not with me," Mhendi said.

"We've wasted enough time," Lanwood said.

"More than enough," Mhendi said bitterly.

"Then why the devil don't we start!" Mabi snapped.

"We can certainly learn something about leadership and discipline from the commies," Lanwood said with sudden heat.

Mhendi softened suddenly. He saw past the self-deception, down to the real Lanwood; for a brief second it was there in Lanwood's eyes. Lanwood was a frustrated, ageing man, on the verge of self-doubt. He looked quickly at Mabi. Mabi had seen it too. Perhaps he shouldn't have said what he had. Tom needed his defences more than any of them.

"I spoke to Rosslee last night," he said with quiet friendliness. "He asked me to invite our group to their week-end policy conference on the colonies. He says this will give us a chance to help formulate policy. I suggest we go, prepared with a line of our own."

"Ah!" Lanwood smiled happily. "They're uncertain. They wouldn't bother to ask us if they weren't. Their empire's tottering so they're looking for allies among the leaders of their colonial subjects. It is only when they doubt their ability to rule by force that imperialists condescend to inviting the likes of us to 'help shape policy'. Well, what do the comrades think? Shall we go?"

"I vote we go," Mabi said. "With a line of our own as Mhendi said. We've nothing to lose."

"I agree," Adebhoy said.

"You, Mike?"

Udomo smiled uncertainly.

"It would be interesting to see their attitude."

The little caucus was under way. Now they would dream and plan for an hour or more. . . .

. . . At last it was all over.

"That finishes our business," Lanwood said.

They talked for a while longer, then took their leave of Lanwood.

As they left they heard Mary Feld in the kitchen. Adebhoy called out a farewell. She responded without coming to see them off. Lanwood held Mhendi back at the bottom of the stairs.

"Sorry about that business." He spoke casually, not looking at Mhendi, as though of something slight. "She didn't mean it."

"Forget it," Mhendi murmured.

"Personal relations must be subordinated to the struggle."

"Forget it, Tom."

"I'm glad you understand. Only the fight is important. Wish some of you fellows could stay. You know I don't take women seriously but they are useful. The only thing I say is that they mustn't interfere with our work. . . ." He looked at Mhendi at last, smiling casually, holding himself erect.

"That's all right, Tom. So long."

He watched them till they turned the corner out of the mews. Then he slowly climbed the stairs and went back into his study.

"They gone?" Mary Feld called.

"Yes," he called back.

"Anything useful come out of the meeting?"

45

"Yes."

He sat at his desk and began sorting out papers.

"Well? Can't you tell me about it? Or have you been infected by that Mabi's 'men only' spirit?"

"I'm trying to work. There's that article. Udomo's coming for lunch tomorrow."

"I'll be out tomorrow."

"That's all right. I'll prepare it."

"Mhendi's getting impossible."

He listened to her moving about the house. All he had to do was shut the door and he wouldn't hear her. She would be shut out. But he did nothing about it. He thought dispassionately about her. They'd been together a long time now. Since those far-off days in the Communist Party. She'd been young and pretty then, and more than that. She'd left the Party with him, because he'd left.

"Did you hear me?"

"Yes."

"Well, can't you answer?"

"I'm trying to work."

"He'd better mind his step next time or I won't have him here again. You're too soft. You did better work without the group. I think it's a waste of time. They're a lot of prima donnas!"

Nearly twenty years ago since they got together. Twenty years since they turned their backs on the Party.

"And that conceited little Mabi makes me sick."

There'd been that other woman before Mary. Soft and gentle and kind. What was her name now? Good woman, that. What was her name? . . . Memory began rushing back. He shut the door firmly on it. There's no time for sentimentality. A man must do what he must. And to do it he must keep alive. And to keep alive he must have food and a home and leisure. That was most important and she'd supplied that. . . . But I did try to get away once. . . . That was an

attempt to retreat. A defeatist attempt. Glad it failed. Dora
Smith. That was her name. Nice ordinary name for a nice
ordinary person. Pull yourself together, Tom!

He forced himself to look at the papers on his desk, to see
them, to think about them. He read one sentence over and
over, restraining the impulse of eye and mind to jump to the
next, and the next.

He hadn't heard her come in but he knew, suddenly, that
she was standing in the doorway, watching him. He turned
and got up. She had her hands on her hips. She stood firmly,
solidly, her feet slightly apart. She watched him levelly, a
hint of contempt in her eyes.

He knew from all the other times in all the other years
that this was the beginning of a storm of words between
them: words with the sharp, torturing edges of daggers.

"Your silence means you agree with that Mabi," she said.

There's only one way out, he thought wearily, only one way.
He went to her.

"Mary . . ."

"Don't try and get round me in your cowardly way, Tom.
I despise you for it!"

"I don't agree with him."

He reached out and pulled her to him.

"Then why didn't you tell him so?"

She resisted, began to fight when he did not let her go.
But, fighting, the scorn and contempt left her eyes. Something
of the old look, the look of years ago, was there now. It made
him want her as he had done in the old days. Something of
the feeling of the old days came over both of them.

Lanwood thought: One day this will fail and then there'll
be nothing. The thought frightened him. He tightened his
arms about her.

"Mary . . . Mary, I'm terribly lonely, please. . . ."

Later, they lay side by side on the little divan, spent and
relaxed, the storm averted. Lanwood intertwined his fingers

with hers. The woman, feminine and tender now, sighed and said :

"We should've had children when I suggested it years ago, Tom. Things might have been different then."

"We agreed not to. There was the struggle."

"But the call never came for you to go and lead them at home. You were sure it would come. And I trusted your word. I sacrificed everything for something that never came."

He felt the tenderness leaving her. How call it back?

"We could still marry." He knew he had made a mistake the moment he said it.

"It's too late, Tom. There isn't a single reason for us to marry now."

He thought: Yes. The moment of intimacy was over. It had never been as brief as this before. She pulled her hand free. She got up and went out. Lanwood closed his eyes. There was that article still to do. Yes, not a single reason. Not love even. He sighed and got up. There was the article.

4

Udomo got off the bus at Camden Town. He had travelled further than his ticket allowed. He should have got off at Mornington Crescent. The conductor yelled at him, waving his ticket rack. Udomo walked away.

"Go to hell," he muttered.

He waited for the traffic lights to change, then he crossed the street. Two black men stood at the entrance to the Camden Town Underground. They called greetings to him. He responded. He went into the station and bought a ticket to Hampstead.

Perhaps Mabi would be out. He would have to go back to the flat then. Trouble is, a man gets tired of eating alone. No fun in cooking for yourself and eating by yourself. It would have been fun to stay with the students and carry on the discussion. But a speaker can't tell his audience he's broke and can't pay for his meal at their restaurant. Of course, one of them might have offered to pay. But he dared not take the chance. They'd looked up to him as a leader; they'd listened to him as a leader. He had to keep them looking up to him. He'd certainly held their attention. That's the sort of thing one feels. It makes one sure of oneself. The secret is always to find a point on which all feel the same and build on it. The one thing stronger than all the points that divide tribal and clan loyalties, is the will to be free of the foreign oppressor. The thing, then, is to play down the divisions, to ignore them as far as possible, and to play up the foreign oppressor. It had worked all right.

The train, two points of light at first, swept into view, curving like a monstrous snake out of the dark tunnel. The doors opened. He pushed past people, got into a non-smoker and found a seat. The doors clanked shut; the train moved, gathered speed. The rhythmic beat of the wheels lulled him into drowsiness. He stared, unseeing, at a pretty girl in the opposite seat. She mistook this, raised her chin, stared back. But soon she grew embarrassed, looked away and pushed her short skirt as far down her knees as it would go. He remained unaware of her agitation.

Pity Adebhoy was on night duty. But they'd all been wrong about Lanwood's woman. She'd been charming when he'd lunched there that Sunday. And very intelligent. Nice and warm down here. Will have to start thinking of finding a place for when Adebhoy leaves. That Colonial Office chap tried to be funny. Have to get the consent of the Panafrican authorities. Hell! They're the Panafrican authority. Shouting at him had made a difference though. They'd soon done something after that. Not much, but regular, and enough to tide him over. He'd got himself new shoes, shirts and socks, and that had taken all his first allowance. The consent of the Panafrican authorities! Brilliant idea this stencilled magazine.

Fine article Lanwood had done: Mhendi too. Pity he drank so much. They'd all done fine articles really. Lovely idea those facts without comment. Let them condemn themselves out of their own mouths, these imperialists. Good chap, Adebhoy. Hope Mabi's in.

The train stopped, and it was Hampstead. The night-air upstairs was chilly, but only mildly so. Not like that terrible night when he'd first met Lois. Nearly a month now since he last saw her.

He pulled the hood of his coat over his head, pushed his hands deep into his pockets, and walked briskly down the steeply sloping hill.

The door at Mabi's place was open. There were no blocks of wood outside. The little hallway was in darkness so he felt his way to Mabi's door. He knocked.

"Come in!"

He went in. The brightness of the room's lights dazzled him for a while. They made the room brighter than the drab daylight of England, bright as a clear day at home when the hard sun beats down on the earth.

Mabi was not alone. Lois was there, sitting on his bed in the corner. In front of her, on the floor, was a pan on a pressure stove; she stirred this continuously.

Mabi stood in a cleared space in front of an easel near the huge window. To the right of him, on a block sat a coloured girl in a dressing-gown.

"Oh, it's you, Mike. Come in." Mabi spoke absently. "Is that front door open?"

"Yes."

"Damn them!" He exploded. "They know this is my model night! Do they want to get me into trouble? Damn them!" He stalked to the door and started yelling at the top of his voice. "What the blooming hell d'you people think you're up to? Leaving the damn door open when you know this is my modelling night! Damn! Bloody damn! Damn you all!"

They heard the door crash shut with an explosive bang. Then Mabi returned and shut his own door with a violent bang. He marched back to his easel.

"Sorry, Kate. All right."

The coloured girl stood up, undid the dressing-gown and shook it off her body, then she climbed on the block and relaxed her body into drooping dejection. Mabi watched her critically.

"Slightly to the right, Kate."

The girl obeyed.

"That's fine. Keep it."

Udomo felt out of place. This was a world where he never knew what to do, where to sit, whether to speak or remain silent. And a woman's nakedness, here in England, startled him. At home, in Africa, it would have been natural. He avoided looking at the naked girl on the block.

"Better come and sit here," Lois said.

He hung his coat behind the door and picked his way carefully to the divan.

"How'd it go?" Mabi said without turning.

"The meeting? All right."

"Fine. Talk to Lois." He finished the sketch, sprayed fixative on, dropped it on the floor and started a new one. "I want your back now, Kate." The girl turned on the block. "Shan't be long now."

"Bit strange to you?" Lois said.

"Yes," Udomo replied.

"It always is. But one gets used to it if you live among artists. I never could pose, not even for my husband. Tried it once but it was an awful failure. They look at you too coldly, all curves and planes instead of a person."

"What's he doing?" Udomo asked.

He looked quickly at Lois' face. The bright light showed up the spidery web of lines at the sides of her eyes and the corners of her mouth. She could, leaning forward like that,

51

be an African woman stirring her pan. She turned her head and smiled.

"No need to whisper. He's too absorbed to take in anything."

"I can hear you," Mabi said. Kate's flat back and protruding buttocks began to take shape on the sheet in front of him.

"What did Michael ask?" Lois said.

Mabi did not answer.

"See," Lois said.

"Yes," Udomo said.

"I hear you've livened the group up. Tom rang me the other day to say what a find you are. That's high praise, coming from him. What have you been doing? Last time Richard came round he said you were too busy to come."

"I was cutting stencils," he said.

He looks tired, she thought. But more relaxed now, less imprisoned.

He looked at his hands, then at her.

"Tom was right," he said. "It's hard work."

"What of your studies?"

"I do them too. They're not as important."

"Don't the others help?"

"When they can. But they've their own work."

"How many stencils must you cut?"

"Fifty-six. I've done eleven."

"My God! And are you supposed to do this by yourself?"

His face creased into that boyishly sheepish smile.

"It was my idea."

Oh God, she thought. A sense of helplessness took hold of her. She fought against it, tried to throw it off. Let them be the liberators if they must. It's their affair.

"Why did you have to do it?"

He heard the helpless protest in her voice. He looked searchingly at her. The violent force of his personality hit her again, as it had done that night.

"Because I must," he said quietly.

She lowered her head and stirred the stew.

"Yes," she said. "Better bring some of those stencils around. Jo and I can help. We've got one typewriter. Perhaps you can find another."

"Will you?"

She dared not look at him now. The shutters would be down. His eyes would be shining. He would seem larger than life itself. There was no need to look to know all that.

"I said so," she said coolly.

"When can I bring them?"

"After school tomorrow."

"Hear that, Mabi!" He was beside himself with joy. "She'll help! I could kiss you, Lois!" He realised what he had said and stopped short.

He turned his head with slow deliberation and looked at her. She looked back at him, calmly, quietly. In the end, it was he who shifted his eyes to a spot to the right of her. But she felt no sense of victory. You're a fool, Lois, she told herself bitterly; a bloody awful silly fool.

"What's that?" Mabi said absently.

"It can wait," Lois said. "Finish before the stew turns to pap."

There was silence, then, in the big brightly lit room. The scrape of charcoal against stiff paper only accentuated the silence. The gentle bubbling of the stew only enhanced it.

Udomo thought: I've called her by her name and I do want to kiss her! I will make her look at me. I will will it. Look at me, woman. I want to kiss you. Look at me! Look at me, woman. I want to kiss you. Look at me. Lois. Lois. Lois. Lois.

Lois thought: This is utterly silly, utterly silly. I'm too old for this sort of thing; he can't talk; he's awkward. He has nothing except animal vitality. He's incapable of tenderness.

Look at me, woman. I will you to look at me.

Utterly incapable of tenderness.

Lois, I will it! Look at me, Lois! Woman!

She glanced quickly, fleetingly, at him, then away again. He relaxed inwardly. The ghost of a smile played on his lips.

At last Mabi finished.

"That's enough, Kate." He flung the piece of charcoal on the table, stretched himself and yawned.

The girl got off the block and went behind an improvised screen.

"God." He made it a long drawn-out sigh. "Time?"

"Nearly ten," Lois said.

Mabi came and flung himself on the divan between Lois and Udomo.

"Better eat," Lois said. She raised her voice. "You eating with us, Kate?"

"No thanks." There was a singing lilt to the girl's voice. "I must get home."

Lois got plates and forks out of a little cupboard and dished up. The girl, dressed now, came from behind the improvised screen. Naked, she had been fat and dumpy; dressed, she was trim and graceful. Mabi bounced up, took an envelope from the table and went out with her. When he returned the food was ready. He turned off some of the lights, softening the harshness of the room.

They ate, sitting side by side on the divan, balancing the plates on their knees.

"Satisfied?" Lois asked.

"Not bad," Mabi said. "Now I've got to make the damn wood come alive. Anyway, how are things with you, Mike?"

"Lois has offered to help cut stencils," Udomo said. It was easy to use her name now. He glanced at her.

"Lois is an angel, Mike. One of the best."

"Lois sprouts wings," Lois said.

"We're all very fond of her," Mabi continued seriously.

"Can we borrow your typewriter?" Udomo said. "Then Jo can help too."

"Sure."

"That's fine."

"Don't drive Lois too hard," Mabi said. "We're fond of her. We don't want anything to hurt her."

"Shut up, Paul," Lois snapped. "Anybody would think I can't take care of myself."

"Can you, my dear?" Mabi was at his most didactic.

"There's no need to. There's nothing."

Udomo withdrew into himself. Mabi was talking for his benefit. He would be patient now.

"Do you think she can take care of herself, Mike?"

"I won't sit here being discussed as though I were some subjected African woman!" She couldn't really be angry with Mabi. She knew him too well, was too fond of him. "You're tired, Paul, and so's Michael, and so am I. Finish and then we'll go."

"But I want to tell you about my people, dear."

"You've told me before."

"Not this. Mike, here, will confirm it. Did you know my people are considered the most primitive and backward of all the people of Africa? Even our fellow countrymen in Pan-africa look down on us. When the people of the plains want to express contempt for someone they say he's behaving like a mountain man. Right, Mike?"

"You're tired," Lois said gently.

"Yes," Mabi sighed. "Take her home, Mike. And never mind me, I don't know what's the matter with me."

They turned into Haverstock Hill and climbed the slight incline that grew steeper higher up. The night was clear; there was no wind. The stars stood out sharp in the black sky. The moon had fattened into a near half-moon. Occasionally, cars flashed by; occasionally, people passed. But in the main the streets were empty, the place silent. They neared Belsize Park underground.

"You can get a bus here," Lois said.

"I'll see you home," Udomo said.

They crossed a street and walked past the Kosher shops. The café opposite the station was open.

"Let's have tea," Udomo said.

She thought: He sounds and feels very quiet. He has a capacity for silence.

"All right," she said.

They entered the café. She led the way to the corner table near the electric fire. She knew he would welcome the warmth. A tired waitress came and took their order.

She leaned back and waited for him to speak, watching his face. It was his eyes, really, that gave his face that hint of sullen sadness. Funny how they all seemed so terribly sad in repose. Could it be the nature of Africa that they carried with them wherever they went? Is Africa a sad continent? Not just about its problems, but basically? All the Africans she'd ever met had this sadness in repose. And yet, when they laughed there was nothing but sunshine.

"What are you thinking?" he asked.

He was able, now, to look into her eyes and still be tranquil.

"About you," she said. "I mean the five of you: and about Africa."

"You must visit it one day," he said.

"What is it really like?"

She'd known he'd smile at that.

"Like any other land," he said. "Only, dearer than any other to us who were born there."

The tired waitress brought their tea.

"You haven't answered me."

She watched the long look of memory grow in his eyes. Perhaps he would talk now.

He spoke slowly, feeling for the words and testing them as he spoke them; not seeing her face though he looked straight at it.

"Africa? She is a little like a heart. You've seen the shape of her. It's like a heart. Africa is my heart, the heart of all of us who are black. Without her we are nothing; while she is not free we are not men. That is why we must free her, or die. That is how it is."

And now he looked at her with seeing eyes, half-challenging, half-defensive. She stifled the argument of reason that rose in her. Could one argue against a mystique? And even if one could she did not want to.

"I see," she said quietly. She poured the tea.

"It is something no white person understands," he said.

He was free now. The shutters were down. And yet there was no violence. He seemed, suddenly, the most charming person she had met in a long time. He took her hand when she put the cup in front of him. He squeezed it lightly, gently.

"I'm glad you asked me," he said. "You made me think about it. Now I know it. It is the most important thing."

She shivered inwardly and looked away from him. Perhaps he was freer with words when he spoke in his own language. He was an educated man who had earned degrees. Why did he give off this sense of muteness when he felt deeply? Had he never expressed deep feeling to another person before?

He turned her hand over and looked at the palm.

"It's small," he said.

"All women's hands are small," she said.

"I never noticed before," he said.

"Then you've never been in love."

"Never," he said. "Are you in love with Mabi?"

"I wish I were. And he with me."

"You like him a lot."

"He's my kind of person."

"An artist, like your husband?"

It's coming, Lois thought.

"Not for that reason. He's just my kind of person."

"I like you," he said.

"I'm glad." She poured more tea.

"I mean in a special way." The words choked him.

She looked up quickly.

"It's only loneliness, Michael."

"I am lonely, yes."

"Then find yourself a nice young girl. Paul knows dozens. He'll introduce you."

He waited till she looked at him, then he said:

"I want you, Lois."

A wave of anger passed over her.

"Why me? Do you love me? Or do you think I'm easy for an affair?"

"I like you," he said quietly.

"Do you sleep with every woman you like?"

"No."

"Then why me?"

"You're angry." His smile was full and real. It lit his eyes. "I like you when you're angry."

She tried to contain the wave of anger.

"Stop this, Michael. I'm nearly forty. I had all the affairs I wanted when I was young. I don't like affairs; they're messy and untidy. I don't want a man . . ."

"Every woman wants a man," he said.

She shut her mouth and stared at him.

"You know it's true," he said quietly.

"Please stop it." She felt worn-out suddenly, battered by this man's calm confidence. "We'd better go."

He picked up the typewriter, paid, and followed her out.

The cinema crowd spilled out. In a little while they were clear of the crowds. They turned up Lois' hill.

"Still angry?"

"No," she said tiredly.

At her door he kissed her hand. "I read women liked that," he said.

Her mind saw the comedy of it. But she could not laugh.

"Good night," she said quickly.

"Good night, Lois. See you tomorrow."

Tomorrow, she thought; oh, Lord! tomorrow.

She shut the door and searched in her bag for a cigarette. She leaned against the door and lit it. Jo Furse was still up. The kitchen light was on. She heard a man's voice. Jo had company.

"That you, Lois?" Jo called.

"Yes."

"Come and have some cocoa. Henry's leaving soon as he's had his. Been to the theatre."

"I won't, thanks. Just had tea and I'm dog-tired. Good night."

She walked past the kitchen and went into her room. She lit the fire and sat on the bed. After a while she got up and went to the mirror. She stared at her reflection.

What are you afraid of, Lois? You always pretend that you have a clear mind. A clear mind that sees things for what they are. Nothing will happen that you don't want to happen. You don't want this to happen. Well, then, it won't. *It will.* Only if you want it to. *I don't.* Then it won't. *But it will.* That'll be because you want it. *No, I don't.* Yes, you do. *No, I don't.* You make me tired. Either it happens because you want it to, or else it doesn't because you don't want it to. *Come into my parlour, said the spider to the fly. . . .* Don't flatter yourself. You're no helpless chicken. You're a woman of experience. He's a straight-forward unsophisticated sort of chap about these things. He'll take a walking ticket if you give it to him straight. *You don't know him.* Blah, blah, blah. *Come into my parlour, said the spider to the fly.* Fool yourself if you must, but don't try to fool me. But, of course, it is part of the smutty Anglo-Saxon puritanism that the blame must always be on someone else and all the better if he's some lesser breed without the law. Use the old line of I didn't want to do it and I didn't know what I was doing. *But why am I so afraid?* You know why. You seem to have forgotten how to think. *Because I was hurt.* A conditioned reflex. *Then it isn't him?* Answer yourself.

She put her hand to her temple. She turned away from the mirror. She sat on the bed and picked up the telephone. She dialled Mabi's number. The phone rang at the other end. She put it back on its rest suddenly.

"No one else can decide," she said aloud.

She crushed out the cigarette and began to undress.

The doorbell echoed through the flat. Lois walked briskly to the door. It was Udomo. She flung the door open and smiled.

"Good afternoon," she said gaily. "'Come into my parlour,' said the spider to the fly.'"

"I brought the stencils," he said.

"Jo won't be in till late," she said.

He followed her into the big room.

The warm afternoon sun shimmered in through the french windows, filled the room with a gaiety and light that matched Lois' new mood. Outside the windows, the new spring grass made a bright carpet on the earth. And on the trees, beyond the carpet of grass, the buds were choking fat to bursting point. The period of blossoming was at hand, and earth and air held a gentle tenderness.

Udomo dumped his parcel on the floor.

"The warmest day of the year so far!" Lois exclaimed.

"And you are happy," he said.

He started to undo the parcel, going down on one knee. She came near and stood looking down at him.

"I am," she said.

Her voice made him look up.

"You wanted to kiss me last night," she said quietly.

He rose slowly.

"Yes," he said.

60

Her eyes told him he could. He took both her hands in his. How they trembled. She was a woman, now, soft and warmly giving as a woman. He pulled her to him. She resisted briefly.

"I don't want just an affair," she whispered.

And then she was in his arms. . . .

They lay side by side in her bedroom later. A chink of sun-light filtered in through the tiny gap at the top of the drawn curtains and played on the foot of the bed, dancing with mad caprice. And outside the window a bird sang with a gay, passionate intensity.

Lois listened to the bird-song and tried to identify the smell of Udomo's hair. A brown smell it was. Burnt leaves, she decided. That was it. Burnt leaves. A lovely smell. She'd not expected such great gentleness from him, like caressing poetry. Gentle Michael. What had she been afraid of, she and Mabi? Not of this utter peace. That violence she sensed must have been imagination. There'd been nothing violent about him. And now this quiet. Which is the greater joy, the loving or the moment of peace after? She was glad she'd put off having her hair cropped. It meant something to him. Better let it grow now. He's so relaxed now. She felt it even in his big arm under her head. And so beautifully shaped.

He stirred and moved his head slightly. She ran her fingers over his broad chest. She thought: Reaction sets in with some men afterwards. Would it set in with him?

"Michael. . . ."

"Yes?"

She was going to ask him if it had been as he wanted it, but she changed her mind. She knew he was happy.

"Just Michael," she said.

His voice was drowsy. Really, they ought to go to sleep now.

"Lois," he murmured, "I want to thank you."

"Oh my dear." She nestled closer to him . . .

She woke suddenly, quietly. He was still asleep. Those stencils, she thought. She eased his arm off her body, and looked at the bedside clock. They'd slept for nearly two hours. The sun had moved. The shaft of light no longer played on the foot of the bed. She got up, went to the bathroom and started a bath. While it ran she made tea. Then she bathed quickly, dressed and took the tea to the bedroom. She pulled the curtains and light streamed into the room.

A man in her bed after ten years. He looked so relaxed in sleep, so like a child. A corner of her brain whispered: You can't really see him any more. But she hardly heard, or, if she did, it did not register. She sat on the edge of the bed and put her hand on his bare shoulder.

"Michael. Wake up, Michael."

He stirred. Then, suddenly, he jerked awake and sat upright. He looked about wildly. She gripped his shoulder.

"It's all right, Michael."

"Oh, Lois." The relief in his voice made her feel deeply tender. She restrained the impulse to put her arms about him.

He smiled and she thought: No reaction.

"Have I slept long?"

"Two hours. You needed it. Here's tea. I'll get a bath going for you, then I'll start on those stencils."

She went to the door.

"Lois."

She turned and looked at him. He was caught up in a new wave of desire.

"We've to do those stencils," she said softly and went out.

She was hard at work when he came in from his bath. He came and stood behind, putting his hands on her shoulders. She looked up briefly but did not stop typing. He ran his fingers through her hair, brushed his cheek against hers, then he went to the other end of the table and sat facing her across the typewriter. He inserted a stencil in the machine, memorised a line of Mhendi's manuscript, then picked out the letters on the keys.

For two hours the clicking of the typewriters was the only sound in the room. Then Lois sighed and straightened her back.

"I'm for a break. Why the devil must Paul write so much! Tea?"

"Yes, please."

He went on typing while she made the tea. The sun had gone down and the late spring darkness had come. The lights were on in the room but Udomo had not noticed Lois get up to put them on. He stopped typing when she brought the tea. They sat side by side.

"Tired?" she said.

"Not now," he said.

She looked into her teacup; a smile played on her lips.

"I was frightened of you," she said.

"And Mabi helped your fear," he said.

"I think he's a little afraid of you too."

"And I of him, but don't tell him. And now, do you still fear?"

"Not in the same way."

"But why do you fear? Why?"

She put her hand on his. She tried to smile. The corners of her mouth twitched. She sighed tremulously.

"Because I think I'm in love with you, Michael."

"And you're afraid of that?"

"I'm that sort of woman." Try not to slop, Lois. "I'm one of those women who must give everything or nothing."

"That is as it should be," he said.

She wanted to tell him of John then, of the humiliating torture his going to that other woman had been. Instead, she said:

"More tea?"

Then they went back to work. Jo Furse came in at ten and prepared supper. She felt unwell and went to bed after supper.

Lois and Udomo went back to the stencil cutting. Just before midnight Lois said:

"You'll miss your last bus if you don't go now."

"I want to miss it."

"Then miss it."

"What of Jo?"

"You won't shock her."

He burst out laughing, a happy rumbling laugh that started in the pit of his stomach. It brought a smile to her face. He got up and pulled her into his arms.

"I love you, Lois."

"I've waited to hear you say that."

5

"Name?"

"Paul Mabi."

"Organisation?"

"The Africa Freedom Group."

"All right. Put your question."

"Mr. Chairman: I've listened with very great care to the speaker, especially when he spoke about . . ."

The chairman banged his gavel.

"Please put your question without any introductory speech."

Lanwood jumped up.

"On a point of procedure, Mr. Chairman."

"Mr. Mabi will now put his question. You'll have a turn."

"But this is a point of procedure, Mr. Chairman. I'm Lanwood, leader of the Africa Freedom Group delegation."

"And I'm the chairman! Please sit down, Mr. Lanwood!"

Udomo jumped up, waving his arms.

"This is an insult! I protest!"

Pandemonium broke loose. Africans bobbed up all over the crowded conference hall. They shouted at the chairman. The secretary of the colonial group of the Progressive Party spoke urgently into the chairman's ear. Mhendi's voice bellowed above the noise:

"Walk out, boys! We won't be insulted!"

Africans began to move everywhere. The chairman banged his gavel. "Order, ladies and gentlemen! Please!"

"To be insulted again!" Adebhoy yelled.

"I'm sorry!" the chairman shouted.

The general African exodus came to a halt.

"I want to apologise if I've offended Mr. Lanwood! I did not mean to. You know how it is."

"We know . . ." a voice jeered.

Mhendi waved them back. When they were all back in their seats the chairman banged his gavel.

"Mr. Lanwood has a point of procedure."

Lanwood was at his most suave.

"I accept your apology in the interest of constructive co-operation, Mr. Chairman. It is good to see you trying to learn the lesson of good manners you are always so anxious to ram down colonial throats. . . ."

The chairman's face turned beetroot. The secretary put a restraining hand on his arm.

". . . My point was simply that the chairman seemed unduly harsh in his ruling on Mr. Mabi. He didn't even give Mr. Mabi a chance to show if he intended making a speech before clamping down on him. This, surely, was prejudging the issue. I've attended enough conferences to know that this is not normal procedure." Lanwood sat down to wild applause from the Africans.

"Will Mr. Mabi please put his question."

"Well, sir, as I began to say, I listened very carefully to the speaker, especially when he spoke about deciding when the people of the colonies would be fit to take control of their own affairs. Now here is the question: By what God-given right are you, the English, empowered to decide the fitness or otherwise of people to run their own affairs?"

The Africans shouted their approval. The speaker rose.

"Mr. Chairman: The short answer to Mr. Mabi's question is that I certainly don't think we have any God-given right, as he puts it. . . ."

"How would you put it?" a voice shouted.

"I would not put it, sir. But we must face facts. The facts are that God-given right or not, we are in charge of these colonies. We are responsible for them and it is our duty to discharge that responsibility. It is in that context that we must decide what is best for the people of the colonies. And it is an earnest of our sense of not having any God-given right that we have asked you, the Africans here, to co-operate with us in deciding what is best for the colonies. . . ."

"How did you acquire this 'responsibility'?" someone shouted.

The chairman banged his gavel.

"I don't mind answering that, Mr. Chairman," the speaker said. "Of course we acquired our empire in the way all empires are acquired—by conquest. But it does seem to me, and I say this without any sense of arrogance, that our African friends lack a sense of history. They seem to think that they are the only people who've ever been conquered and occupied. Conquest and occupation are as old as the known story of mankind. We, in these islands, have ourselves been occupied. Britain was once a Roman colony, was once invaded by the barbarians from the German forests, and was last conquered by the Normans. But we gained from these conquests. They helped to make us what we are today. If our African friends would bear all this in mind, would remember that they are not unique in the history of the world, they may yet learn and gain much from this period of imperialism which is rapidly coming to a close and which we are as anxious to bring to an end as they are."

The English section of the audience applauded warmly; the Africans remained silent.

The next speaker was the secretary of the colonial section of the Progressive Party.

"Mr. Chairman: It seems to me that the first question we should ask ourselves here is this: What is the relation between political and social advance in the colonies? It seems to me that we will miss the heart of the problem if we do not answer that question realistically.

"As we see it, real political progress is dependent on advance in the economic and social fields. There can be no political progress without that. Trade unions, co-operatives and democratic local government structures are essential, not only because of their direct effects on the standards and conditions of living, but also because they are organised expressions of public opinion interested in the maintenance of democratic procedure. Believing this, we, as the party in power, have done certain things. What have we done?

"We have introduced legislation insisting that where grants are made under the Colonial Development and Welfare Act the laws of the colony should provide reasonable facilities for the establishment of trade unions. We have appointed trade union advisers. The result was an immediate leap in the number of organised workers in the colonies. This growth is still going on. Similarly, co-operatives have grown in number and importance. We have spent enormous sums for the benefit of the colonial peoples. Millions of pounds—the figures are on record for those who want to check them—on medical and educational services, on housing, on improving road and rail services, on improving agricultural methods, on building deep harbours in some places and fighting soil erosion in others. Over 150 million pounds has gone into this work in the past ten years.

"Where did all this money come from? It came from the ordinary tax-payer in this country. We are no longer a rich country; we are no longer the first power in the world. So to find this sum of money was a real hardship for the British tax-payer. Yet it was found, and willingly. Why?

"We come now to the point of the question. The idea behind the spending of all this money, behind all our efforts, is a simple one, but a very true one. We believe that the practice of government, especially democratic government, is a most difficult practice that needs to be learnt with very great care. It is not enough to hand over power to a few specially selected or particularly vociferous local individuals. Such people, if we were to hand power to them, cannot be called to account by unorganised masses with no tradition of national democratic procedure behind them. So we decided to create, to build up, a tradition of participation in local affairs through trade unions, local government and co-operatives. The end in view is the transfer of sovereignty. But that is the final step, not the first. This situation, I know, leads to acute frustration in individuals who are educationally and politically far in advance of their fellows. We've had some of that frustration expressed here today. These individuals accuse us of being undemocratic, whereas in fact we are working towards democracy for their countries. We may understand and sympathise with these frustrated individuals, but our clear duty is to the masses of the colonial peoples rather than to a small and politically ambitious group of individuals. To hand over the masses to these individuals before the masses are sufficiently educated to control and restrain these individuals by the proper exercise of their rights would be to betray our trust and responsibility to the colonial masses. I see nothing to be ashamed of in all this or in our record. Our motives are noble, our deeds are on record, our end is declared. The challenge is not to us but to those individuals. Let them join with us in the great task of preparing their people for the ultimate transfer of power. That is the way out of their frustrations: that is the way they can truly serve Africa and their peoples."

A score of hands shot up before the secretary was properly in his seat. Lanwood, Udomo and Mhendi were on their feet, snapping their fingers. But a woman got in before them. She was a tough lady Progressive who sat in the Commons and was recognised as an expert on colonial affairs. She endorsed and amplified the secretary's statement, then went on:

"The truth is, and you all know it, that all our troubles in the colonies are not caused by any universal discontent among the mass of the colonial people but by a small, unrepresentative and vocal minority. A small handful of people are exploiting the ignorance and fears of their own people for unworthy motives. They are demagogues who see us standing between themselves and the unrestrained exploitation of their own people. There is one of them here in this hall today who was responsible for that terrible blood-bath in Pluralia five years ago. It is time we turned and accused these people, Mr. Chairman, instead of always being on the defensive. It is time we stopped being frightened of a vocal and irresponsible minority who do not speak for their people. I dread to think of the poor ignorant peoples of the colonies being delivered up to their mercies. I am convinced that if power were handed to these people they would oppress and exploit their people with a ruthlessness that would make our so-called oppression look like heaven.

"I was in Panafrica this past winter, Mr. Chairman. I discovered at first-hand, then, what the so-called educated Panafricans thought of their uneducated brethren. They talk of them as people out of the bush and treat them with a contempt we have never managed. Let me tell you of a little incident. I spent a day, a Sunday it was, with a couple. The man was a highly successful lawyer, trained in this country. His wife had been a nurse here. They had three servants. And throughout the day they never once treated any of those servants as though they were humans with any feelings. They were forever complaining of the laziness of their servants while the servants themselves were still in the room. At lunch-time the steward who served us had to wear white gloves. The charming woman told me in his presence that all the people from the bush were too filthy in their habits to be trusted to serve except in sterilised white gloves. I looked into the boy's face and saw the expression one sees on the face of a whipped dog. Later, the fine lawyer abused another 'boy' in my presence in a way I've never seen an employer in this country abuse a servant. And this was no isolated case. . . . No, Mr. Chairman! We must face the fact that the mass of the Africans would be worse off under this minority that now pretends to be concerned only with their freedom. I have very little doubt in my own mind that if the mass of the Africans were truly free to express their wishes, the overwhelming majority would opt for our continued presence until they feel strong enough to cope with their so-called black élite!"

It was three minutes before the chairman restored order. Mhendi remained insistently on his feet. When the chairman pointed at another African Mhendi said:

"The lady has referred directly to me. I claim the right to reply."

"I've called a speaker," the chairman said firmly.

"I waive my right, sir," the African said.

"I'm a little tired of all you people," Mhendi said wearily. "I'm tired of all your talk about multi-racial commonwealths and freedom and protecting our so-called backward brethren from us. I'm tired of the whole lot of it because I've heard it so often. I'm even too tired of the familiar arrogance behind the last speaker's words to be really angry about them. The lady accused me of being responsible for the deaths in Plur-alia. Of course I am! It's a burden I carry alone. She cannot help me carry it by all her fine words. But I do not object to the accusation. What I do object to is its source. And instead of trying to compete with the lady in the game of political jiggery-pokery, I want to tell you why I object to the source of the accusation. I'll be brief, I promise you. I know it is a waste of time.

"If any one of the people who started your movement, those pioneers of yours who went to jail and went hungry and were transported for the sake of your movement, if any of them were in this hall today, they would have been ashamed of what has happened to the movement they started. They knew the meaning of freedom. Maybe it was because they didn't have it. Maybe it is only those who are without it who know the meaning of freedom. And yet, you seemed to know the meaning of freedom when you were fighting your war against the continental invader. Shedding your own, as well as other people's blood became legitimate then. Certainly, I would concede you that you are better politicians than the pioneers of your movement were. They would not have had the effrontery to send out an army to crush the expression of the national aspirations of a people and then turn on its defeated leader and accuse him of responsibility. I'm sure they would not have had the nerve to talk about a multi-racial commonwealth of free and equal partners knowing all the facts of the Pluralian situation today. I think I would have wanted to argue back if one of *them* had accused me. I certainly don't want to argue back at this lady. I hope she gets promotion. I think she would do well as a Secretary or Under-Secretary of State for Colonial Affairs. I thought earlier on that she must have known, while speaking, of the shooting down of my wife and other women a few weeks ago for refusing to be removed from our ancestral lands. And I thought: If one of those pioneers were in this hall today, he or she would have come up to me and said, 'Mhendi, I've heard the sad news of your wife and the other women and in spite of all our disagreements I want you to know how sorry I feel.' At first I was hurt that not a single one of you Progressive people came to me and said anything about it; then I thought: No, I'm not disappointed, I'm glad. These people have ceased to be the heirs of those pioneers. It is fitting that even in personal relations there shouldn't be the great warmth that was such a strong feature of the lives of those old pioneers. That's all I want to say, Mr. Chairman. I know it is no contribution to the efficiency experts seeking new techniques to carry out a job. But then, I'm unemployed and so not concerned with jobs. I still read the old pioneers of your movement. Do any of you?"

Mhendi sat down, then he jumped up again. "Mr. Chairman! There is one small thing I have forgotten and which I must say, for it is more important than all the others. If any of my remarks are at all reported, I should very much like my thanks to be included to all the ordinary, non-political decent people of this country whose protests stopped their government from delivering me up to my enemies when the government of Pluralia demanded my return. I am deeply grateful for that."

There was a long, uneasy silence in the hall after Mhendi sat down. The British section of the audience felt awkwardly embarrassed. The Africans could not make sense of Mhendi's speech. They were Panafricans in the main, and knew next to nothing of Pluralia. They had expected a fiery outburst from the great Mhendi, not this quietly sad and deliberate statement. They turned and looked wonderingly at him. Mabi, who sat beside him, put a hand on his arm.

Even the chairman was embarrassed. He cleared his throat uncertainly.

"I hope our following speakers will keep to the point under discussion, and I can assure Mr. Mhendi that, whatever our differences, we are not as cold-blooded as he seems to think. . . ."

He sat down as though uncertain of what to say or do next.

Mhendi lit his pipe and leaned back. Lanwood rose.

"Mr. Chairman . . ."

"You have the floor," the chairman said.

"For the record, I'm Thomas Lanwood, leader of the Africa Freedom Group.

"My colleague, Mr. Mhendi, has just injected a whiff of the subjective reality of colonial politics into this conference hall. I'm sure you will understand that as a man recently bereaved our colleague suffers under intense emotional strain. So I propose to objectivise what he tried to say, and to develop it.

"I want, first of all, to address myself, through you, to the lady who spoke so scornfully of the black élite. But before I do so I want to say, in passing, that in all my years of attending conferences I have never encountered such vulgar chauvinism as she expressed in her references to Mhendi . . ."

The lady jumped up.

"I protest, Mr. Chairman! The speaker's insulting . . ."

Other whites joined in her protest. The Africans applauded.

"We listened in silence to your insults!" Lanwood roared above the hubbub. "Now listen to us!"

"There's no need to be personal," the chairman shouted, banging his gavel.

This led to a new uproar. The secretary conferred urgently with the chairman and others on the platform. Black and white, in the body of the hall, yelled at each other. Lord Rosslee, the young peer who had been at Lois' party, took over the steering of the conference.

"Ladies and gentlemen!" Rosslee boomed. "Comrades! Please!"

He raised both hands and waited. Quiet gradually settled in.

"When passion comes to conferences reason goes out. Let it not be said that our conference was without reason, I beg you. I know that our friend, the lady member of Parliament, won't mind my saying that most of us on this platform felt she spoke too harshly about the black élite. But she is as entitled to her opinions as is Mr. Lanwood, and she had a fair hearing. Now let us give Mr. Lanwood a fair hearing. Carry on, Mr. Lanwood."

"Thank you, Mr. Chairman," Lanwood said. "I feel I would have failed in my duty if I had not referred—in passing, mind you—to such an exhibition of chauvinism from a member of the party of progress in this country. But now to the concrete point the lady raised. You must, she said, go onto the offensive against this ambitious, unscrupulous minority. In other words, you must go onto the offensive against us, for we are the people she is talking about. Fine! Now we know where we are. We are in the arena of naked imperialism, of divide and rule. Divorce the leadership from the mass of the people, create hostility towards the leaderships in the minds of the people, that is her policy. One thing can be said for her: she's honest. We know where we are with her!

"We can't say the same for your secretary, Mr. Chairman. He would beguile us with impressive figures for roads, schools and hospitals. On paper they sound fine. But we are not paper experts. We know the reality of the lives of the people. And the reality does not measure up to this wonderful picture of achievement. But, even if all his paper achievements were so in fact, does that answer the question of freedom?

"The one thing you people seem congenitally incapable of understanding is the question of freedom. There is no substitute for it. The colonial peoples are on the march, Mr. Chairman, not in the direction of uplift, either economic or moral, but in the direction of freedom, in the direction of determining their own fate and their own destiny in their own way. We've been accused of being negative and destructive. I'm not ashamed of admitting that is so. I would begin to question my motives, my integrity, if you ceased accusing me of being negative and destructive. It is the traditional function of the most noble and most heroic sons and daughters of an invaded and occupied people that they should harass the enemy, blow up his bridges and trains, cut his communications, put sand into his machines. It is only the psychologically enslaved or the traitors who behave otherwise. We must be negative and destructive until we are free. You ask for our co-operation. Good! Here is the one and only condition for our co-opera tion: when you are ready to discuss with us the date for your withdrawal from the colonies, then, and only then, will you get our willing co-operation! The slave does not co-operate with the slave-owner! We spurn your invitation! We give you warning, frankly and publicly, that we intend to break our chains! The battle is joined!"

The blacks rose to their feet as a body to acclaim Lanwood. Whites jumped up from all parts of the hall, raising their hands for an opportunity to reply. On the platform, the secretary tugged at Rosslee's sleeve.

"Let me reply to him."

"Let them talk themselves out," Rosslee said. "They'll be easier to handle later on. I know them."

"They'll disrupt the conference," the secretary said.

"No," Rosslee said. "I know them. Let them talk. That chap at the back's one of them, isn't he? Think I met him at a party."

"He's new," the secretary said. "Udomo, I think his name is."

"Of course," Rosslee said. "I'll call him."

Hands were raised everywhere as the chairman rose.

"The gentleman in the corner at the back first caught my eye. . . . No, not you; the African gentleman. No, not you. The one to the right of you. Yes, yes, you, sir. Name, please."

"Udomo! Africa Freedom Group. . . . Mr. Chairman!"

Udomo felt all eyes turned to him, felt the people watching and waiting. He began to tremble. He clenched both fists and raised them to the level of his shoulders. He held his breath. Words began to form and hammer at his brain.

"Mr. Chairman! Someone in this hall . . ."

He had difficulty with the words. He was forcing them out with all the strength of his body. The audience felt only the strength. They watched intently as his face contorted with passion.

". . . Someone in this hall mocked at Mhendi because his revolution failed to throw off the yoke of slavery!" He raised his clenched hands a little higher and beat out the words as he spoke them. "She was not concerned about the dead! There is too much blood on your hands for you to be concerned about a few more dead blacks!" He paused and listened to the utter silence of the room. His voice rose. His lips twisted: "She was gloating! She was gloating because another native attempt had been crushed! She was warning us what to expect! Well! We will not forget! But next time . . .! But next time . . .!" He hissed it out yet again. "But next time!" He raised his right, fisted arm high above his head. His head shot up. His eyes glowed. "We will not fail! Even if there's a sea of blood! We will not fail! Now! *You* have been warned! We will not fail!" He stood like that for a long time: clenched fist high above his head, aware of the faces turned to him, aware of the great silence in the hall, aware too, now, of the violent trembling of his body in the great silence. Then he sat down suddenly, utterly spent.

The silence lingered on for a spell, then African voices burst in a great roar of approval. And the English people, freed now of Udomo's force, began to talk among themselves. Even Lanwood, Mhendi and Mabi were yelling with the rest of the Africans.

On the platform the secretary exclaimed:

"My God!"

"Yes. He's got it bad," Rosslee said.

"He's dangerous; he's mad."

A wicked glint showed in the tall peer's eyes.

"Wouldn't you feel like that if we'd been occupied by the continental invader?"

Before the secretary could answer, Rosslee was on his feet, banging his gavel.

Udomo looked at the platform. The blurredness had gone from his vision. He could see people again. The awful shaking had stopped. Strength flowed back into his body. That chairman lord was smiling. He turned his head. Lanwood had been looking back at him, trying to catch his eye. Now Lanwood beamed his approval. Udomo smiled and nodded. The chairman began to speak. . . .

Mhendi said:

"Mike. . . ."

"It's late," Lanwood snapped. "Go to sleep. We want to be fresh for the final session tomorrow."

"What is it?" Udomo called.

"Let it keep till tomorrow," Adebhoy protested.

"Come here for a minute," Mhendi called.

"Oh God!" Lanwood protested.

Udomo got out of bed and went through the open door that joined the two bedrooms. He, Lanwood and Adebhoy shared the bigger bedroom; Mhendi and Mabi the small one. The moonlight, filtering in through the open windows, was bright enough for him to see his way.

He sat on the edge of Mhendi's bed.

"You awake, Paul?" Mhendi said.

"Yes."

"Tell Mike what you told me about the way through the jungle."

Mabi said:

"I told Mhendi the old people up in the mountains say there's a way through the jungle. They're quite sure of it."

"Well?" Udomo said.

"Don't you see . . . ?" Mhendi tried to suppress his excitement.

"No," Udomo said.

"Pluralia is on the other side of the jungle," Mabi said.

There was a long moment of silence. Then Udomo nodded in the dark.

"Yes," he murmured softly. "Yes, I see. But are you sure?"

"The old people won't say it without reason," Mabi said.

"You'd have to win freedom first," Mhendi said. "Only then will there be a way back for me. D'you see that, Mike?"

"Yes," Udomo said. "Yes, I see. . . ."

"It's my only hope," Mhendi said.

Udomo felt for Mhendi's shoulder, gripped it.

"We'll fight for it to come true, brother."

"My only hope . . ." Mhendi repeated.

Udomo tightened his grip on Mhendi's shoulder. They were silent for a long while. Then Udomo stood up.

"I promise you, brother," he whispered.

Then he went back to the big bedroom.

PART TWO

THE REALITY

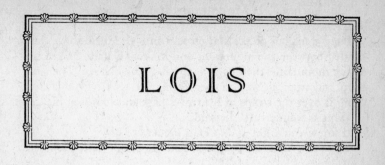

LOIS

The train from Paris came to a stop. Lois shaded her eyes against the glare of the Mediterranean sun. People began to spill out of the carriages. She decided to be calm: no rushing about among the passengers. He would come and she would be there, waiting. No need to rush. She stood back from the other people: she looked up and down the line of carriages, dismissing each face that was not his. He would come and she would be there, waiting. A nerve point in her neck began to throb. She realised how desperately she had come to care for him in the past five months: there was something impersonal about the realisation, as though it were connected with some-one else, not herself. He would come. He would come. Yes, he would come and she would be there, waiting. She put her hand to her neck to try and still the throbbing. He would . . .

There he was!

"Michael!"

And then she found herself running to him. She forced her-self to slow down to walking pace. She had shouted! Like a silly, empty-headed, lovesick kid!

"Lois!"

He came to her. She had a blurred impression of great size, bright eyes, a huge smile and flashing white teeth. Then she grabbed at him and buried her face in his shoulder.

"Oh, Michael. . . . My dear, my dear."

"Hello, Lois."

They went out of the station and into the little town that nestled between the mountains and the sea. Udomo looked up at the mountains, then back at the flat glasslike sea. The sun, hard and tropical, was on everything. He took off his jacket, flung it over the straps of his travel bag, and loosened his tie.

"This is wonderful!" he said.

"I knew you'd like it. . . . Had breakfast?"

"At those first-class prices! You shouldn't have done it, Lois."

"It was the only way I could get you here, so I bought the ticket and posted it to you."

"But all that money."

"What's the good of having money if you don't spend it? You can't take the stuff with you. And I did so want to do this, so please don't nag."

"You're no good!"

"Then I'm no good! Come, there's a café. Careful of that car. They drive on the wrong side of the roads here."

They crossed and sat at a little pavement table under a huge multi-coloured umbrella. Lois ordered a breakfast of fruit and coffee.

The sun and air had turned Lois a golden colour, had given her skin a glowing freshness. And, freed now of the need to dress for warmth, she had on a gay cotton dress that fitted tightly down to the waist and flowed out into a full skirt.

"You are lovely," he said.

"I'm glad. . . . Now stop looking at me like that, Michael. It makes me feel like a silly girl and I'm liable to kiss you or burst out bawling in public."

"I wouldn't care."

"Well, I would. Don't you forget I'm an inhibited English-woman."

"You're a lovely one."

"Stop it, Michael!"

She reached across the table and gripped his hand. The grand-daddy of an old waiter who spoke French with a heavy Italian accent beamed at them.

They walked through the town after breakfast, climbing the sloping land in the direction of the mountains. Soon they left the tourist section, the sea-front hotels, behind them. The town proper was no more than an overgrown peasant village. Sea-front ostentation gave way to peasant poverty. The people here were lean and dark. They moved and talked with a freedom that reminded Udomo of home.

"It is like home," he said. "At home the sun is like this, only hotter; and the people are like these, only more so."

"I'll visit you one day," Lois said.

"You'll love them," he said.

Restraint left her here. She took his hand. They climbed the sloping land hand-in-hand. At last they were clear of the town, above it. Beads of sweat glistened on Udomo's brow. His shirt clung damply to his body. Lois went down on a patch of grass beside the track that wound up to the mountains in one direction, and down to the town in the other.

"Halfway house," she said.

Udomo flopped down beside her and mopped his brow.

"Wheee! It's hot! I'm sweating like a pig! Why aren't you?"

"I'm used to it. I grew up in it."

"But I was born in Africa!"

"Your sun is different from mine. Mine is a crisp, dry sun. Yours is a damp, sticky sun. You're used to the one, I to the other."

He grinned and began to reach for her. But the sound of voices stopped him. Down the track came two peasants leading a line of loaded asses. They called out greetings as they passed.

Far away at sea, a long ship seemed motionless till it suddenly dipped behind the skyline of the sea. And all that immensity of living water slept placidly in the morning sun. No white spray of breaking waves showed anywhere along the coastline.

"Time to move." Lois jumped up.

On either side of the track the land was terraced. Vines grew on these terraces; miles and miles of vines going up and sideways.

They came to a dip in the steep slope of the land. A smaller track cut across the large track up to the mountains. They turned right along it.

"There it is," Lois said.

The cottage stood in a large fenced-off piece of flat land. There were neglected fruit trees, an overgrown stretch of lawn at the side of the house, the remains of what had once been a child's swing; and in front of the house weeds had claimed what had once been a rock-garden.

Lois hurried on and opened the door. She stepped just inside the door, then turned and faced Udomo. Her face, suddenly, was that of a child.

"Welcome to my inheritance, Michael!"

He dropped his bag, stepped across the threshold, and folded her in his arms. She looked up after a while and her eyes were wet.

"You do do the right things, Michael."

"It's important to you, this?"

"It's my dearest possession on earth."

He ran his hand through her hair, grown long now.

"Say you love me," she said.

"I love you," he said.

"Oh, my dear. . . ."

They lay side by side on the soft grass at the side of the house. The sun had lost its fierce metallic hardness and rested on the edge of the western end of the immensity of water. Only the highest mountains, it seemed, now caught the full glare of it. They were the only areas of light in the slowly darkening land.

Lois had found a rusted old scythe and Udomo had, after a long sleep, used it with skill. Now where they lay had the appearance of a cared-for though yellow lawn.

Thin, short-tailed young lizards darted up and down and sideways and round on the wall of the house. The puffy, long-tailed oldsters sunned themselves more placidly; only moved to shoot out their tongues and capture some foolish insect that had ventured too near.

"Listen," Lois murmured.

The din of the creatures of the grass grew in intensity with every moment of approaching darkness. A dark shadow crept slowly up the side of the mountains, blotting out the light.

"It's like home," Udomo grunted lazily.

She rolled over, raised herself on her elbows and looked into his upturned face.

"It *is* home, Michael. Oh, if only we could spend all our days here!"

He opened his eyes. She saw the warning in them.

"Don't put up the shutters, Michael."

"You know I must go back."

"There is no must about it."

"I must. You know that."

"Yes. But let me dream without putting up your shutters. It *would* be wonderful to spend all our days here. Let me dream. I know you will go after your dream of liberation, but let me dream this might be home for us forever."

The shadow had reached the lower mountain peaks. Only the rim of the sun still showed beyond the edge of the sea. The clear blue of the sky took on huge tinges of darkness. The din of the creatures increased.

"You speak like a woman now."

"Oh, darling, I am a woman! Very much a woman. More woman than I like. So let me be, let me dream, and I know it's a true dream that we could be happy here." A tinge of bitterness crept into her voice. "But I also know that you would grow restless for that other dream of yours. I wouldn't want you here then, Michael. For then there would be no real happiness."

His eyes shifted from her face to the darkening sky.

"Lois. . . ."

She felt that his range of thought had taken him away from her. This was the way he looked when he thought about his great dream. That abstracted touch to his voice was part of it.

"Yes?"

"I was thinking . . . Perhaps . . . If things go as we plan . . . When we've won our freedom . . . I was thinking you would come to me then, perhaps . . ." His eyes shifted back to her face.

We are close now, she thought: closer than human bodies can ever be: as close as only human spirits can get in rare moments. She didn't know what to say.

"What am I to say, Michael?"

"Just yes."

"Yes, Michael, yes."

"Shall I tell you about our Congress? It was a greater success than we hoped for."

"No," she said firmly. "These days are mine, all mine, and I'm not going to listen to one word of politics. We'll swim, we'll go down into the town, up into the mountains, we'll clean up this place—but we won't talk politics. Your secretary has resigned until we get back. Agreed?"

"All right."

"I want your promise."

"I promise. . . . Just one thing. Mabi told me to tell you he's coming here for the week-end we go back."

"Fine. . . . Now, what shall we do tonight? We can go down

86

into the town and dine at one of the hotels, or we can visit some friends of mine, or hire a motorboat and sail along the coast to the real tourist centres with their millionaires, film-stars and gambling hells. What's it to be?"

He reached up, grabbed a fistful of her hair and pulled her face down on to his chest.

"Let's stay just where we are."

"The right answer again, Michael! But listen to the mosquitoes. They'll feast on us."

"Then we'll stay indoors. . . . Oh, damn!" He smacked at his forehead.

Her peals of laughter stopped abruptly. She smacked at her neck. They hurried into the house. Darkness and the creatures of the night took possession of the world.

"Glad you came?"

He turned from lighting the lamp.

"Very glad. Now come here."

She saw the sudden kindling of desire in his eyes. She went to him.

"Me too," she said softly.

The moonrays filtered in through the windows and bathed the room in soft light.

"Asleep, Michael?"

"No."

"Must have made our supper too rich."

"It was very good."

The mosquitoes sang angrily just beyond the net that covered the bed.

"Tell me about your people. Your mother still alive?"

"Yes."

"And your father?"

"He died since I left. Not very long ago."

"Then your mother's alone now, or are there other children?"

87

"There are the other women. My mother was my father's third wife. I was her only child. My father had a small farm but the son of the first wife has that. It is like that with us."

"You hear from your mother?"

"She can't read or write. I was only the second boy from our village who went to the mission school. It was a very small village and they were all simple and ignorant people. . . ."

His voice drowsed off so she let him be. The moonrays reached his face. She raised herself and lay watching him far into the night. Then she put her hand to his cheek and fell asleep.

2

Mabi made a funnel of his hands and shouted out to sea:

"Lois! Mike!"

They were a long way off, only their heads bobbed above the sea. He shouted again, louder. Lois raised her arm to signal they had heard. They began to swim landward.

Mabi walked back from the edge of the sea to the rug in the shade of the huge boulder where they had left their clothes and food basket. He took off his shirt and lay on the rug. The morning sun was gently warm. A slight breeze fanned his body. He shut his eyes and studied the red haze of blood that flowed through the skin over his closed eyes. The little floating specks seemed very lively. Would they be white or red corpuscles? And was there a Paul Mabi among them? And a Lois Barlow? And a Michael Udomo? Was his body just another universe for another form of life? What, anyway, is blood? God, he was tired. No joke travelling from Paris sitting upright. Even those damned cushions began to feel like rocks. He heard their voices, opened his eyes unwillingly and sat up. He looked up and down the beach. Only a few kids a long way away. Then he looked at them.

They came to him hand-in-hand, shining in the sun and

dripping water. Udomo's deep brown had turned a glowing black; and Lois was a radiant golden coppery brown. He thought: The lovers. Catch them like that, pour it into wood that would last a hundred years and call it 'The Lovers'. It would have to be a black wood and a pale golden-brown wood. But how would the hands be married? That would present a problem.

"Hello, Paul!" Lois called.

"We were at the station Friday and Saturday," Udomo said.

"But you didn't come," Lois said. "So we gave you up."

"So you're still in love after ten days alone."

"Oh, Paul! You're not in *that* mood! It's such a lovely day and it's so nice to see you." Her eyes glowed with happiness.

Udomo towelled himself vigorously.

"Doing that damned train journey upright's enough to make anybody sour. And then I climbed all that way only to find that you weren't at the house. What time d'you get up?"

"Had breakfast?" Lois said and began to unpack the basket.

"We really didn't expect you today, man," Udomo said. "You know we are travelling back tonight."

"You didn't either of you answer my question."

"What question?" Lois said.

"I asked if you were still in love after ten days alone."

"I thought you made a statement."

"All right. Comment on it, then."

"You're being difficult, Paul. Here, have some food."

Mabi laughed suddenly, without humour.

"Yes, I am being difficult. You both looked so happy coming out of the water, it made me realise how alone I am. Sorry."

"Oh, Paul." Lois brushed her cheek against his. "There are all those girls of yours. And most of them very nice."

"Forget it. But seriously, it's good to see you both. Now I'll tell you why I came. I'm going up that mountain. I may not have another chance to do it, and I do want to see that village again."

"What village?" Udomo said.

"Didn't you tell him?"

"I thought I did," Lois said. "Didn't I?"

"No."

Mabi saw the tender look that crept into her eyes when she looked at Udomo, and the response in his eyes. He pointed up to the centremost of the row of mountain peaks.

"There's a Saracen village up there. It dates back to the days before the crusades, when the Mohammedans invaded and conquered southern Europe. One day there'll be a hall in Africa which I hope will be called the Africa Museum. In it, I hope, will be found the whole record—in books, painting, sculpture, music and all forms of craft work—of African achievement. And on the walls of that hall I hope to do some murals, of which this Saracen village will form a small part. That's why I want to see it again."

"We'll come along," Udomo said.

"Then we'd better get back to the house," Lois said. "But will you make it, Paul? You're awfully tired. You should've come a day earlier."

"Those Paris cafés have a strong hold," Mabi said. "There was a lovely girl with green eyes and hair like straw called Monime. . . ."

"And then you complain about being alone," Lois laughed.

"You ought to know one can be alone even in bed with someone. Still, it was lovely while it lasted and I expect I'd much rather have it so. Remember this?

> *Come fill the Cup, and in the Fire of Spring*
> *The winter-garment of Repentance fling:*
> *The bird of Time has but a little way*
> *To flutter—and the Bird is on the Wing."*

A line of fleecy clouds drifted across the sky. And all the world seemed calm.

"Yes," Lois said. "But I prefer another quatrain, perhaps because it echoes my heart; but then, don't we always do that? My heart responds to

> *Here with a Loaf of Bread beneath the bough,*
> *A Flask of Wine, a Book of Verse—and Thou*
> *Beside me singing in the Wilderness—*
> *And Wilderness is Paradise enow."*

She shifted her eyes from Udomo's face to Mabi's.

"That's my mood and my prayer," she said quietly.

Mabi stared away to sea. Udomo watched Lois.

"You make me feel an intruder," Mabi said softly.

"No, my dear. I'm just being a woman, and honest."

"Just at this moment I envy you very much, Mike," Mabi said.

Udomo grinned.

"You had all the time in the world."

"Yes. And I didn't take it."

"And you wouldn't," Lois said. "Even if you had it all over again. You're afraid of ties, that's your trouble, Paul."

"Not in the way you mean," Mabi murmured.

Lois stared at him and something of his mood reached her. She got up suddenly.

"We'd better go if you want to climb that mountain to-day."

Mabi stopped halfway up the mountain. Sweat ran down his body in tiny streams. Lois climbed to where he waited. Udomo followed.

Mabi mopped his face and squeezed out the damp handkerchief.

"What about a drink?"

Udomo slipped the knapsack from his back and passed it to Lois.

"Water and wine or water?" Lois asked.

"Water and wine."

"Michael?"

"An orange, please."

She gave Mabi a Thermos flask and rolled two oranges against the rock on which they sat. All about, all they could see, were the soaring mountains of the Maritime Alps, fading away, in the distance, into the misty blue of the bright sky.

"I hate mountains," Mabi said.

"Men climb them," Lois said.

"They're a challenge," Udomo said.

Lois laughed. A hint of mockery crept into her eyes, played about her lips. She took Udomo's hand. She said:

"Man is forever trying to escape his instability through conquest. It is self-knowledge that compels him to climb mountains, to want to conquer space and travel to the moon. It is all an expression of his desire to escape himself and his basic instability. He hasn't made peace with himself and until he does he will go on making revolutions, climbing mountains, flying to the moon and exploding huge bombs. . . ."

"What of woman?" Mabi said.

"She's made peace with herself. You have the odd woman with her eyes on the moon. But on the whole we are reconciled to our earthbound fate. For us the pattern is in tune with the seasons of the earth. Perhaps it is because we reproduce the pattern of the evolving earth in our own bodies. Whatever it is, we hanker less after immortality. We don't climb mountains, we don't dream of journeys to the moon and further, we don't explode bombs. Instead, our energies go into the making and nurturing of human life. It must be that we are basically freer than men, for it is only the unfree who hanker after freedom from this or freedom for that. The free do not have to prove their freedom; the strong do not have to prove their strength. . . ."

"We'd better go on," Mabi said.

He pushed the flask into Lois' hand and set off again at a brisk pace up the narrow, winding mountain track that grew more difficult as it went up. They scrambled up after him.

The track began to narrow as they climbed, the incline to grow steeper. Soon the track grew too narrow for them to walk side by side. Udomo fell in behind her. And Mabi, a long way ahead, scrambled up as though in great haste.

Mabi was getting farther away from them. Lois moved faster, her feet slithering over pebbles now. But she felt safe; Michael was behind her and she knew the measure of his strength. He would see that no harm came to her. A woman is not whole until she has a man and the protection of a man. Never whole.

Mabi stopped and looked back. Then he went on, out of sight round the curve of the mountain. She thought: He's in the sun now and it will do him good. Behind her, Udomo climbed with a sure-footed steadiness that filled her with comfort. There was a gentle throbbing at her temples: but Michael was behind her and all was well. She felt both cold and sticky with sweat; but Michael was there. They moved into the area of sun where Mabi had paused. The sea now lay far below them to the left. Looking down, she grew dizzy. She stopped and shut her eyes. Then Udomo's hand was on her shoulder and she was all right. She turned her head, touched her lips to his hand and went on.

"Don't look down," he said.

"I'm all right," she said.

The top was in sight now. Mabi leaned over the rough rock parapet and called down:

"Come on!"

He watched them for a while, then disappeared from sight.

At last they reached the top. Mabi sat in the sun with his back against the ruins of what had once been the walls of a room.

Lois staggered wearily to where Mabi sat. Udomo shook the knapsack off his back and surveyed what had once been a Saracen village.

"But this is so small," he said. "Why did they come up here?"

"To avoid being attacked in the dark. They were invaders, don't forget," Mabi said.

Udomo shook his head and laughed. He walked about among the ruins.

"It's hard to believe. How many were there?"

"Nobody knows," Lois said. "They probably camped on the mountains in groups of twenty."

"With their horses?"

"Yes."

"God, they must have been crowded! And horses coming up that track!"

"Don't forget they were the invaders," Mabi said again.

"We should've driven our invaders into the mountains," Udomo said.

"And this is all that's left of them," Mabi said dreamily. "Just ruins on a mountain top. The invaders came and the invaders went. And this is all."

"Not quite all," Lois said. "Something of the invaders remains in the dark colour and temperament of the mountain people. And you'll find it in their music too."

"Yes," Mabi said slowly. "But of their physical conquest only these sun-bleached ruins remain."

"But still, they conquered once," Udomo said.

"And what is the worth of that conquest?" Lois said.

"It is proof that men lived and had spirit," Udomo said. "It is proof that they were men, and because they were men they had to act."

Mabi looked up at Udomo and thought: Up here that power he has seems to leave him. He's ordinary up here. Mabi began to fill his pipe. Lois reached for the knapsack and brought out fruit and food and drink. They all seemed unaware of the burning sun.

"And this," Mabi said dreamily, "is the proof of their action. These bleaching stones. And perhaps there were some human and animal bones here too that are now bleached to dust and pebbles. Remember this, Lois?

> *And now they wait and whiten peaceably,*
> *Those conquerors, those poets, those so fair:*
> *They know time comes, not only you and I,*
> *But the whole world shall whiten, here or there;*
> *When the great markets by the sea shut fast*
> *All that calm Sunday that goes on and on;*
> *When even lovers find their peace at last,*
> *And earth is but a star, that once had shone.*

These are the relics of a former conqueror. What's the point of it all?"

"Simply that you're alive, Paul," Lois said. "Alive and caught up in it."

"As in a game children play. . . ."

"Yes, my dear. As in a game children play. There is no immortality. That is why—I don't mind your knowing, Paul— that is why I offered Michael present fulfilment. I would like him to stay here with me. I know we could be happy: we could have children and a good life for as long as we have life. This seems truer and more real to me than your dreams of liberation. If I thought for one second the realisation of your dreams would really change the world I would not dare to ask this of him. But I know . . . Oh, never mind. . . ."

Udomo came to her then. He sat down beside her and put his arm about her body.

"It is not a dream," he said. "Or, if it is, it is more real to me than what you call reality. I never had a chance to read poetry, like you and Mabi, but I know it is beautiful for both of you. Well, for me the freedom of my people and the dream of that freedom is as beautiful. I know you think I think of nothing but politics. But it's not really politics. It's my people, Lois. That is my poetry."

Lois freed herself from his embrace, got up and walked to the parapet.

"And I'm caught between you," Mabi said.

Lois leaned against the parapet and stared down at the green earth far below. Beyond the earth was the sea, looking black from this height. She thought: Odd how without pride I am now.

Mabi looked from Lois to Udomo. I was wrong, he thought. Even up here he seems larger than other men, surer than other men.

Lois turned and came back to them.

"All right, Michael. I have you here and now. This is present fulfilment. I'll not try to stop you when the time comes for you to go."

She sat down beside him. He fondled her hand.

"It's what is in our hearts that's important," Udomo said. "One day you will come to us, to me. If I go it will not mean that I'm going from you for good. You will come to me. We agreed."

"But you may fail, Michael. You may get killed."

"We will not fail," Udomo said.

"No," Mabi said. "I don't think we'll fail—now."

"And you may change," Lois said. "I want this undefiled or not at all. I want it clean. It is the cleanest thing I ever had."

"That's why I fear you women," Mabi said. "You turn men into gods and build your lives on them and I am much too weak for that."

"I will not change," Udomo said.

"That's not what she means, Mike!" Mabi snapped impatiently.

"We'd better eat and move," Lois said. "Else we won't get down in time."

"Lois," Mabi said softly, "even Mike is only a man."

"Go on and eat," Lois said. She leaned against Udomo.

3

It was a bleak and frosty September evening, a week after their return from the south, that Adebhoy left for Panafrica. They all went to the station to see him off—Lois, Jo Furse Lanwood, Mhendi, Mabi, Udomo. Udomo carried a parcel of a hundred copies of the latest issue of *The Liberator*, their stencilled magazine, for Adebhoy to take with him. They clustered around him as the minutes to departure ticked away. And Adebhoy's face was wreathed in a permanent, happy grin.

"Don't forget you're our John the Baptist," Lanwood said. "Prepare the way well for our coming."

"Take care," Lois said.

"And write sometime," Jo Furse said.

"Thanks for the good times, Jo," Adebhoy said. "You women took care of us, and you took care of me. Thanks. And you too, Lois, thanks. Take care of my home-boy."

They were all a little drunk, even Lanwood and Udomo. They had drunk two bottles of champagne.

"Prepare a home for me," Mhendi said. "And put a sweet simple woman in it."

"I will, brother, I will!"

"Mind the doors!" the guard's voice echoed.

Adebhoy turned to Udomo, and now the grin was gone. His eyes were cold and serious.

"Well, home-boy . . ."

"Yes," Udomo said. "Remember I'm waiting."

They clasped hands. Udomo felt Adebhoy's free hand push something into his pocket.

"You'll need it more than me, home-boy."

"It's the other that's important."

"I won't forget, home-boy. I won't fail you."

The guard hurried down the platform shutting doors.

"Oh, Dick . . ." Jo Furse spoke as though she had just realised he was really leaving. She hugged him impulsively, then turned away.

Adebhoy shook them each by the hand.

"Hurry up!" the guard shouted and blew his whistle.

Adebhoy got in. The train began to move.

That's how he'll go, Lois told herself. And then she knew Mabi was beside her, watching her intently.

"That's how he'll go," she whispered.

"That's how we'll all go. We belong to Africa, not Africa to us."

Adebhoy reached the window and poked his head out.

"We depend on you!" There was passion in Udomo's shout.

Adebhoy nodded silently and waved. He waved till they could not see his white handkerchief any more.

"This is the beginning," Lanwood said.

Udomo pushed his hand into his pocket and felt the wad of pound notes Adebhoy had put there.

"Yes," he said. "This is the beginning. Let's go."

Lois pushed her arm through his as they left the station.

Udomo moved his things into Lois' flat that night.

A month later Jo Furse lost her job.

She came into the sitting-room in her dressing-gown the first morning of her unemployment. Udomo had turned the corner near the french windows into his study. He now sat reading Adebhoy's first letter.

"Hello, Mike. Had breakfast?"

He looked up briefly.

"Hours ago; with Lois."

"I'm going to sleep late a few days. God, it's good to be free of jobs! Don't think I'll even try to get one this week. Like some coffee?"

"Please."

She went to make it.

Nothing much in this letter, Udomo decided with disappointment. But really, Adebhoy had only just arrived. It was unfair to expect any more than news of his arrival. Still. . . .

He pushed the letter aside and turned his attention to the copy for the next issue of *The Liberator*. If only they could have it printed. Cutting those damned stencils took all his and Lois' time. Still, that would come. He worked steadily till Jo Furse came in carrying a tray with coffee and her breakfast on it.

"Oooo! What luxury!" she exclaimed.

She put the tray on a stool, heaped cushions on the floor and sat on them, leaning her back against the french windows. Her long corn-coloured hair tumbled all over her face and shoulders. Her dressing-gown fell open, revealing one thigh.

"This is the life for me! Wish this had happened while you were down in the south. I'd have joined you. God, how I need the sun!"

Udomo raised his eyes from the papers and looked at her, at the long slender naked thigh.

"You ought to get dressed."

She roared with laughter.

"Oh, Mike! Don't pretend to be prissy with me."

"I have work to do."

"And I distract you?" She sounded happy.

"Yes," he said coldly.

"Don't you like me?"

"I like you but I have work to do. You can help me if you like."

"Oh, not today!"

"Then go away and let me work."

She studied him from under lowered eyebrows.

He turned back to his work. But his concentration, now, had grown weaker.

"Michael. That's what Lois calls you, Michael. And she makes it sound as though she's singing a song. Michael."

He raised his eyes and tried to keep them away from her thigh, but they would stray there.

"If you don't let me work now I'll tell Lois when she returns."

"Big strong Michael will tell Lois," she mocked. "All right then. Tell her! What will you tell her? That if sex weren't in your mind it wouldn't have come into mine? That's true, you know."

"Would you betray your friend?"

"And you, Mike, would you betray your mistress who adores the earth you stand on?"

She rose. Watching her, Udomo grew drunk with the thought of her thigh, now concealed, with the thought of her tumbling corn-coloured hair, her youth. She picked up the tray and went to the door.

"Jo. . . ." He felt his body tremble.

She turned.

"What do you want?"

"Lois is your friend."

"And your mistress."

"That is not a nice thing to say."

"It is the truth."

"She's a good person."

"Yes. I'm going."

He got up and moved to her.

"It's too late."

"I know it's too late. You've already betrayed her."

"Why did you do this?"

"Because I'm a woman; because I'm young; because I'm jealous of all the love all of you give her; because it's good to know I can do it, and because of you. . . ."

He touched her and felt the violent trembling of her body. His began to tremble too. He put his arm about her. Then he took the tray from her and put it on the chair. She sighed, opened the door and led the way to her room. In her eyes was a look compounded of triumph and despair. She entered her room. She turned to him, raised her eyes to his, and, suddenly, a terrible fear assailed her. . . .

They were both typing steadily when Lois came home from school.

"God! Those brats were difficult today. How are you, Michael?" She leaned down and kissed him on the cheek.

"I'll go'n make tea," Jo Furse said.

Udomo got up and stretched.

"Let's go and see Mabi tonight. I've done enough work."

"Can't, my dear. I've a tremendous amount of homework. But you go. Paul will be glad to see you." She wandered over to the desk. "Ah, a letter from Adebhoy. What's he say?"

"Nothing much; read it. It's about his arrival."

Lois realised her fingers were trembling as she picked up the letter. One day, she knew, a letter would come and then he would get ready and leave. But it would take time. Might even take a year or more. Yes! . . . She hugged the thought about her, like a blanket of comfort, till the trembling of her fingers ceased. She turned to him with new tenderness.

"You look tired, Michael."

"I've worked hard."

"Glad Jo helped."

"Trouble is she talks too much."

"She's young. Be patient."

"Oh, she's all right."

Jo Furse returned with the tea.

"You look as tired as Michael, Jo. Have you two been in all day?"

"Yes." Jo Furse did not look at her.

Vaguely, Lois noticed a new subduedness in Jo.

"You'd better go with Michael to Paul's. Go round by the

Heath. You both need fresh air. I'll have supper ready when you return."

"I'd rather stay with you," Jo said quickly. Her eyes touched Lois' face, then slid away. She felt a sudden need to explain. "I want to get my clothes ready. I think I'll go over to Paris for a few days."

"Go on. The air will do you good."

Jo cast about for some other excuse. But none came to mind. The thought of going to Mabi's terrified her. Mabi would turn his big cold eyes on her and he would know. And then what? No, it wasn't Mabi, it was Udomo she feared. Or was it? Oh God! She became aware of Udomo watching her. She began to tremble. Udomo rose and put down his cup.

"Off you go," Lois said. "I'll have supper ready for nine. Try not to be too late, and give Paul my love."

Jo Furse rose unwillingly, got her coat, and followed Udomo out into the chilly early evening.

In bed, later that night, Jo Furse found sleep a long time coming. . . . Paul hadn't noticed anything. There'd been some other people and he hadn't noticed anything. And Udomo? She couldn't think of him as Mike any more. Udomo. Udomo. Udomo. Yes, she'd go to Paris early in the morning. All he'd said while they walked across the Heath was that he was sorry she wouldn't be here to help him with his work. She'd do anything if only he didn't make her feel so filthy. Made her feel she was dirt. And Lois didn't know and couldn't see. Didn't know and couldn't see. And yet she loved him. Filthy dirt. An easy man to love. Some children have mothers. I never had one. If I had a mother now I would kneel in front of her and put my head on her lap and tell her all my troubles. Some children have mothers. I only had a father who married another woman who made me want to leave home as soon as I could. A filthy dirty little tart, his eyes say. Oh God! Is it wrong to want to be loved? You give because you want and all you get is a filthy dirty little tart in his eyes. Dear Mother whom I never knew . . .

"Oh God!"

She flung the bedclothes back. She put on her dressing-gown and went to the bathroom. The house was deadly still. No light showed under *their* door. She felt for the medicine chest in the dark. No need for the light. Her fingers groped till she found the bottle of Veganin. But now she needed the light. She turned it on. She filled a tumbler of water, placed two Veganins on her tongue, and drank the water. That, she decided, should make her sleep; a long, deep sleep. She went back to her room and got into bed. The bottle had grown cold so she threw it out. She hugged the blankets round her ears and shut her eyes. But still, for a long time, sleep would not come.

In the other room, Lois lay thinking. There'd been something wrong about their loving this evening. Was he growing cold? Had she been clumsy? It had never been as laboured before.

"Michael. . . ."

He's asleep. Better let him sleep. Must be that he was over-tired. This is a delicate thing, to be watched, to be handled with great care. Not like a glass of water. They would have to get over this awkwardness of not talking about it, or they might mess things up. Just now there was the danger that if one thought the other wanted it the one who thought so might force himself or herself, though really unwilling. This desire always to please the loved one is one of the great dangers of loving, especially in the early phases. We must talk about this, my dear. She turned on her side, adjusted her head and closed her eyes. . . .

Jo Furse awoke with a start.

Udomo's head seemed up near the ceiling. He flung the bedclothes from her and stood looking down with his hands deep in the dressing-gown pockets. Fleetingly, as something vague and far away, she recalled going with Lois one Saturday afternoon to buy the dressing-gown . . . Lois!

"Lois!" she murmured.

"She's gone. It's late. Nearly ten." He sounded bitter.

He undid his dressing-gown. The thought of protest crossed her mind. But then she was caught up in waves of excitement. Be kind, please. She said it out loud:

"Be kind to me, please, Michael."

She moved to make room for him. And only she was trembling now.

4

Udomo raised his head and listened. Had he heard something at the door? There was no sound, no one was opening the door. But there had been a sound. He pushed back his chair, got up and walked briskly out of the room. Yes, there had been a sound. The postman had been. He recognised the greenish-blue air letter that lay on the mat. It was from Adebhoy. He curbed his sudden excitement. It might be like all the others. For three months now each greenish-blue letter that came had filled him with hopeful excitement; and each time it had been the old story. Not yet. Not yet. Had he been wrong about Adebhoy? No; no. These things take time. But Christ! why so much time! Anyway, don't be excited. It would be like all the others. Like all the others.

He stared at the letter. If only . . . He bent down and picked it up. He went back to the room with it, out of the coldness of the passage. God, how cold it is! Not even the full heat of the gasfire really defeated the cold. He walked round the desk and stared out of the french windows. Outside, huge snow-flakes wafted down with lazy ease. They seemed to settle delicately on the earth. Certainly, they did not fall. And the earth lay covered in a blanket of white, light as whipped cream.

He turned his eyes from the wafting snow and tore the letter open.

"Dear Home-boy,

"This one will be very brief for I must go and operate in half an hour. It is just to tell you that things are really moving at last. I'm having a conference with three merchants next week and I think something will come of it. They have the money to put into a paper and I will persuade them that it is in their interest to do so.

"I know how strongly you feel that we must get the co-operation of the chiefs and elders. But they will not co-operate. I've tried to persuade them for three months now but they're only interested in their own positions and their seats in legco and being invited to the Governor's parties. They're no good, home-boy, so we've got to do without them. We might never start anything if we wait for them. They have no interest in freedom for the people or our country. They are corrupt. If I can persuade these three merchants they will give the money and you can come and we can make a start. I hope you will agree with me that this is the best plan because I can see no other way to get you home. Write to say you approve. . . ."

The rest was personal: messages to Lanwood and the others and a little about his life. Write and say you approve. . . . Udomo read it again. Write and say you approve.

"Damn those chiefs and elders!" Udomo shouted.

He went to his desk and sat down. So they wouldn't co-operate. Not even for the freedom of their own country. Well, if they wouldn't and the merchants would, then it is with the merchants we must deal. But the *people*, would they follow without the chiefs and elders? Would they? But if there's no other way. . . . The people would have to be won from the chiefs and elders. That's the way.

Udomo found a blank air-letter form and slipped it into the typewriter. He thought for a while, then pulled out the form, slipped a carbon and a sheet of blank paper underneath the form and put it back. He wrote:

"Dear Dick,

"Your letter has just arrived and I am replying straight away so that you can carry on. You know why I think it is important for us to have the chiefs and elders with us at this stage, but if they will not join with us then we must carry on without them. This will be difficult as the people are in their hands. But we will find a way of getting the people. Try and get your merchants to pay my passage home. Tell them we can discuss and plan everything when I'm there. But it is important for you not to make them any serious promises if you can help it. You know what I mean. Promise them positions like the patron or president or even treasurer of the party when it is formed, but don't promise them anything on policy. Tell them it's best to talk about such things to me when I'm out there. I will inform the group here, but you carry on and . . ."

The flat door banged shut.

Udomo sat back and waited. Rather early for Lois, he thought. And then, suddenly, he wondered what would happen if she lost her job. Did teachers ever lose their jobs?

Jo Furse came in.

"You're early," Udomo said.

She moved to a chair and sank wearily into it.

"Anything the matter?" he said.

She raised her eyes to his face. He saw the dark misery in her eyes then. Her face was drawn, thin and haggard. He'd been aware that she'd grown thin these past months, but it was only now that he saw how thin.

"You must help me, Michael," she said.

The despair in her voice compelled his attention.

"What's the matter?"

"I was sick at the office," she said. "At the office this time.

I've tried everything on my own. Now you must help me. I tried to do it by myself. I didn't want to bother you. But it's no good. You must help me, Michael."

"What are you talking about?"

"I'm pregnant."

It was a long time before Udomo said:

"No!"

"I tried to get rid of it by myself."

He bounded across the room and towered over her.

"No!" His voice rose to a shout. "You lie!"

He stared into her eyes and knew it was true. He fought down a wild impulse to strike her.

"Why didn't you tell me before?"

"I tried to get rid of it by myself."

He went back to his desk.

"How long is it?"

"Nearly three months."

Rage and fear, intermingled, possessed him.

"You damned fool! You bloody fool! You should have told me!"

"I knew you'd curse me. That's why I tried by myself."

I must be calm, he thought: I must think clearly.

"Who knows?"

"Nobody."

"You've not seen your doctor?"

"No."

"You've told nobody?"

"No."

"What would you say if Lois found out?"

"She mustn't."

"What would you say if she did?"

"I don't know."

"You must know!"

"What do you want me to say?"

"It's somebody else."

"She'd know, Michael. It would be a coloured child and it would be your child. She'd know."

"Only if there's a child. But there won't be."

"Then why . . . ?"

"She might find out you're getting rid of a child or have got rid of one. You'd have to explain then."

"Tell her the truth, Michael. Ask her to help us. She'll forgive you if you're honest with her and ask her to. She loves you, Michael!"

"You should've thought of that the morning you showed me your thigh and invited me. Shut up, damn you! You said you could take care of yourself. . . . It's somebody else. Understand?"

"Haven't I paid enough, Michael?"

"It's somebody else. Understand?"

"Yes. I understand."

"Now leave me. I want to think."

Jo Furse went to the door. She hesitated there, then turned and looked at Udomo.

"Michael. . . ." She thought: I used to call him Mike.

"Yes . . . ?"

"Have you no pity for me and the hell I'm going through?"

Udomo watched her for a while, coldly. Then his face relaxed. The hardness went out of his eyes. He rose and went to her. His face softened, a smile of sympathy curled the corners of his mouth. He put his arm about her shoulders.

"I'm sorry, Jo. I didn't mean to be harsh. But this is frightening. It came as a shock. That's all. We'll get rid of it and you'll be all right, I promise you."

"And Lois mustn't know, Michael. You're right about that. She's been so good to both of us. And she loves you so much. You really think it will be all right? It's not too late?"

"Everything will be all right if you do as I tell you. And remember, if Lois does find out afterwards, somebody else was responsible. If you think about it you'll see that's best for all of us."

"I'm terribly ashamed, Michael. Nobody in the world has been as good to me as Lois."

"A good reason why she shouldn't know. Now I must think about the best person to help us."

She left him then, more comforted than she had felt for a long time.

The look of sympathy fell from Udomo's face as the door shut. He went back to his desk, closed his eyes. He thought of all the African medical students he knew in London. And as he thought, each one passed vividly before his mind's eye. He examined each with a cool critical detachment; he saw each face clearly, the kind of person each was, the degree of loyalty each would give, the reliability of each. At last he opened his eyes. He reached down under his desk and pulled out a card-index box. He took out a card from behind the letter T. He smiled without humour. He slipped the card into his pocket, put the box back and rose. He went into the bedroom. He wrapped two woollen scarves round his neck and put on the dufflecoat. He heard Jo Furse in the kitchen. He went there.

"I've found our man. I'm going to see him now. I'll try and get him here tomorrow. You'd better get to bed before Lois comes. Say you're ill. And don't go to work tomorrow."

"Will it be all right?"

"If you do as I tell you."

He pulled the hood over his head and went out into the wafting snow.

Lois banged the door shut, stamped her feet and shook the snow off her coat. She leaned against the wall and untied her boots. For all their fur-lining, her feet were icy cold. Her fingers were stiff.

"Michael!" she shouted gaily. "Help, Michael! Your woman

is frozen stiff! Hope you've got that cuppa ready! God! It's miserable out!"

"He's not in!" Jo Furse called from her room.

"Why, Jo!"

Lois went to Jo's room.

"What's the matter?"

"Had a vomiting fit at the office."

Lois sat on the edge of Jo's bed. She took one of Jo's hands in her own.

"This has been coming on for an awful long time, hasn't it? I've been watching you wasting away for months now. I've hoped you'd talk to me. You've never kept things from me before. Is it a man? Feel like talking about it?"

"Get yourself a cup. This pot's freshly made."

Lois fetched a cup and poured herself some tea.

"Michael went out shortly after I came. Said to tell you he'd try not to be too late."

"Tell you where he was going?"

"No. Only said he had to see a man."

"It'll be agony for him. He hates the cold."

"Oh, Lois. . . ."

Jo Furse's body began to shake with silent sobbing. Lois folded the younger woman to her bosom and rocked her; as a mother rocks a child much hurt. A storm broke inside Jo Furse. Sobs shook her body. The storm grew violent. She screamed in agony of spirit. And all the while Lois rocked her as a mother rocks a child much hurt; rocked her till the storm spent itself, till the sobbing died to a whimper, till the whimper turned to tremulous breathing.

"There, there, my pet. You'll feel better now. I'll concoct something for you and you'll go to sleep. I'm sorry I've neglected you so, my dear. Happiness is such a selfish thing."

"Don't say that, Lois. Don't say that!"

"All right, my dear. I won't. If there's anything I can do, you just tell me."

"You've done more than I deserve already."

"You lie still, my child. Relax. I'll get you something that will put you to sleep. You'll feel much better tomorrow, and perhaps you'll want to talk."

Lois eased her head back onto the pillow, and went to the bathroom. She returned with a liquid sedative.

"Drink this, pet. It'll put you to sleep."

Jo took the glass and drank. Then, suddenly, her face contorted into a grimace of horror.

"I can't go on with this!" she screamed. "I can't! I must tell you!"

"Not now, my pet. Tomorrow will do."

"Now!" screamed Jo. "Now! I can't bear it! Now!"

Lois leaned down suddenly and slapped Jo's face. Jo gasped. Lois crossed the little room quickly and drew the curtains. She took up the tea-tray, switched off the light and went out.

"Things won't look so black tomorrow," she murmured as she shut the door.

Lois went to the sitting-room. Michael had left the fire on. Bless him. She walked about the room. His presence was everywhere, warm and comforting. Poor kid. She's probably caught up with some married man. This was the first serious affair for her. All the others had been youthful experimentation. She'd need all the help in the world. Whatever the experts say, youth and the first real passion is the most hellish time of a woman's life. Odd how the first real passion nearly always is with some unscrupulous man who is married. Poor kid. Bloody awful for her.

She sat down at Udomo's desk. Another letter from Adebhoy. She read it through quickly. Yes, the day would come. But she knew now that it would only be a temporary parting. She would go to him as soon as possible, wherever he was. Her roots, now, were in him, took nourishment from his love and lived.

She read the unfinished reply that was still in the typewriter. Yes, he would go one day. He would go to fulfil his destiny.

But, now, she could think of it without terror. Their hearts were married. And if he lived, and she felt he would live and win, she would go to him.

She looked through his work. He worked terribly hard, harder than all the rest of the group put together. He was the real force. His coming had affected the whole of the group. Before he came they had been a group of wishful dreamers. Now an organisation had come into being. And they had plans rather than dreams. Even Mhendi really believed again. He'd even stopped drinking. And though Tom was still the nominal leader, it was to him, Michael, that they all turned and his word carried most weight. And all in the space of six months. And *The Liberator*, that had started as something mad, now had subscribers from all over the world, for all its being still stencilled. Thank Heaven they could now afford to have the stencils cut and run off by an agency! How he'd danced that day the Colonies Committee of the Council of Nations had quoted from it as an authoritative journal on Africa! It had come over the radio and he'd gone mad with joy and even got slightly tipsy with the others.

Suddenly, briefly, as a stranger, she saw herself sitting at her man's desk.

"God, how you hero-worship him!" she said aloud.

And then the moment passed, and she could not see herself detached from him.

She rose from the desk, went to the bookshelves and got a book. She made herself comfortable near the fire and read until nine. She turned on the radio, then, and listened to the news. After the news she went to Jo's room. She opened the door quietly. Jo was in a deep drugged sleep, snoring aloud. She went to the kitchen and prepared a light supper. She took it into the sitting-room and read while she ate.

At half-past ten she went to bed. She left the fire on. On a very low flame in the kitchen, she left a pan of thick soup simmering. She put two hot-water bottles in his side of the bed. He would be cold and tired and hungry when he got back. He would appreciate these things. . . .

Outside, the snow came down steadily, no longer wafting but falling, thick and fast.

Lois was only vaguely aware of Udomo when he got into bed a little before midnight. She nuzzled close to him instinctively, warming him with her body.

Jo Furse woke. She got out of bed, went to the window and pulled the curtains aside. It was daylight and the snow was still coming down. She looked at her watch. It was after eleven. Lois would have gone and only Michael would be here. She went back to the bed. She'd better dress before going out to meet him.

He knocked on the door. She grabbed her dressing-gown. He came in before she had it on properly. He saw her frenzied haste and smiled.

"Good morning."

"I overslept."

"Lois told me she gave you a drug. Want your breakfast here? Lois told me to keep you in bed."

"No. I want to get dressed."

"My friend may turn up any time now. You'd only have to undress again."

"I don't mind."

"As you wish."

"Will you please go."

"Shy of me?" He smiled.

"Please leave me."

He went out and shut the door behind him. She listened till he shut the sitting-room door. Then she dressed with feverish haste. When she had done she sat on the bed, breathless and tired. A wave of morning sickness assailed her. She rushed to the bathroom and locked the door behind her.

In the other room Udomo's eyes kept straying from his

morning post to the clock. The fellow had said he'd be here
as early as possible after half-past eight. He told himself he
had a lot of work to do. He tried to concentrate on the letters.
He read the topmost one aloud to himself. Still, he couldn't
take in its contents. He got up and walked about the room.
The damned fellow ought to be here by now. He'd waited
all night outside the fellow's rooms. Could he have changed
his mind? He dismissed the thought. The fellow would come.
He was one of the boys. But why wasn't he here now? Damned
nuisance, this interference with a man's work. Bloody fool
woman who can't take care of herself. Must get Lois to get
rid of her after this. She might start getting ideas. Lois said
she was hysterical last night. Yes, best thing would be to get
rid of her before she does any harm. Damn that chap. Why
didn't he come?

He went to the window and stood watching the falling snow.
Then he went back to his desk and tried again. But it was no
good. He could not work. His eyes, now, refused to see the
letters that made up the words. Damn that stupid girl to put
him in this position. Why doesn't the fellow turn up?

In the bathroom, Jo straightened her back and wiped the
tears from her eyes. The fit of vomiting was over. But it had
drained her of all strength. She had to support herself against
the wall to get to the wash-basin. She washed out her mouth
and drank half a tumbler of water. She felt better after that.
I'll go away when this is over, she decided: I must go away.
Must do it without Lois knowing, without her being hurt. But
he will hurt her. Perhaps it will be worse later than it would
be now. Please God, help me to do the right thing. She's the
only one who's always done the right thing by me. If I tell
her, it'll hurt her; if I don't she'll always go on believing this
lie. And the longer she believes it, the weaker she'll become.
And if she discovers it too late it might kill her. She already
worships him. But I can't hurt her. She's been too good to me.
I'm a coward. I know that. But please tell me it's right not to

want to hurt her. I'll go away as soon as this is over. I'll go away and never see her again; and she's the only one who's ever loved me really, like a mother loves a child or a big sister a foolish young sister. Please help me, God.

She unlocked the door. Udomo heard her and came to the sitting-room door.

"That fellow's late, Jo. I nearly forgot. Lois told me to give you breakfast but that fellow said you shouldn't eat anything. I'll make you a cup of tea if you like."

"I'll make it myself."

"I'd like one too. Bring it in here."

She went into the kitchen. He went back into the sitting-room. He paced about the room for a while. He thought: Perhaps he's on the phone. He grabbed a telephone book, thumbed quickly through a section of it. The fellow wasn't on the phone.

Jo brought him a cup of tea.

"Where's yours?"

"I'll have it in my room."

"It's warmer in here."

"I prefer my room."

He looked closely at her.

"Are you always going to be like this now?"

"As long as I'm here."

"Oh. And what do you think Lois will think?"

"I won't be here long enough for her to notice it."

"So you're leaving?"

"Yes."

"When?"

"Today—if I can walk after your friend has been here."

"Why?"

"You really ask that?"

"You've changed. I like you better now. Where will you go?"

"You don't care, so why ask."

"I'm interested. Bring your tea in here and let's talk. It'll help pass the time till that damn fellow turns up."

"I prefer my room."

She left him. He shrugged and drank his tea. He went to the flat door and looked out. The cold drove him back to the warmth of the sitting-room. Damn that fellow! He began to curse the man in his mind.

By one o'clock he was tense, desperate and anxious. He began to doubt the fellow and his own judgement of him. He went to Jo's room, knocked on the door and tried the handle. The door was locked.

"What's the matter with you?" he yelled in a sudden fit of rage.

"Has your friend come?"

"No! Open! I just want to talk to you!"

"I don't want to talk to you. I'll open when your friend comes."

He stalked back to the sitting-room and slammed the door.

The flat door-bell rang at half-past one. Udomo rushed to the door. His fingers trembled as he opened it.

"I'm sorry I'm late . . ." the man began.

"You are here!" Udomo said. "We haven't much time. It's all got to be done by four o'clock. I explained to you why last night."

"I'll do my best. But there might be a risk in it for me if anybody turns up at four."

"It'll only be my woman and she won't harm you. I promise."

"That's all right then."

"Yes, it's all right. Everything will be all right for you. I promise you that."

He led the man into the sitting-room.

"I'll get her," Udomo said.

He went to Jo's door and knocked.

"My friend has come."

She opened the door and followed him into the sitting-room.

116

"No names," the man said quickly. "I don't want your name: you don't want mine."

"Will I be able to have children afterwards?" Jo said.

She watched the man steadily. He avoided looking at her.

"Of course. I'm only going to inject you. We may only need to do one."

"You're sure I'll have children?"

"Of course."

"All right then. Get it over with." She fought back the fear that grew in her.

"You'd better stay here," the man said to Udomo. "I'll call you when I need you." To Jo: "Take me to your room, please."

The man came back into the sitting-room an hour later. Udomo stopped pacing about the room.

"Is it done?"

"I've just given her the injection."

"All this time!"

"No, my friend. Her stomach had to be emptied first. These things take time if one is not to damage a person. It is less easy to get rid of it than to make it."

"How long will it take now?"

"We'll see."

The man had left the door open. Now, they heard Jo groan. The man hurried to her. Udomo started pacing again. . . .

The man came to him half an hour later.

"It nearly came. We must try again."

Udomo looked at the clock. Its ticking went through him.

"Hurry, man! Give her a big one. Lois will be here in an hour."

"Lois?"

"My woman. Please hurry! You know how it is. I don't want her to know."

"I must be careful or I'll damage the girl."

"Yes. But hurry, please!"

At half-past three the man came to Udomo and said:
"This is a hard one."

Jo's groans turned to screams at four o'clock. She began by
wailing as she writhed on the bed. The wailing turned into
long, agonising calls for Udomo to help her. Then they turned
into long, drawn-out shouts of:

"Michael! Michael! Michael! . . ."

Udomo shut the sitting-room door to keep out the screaming
voice. He sat deep in a chair in front of the fire, eyes closed,
praying that this thing might end soon.

No one heard Lois enter. The screaming sent her rushing
to Jo's room. The man, concerned only with his task, looked
up briefly.

"Hot water and as many rags as you can!" he snapped.

"Michael!" Jo screamed.

And Lois knew.

She brought rags and water. . . .

And at last it was over. The man put his hand on Jo's forehead and felt her pulse.

Jo opened her eyes and saw Lois.

"It was Michael," Lois said. It was not a question.

"I'm sorry . . ." Jo Furse gasped. "So sorry."

"She must go to sleep," the man said.

He gathered a lump of flesh on Jo's arm and pushed his
hypodermic needle deep into the flesh.

The silence brought Udomo from the sitting-room. He saw
Lois. His footsteps faltered. Lois looked briefly at him, then
she turned to the man.

"Is it finished?"

"Yes."

"And your work here is done?"

"Yes."

"And the drug?"

"She'll sleep for an hour."

"There's nothing else?"

"No."

"Then go now."

"Lois . . ." Udomo said.

"Go now," she said to the man.

The man picked up his bag and walked past her. He looked at Udomo.

"I'm sorry. I tried . . ."

He went to the door and out of the flat.

"Lois . . ." Udomo began.

Lois looked at him with eyes gone dead.

"I'm going now," she said. "I'll come back in an hour's time. If you are still here, I'll call the police and tell them what you've done. . . ."

"But, Lois! I can explain. It was nothing. It didn't mean anything. That little one's just . . ."

"Don't say it! Look at me. You know I mean what I've said. In an hour from now."

"But where will I go in this cold?"

She took the key from the inside of Jo's door, put it in the hole on the outside, locked the door and slipped the key into her overcoat pocket. She held out her hand to him, palm upwards.

"You've a key of mine."

"Please listen to me, Lois. You know I love you. You know how lonely you were before I came. You told me. Don't let her spoil it. I promise you I'll never . . ."

"If I go without my key I'll send the police here immediately."

The stillness about her frightened him.

"My key," she said.

He took it out of his pocket and dropped it into her hand. She looked at her watch.

"In one hour," she said.

She walked past him. He heard the door open then slam shut.

He went slowly to the sitting-room. He sank into the chair in front of the fire and sat with his head in his hands. After a while, the ticking of the clock came to him, grew loud, louder. He looked up at the clock. She meant it all right. She'd get the police if he were still there. The Police. He jumped up and went to the bedroom. He picked up the phone and dialled the Haverstock Hill taxi rank. He asked for a taxi to be at the flat in half an hour.

He pulled two trunks from under the bed and carried one to the sitting-room. He packed his papers methodically into it. The unfinished letter to Adebhoy was still in the typewriter. He sat down and tapped out: "I'm moving from here now. Don't write till you get my new address. Treat the merchants as most urgent. I shall be homeless from today. And don't believe all you might hear about me. If you have any money I shall need it desperately now. Will send you an address to-morrow. Work fast."

He signed the letter then sealed and addressed it.

He finished packing his papers. He went into the bedroom and packed his clothes into the second trunk. He put the new dressing-gown and slippers on top. At last it was done. He looked about the room. There was nothing else of his. He wrapped two scarves round his neck and over his chest and put on the dufflecoat. Then he sat on the bed and phoned the YMCA and asked them to keep him a room for that night. He said he would be there shortly. He took out his wallet. There were only two pounds in it. He opened the chest of drawers where Lois kept her ready cash. She had fifteen pounds there. He took two. He went to the sitting-room and sat by the fire, waiting for the taxi.

So much they'd shared, he and Lois. So much. Now it was over. Damn that girl! Damn his own stupidity! So much . . .

*   *   *

"Come in!" yelled Mabi.

When no one came in he turned from his work. He flung down the hammer and chisel and stormed to the door. He flung it open. The angry words died in his throat.

"Lois! My God!"

Before he could catch her, Lois crashed to the floor at his feet. He half-carried, half-dragged her to his bed. Then he rushed to the door and shouted at the top of his voice.

"Cath! Quickly!"

He hurried back to Lois. He undid the top of her coat. She had come without her hat. Her hair glistened with melting snow. He rubbed her cheeks, her hands, her forehead.

The woman, Cath, in artist's overalls, clattered down the stairs and came in. She looked at Lois.

"Looks like a fit. See the clenched teeth and rigidity of the body."

"Do something, damn you! Lois doesn't suffer from fits."

"Brandy," the woman said and rushed out.

She returned with a half-full bottle of brandy. They forced Lois' teeth apart and poured brandy down her throat. She choked, spluttered; her body relaxed.

"Now go," Mabi said. "No. Leave the bottle. Thanks."

Cath left them. Lois opened her eyes.

"Oh Paul . . . Help me. . . ."

"My dear . . . What is it?"

Her blank eyes stared at him. Her voice too, sounded dead.

"I walked in on their abortion; Jo's and his. . . ."

Mabi stared into the blank eyes. A shiver passed through his body. Then, slowly, his eyes filled with tears. They ran down his cheeks.

"My dear," he murmured brokenly. "Oh, my dear." And all the guilt of Africa was in his voice.

UDOMO

ONE

I

Udomo leaned against the rails and looked at the moon. He thought: the moon is a woman comforting her children against the dark terrors of the night. Then he thought: no, a woman is near and touches you; the moon is far. Then again: but it does comfort. Be brighter, moon! Then I'll see Africa again.

The throb of the ship's engines was steady, continuous; and the lap-lapping of the dark waters against its sides regular. And above the throb and the lap, deep and low, was the eternal hum of the living sea. And the ship was a solitary point of light on the face of the dark water. The moon, though clear, was too far away to strike reflection here. And somewhere to the left, hidden now by the darkness, was the coastline of Africa.

Mother Africa! Oh, Mother Africa, make me strong for the work that I must do. Don't forget me in the many you nurse. I would make you great. I would have the world respect you and your children. I would have the sun of freedom shine over you once more. It was for this I left you for so long and lived in strange lands among strange people and suffered and was abused and was cold and hungry. It was in order to come back to free you, to free all your children, and to make you great among those who now look down on you. They do not understand your dark ways. For them you are something to be exploited, and your children creatures to be held down. Now this must end. I will end it if you help me. I cannot see you but I can feel you out there in the dark. Tomorrow I will be with you, in you. Do not let me get lost in your many. Help me, watch me, guide me. My name is Michael Udomo. Do not forget it: Michael Udomo, the instrument of your freedom. . . .

He turned from the rails and walked, legs apart, along the narrow deck till he came to the stairs that led up to the first-class deck. He stopped and looked both ways along the deck. No one was in sight. The music from up there now came clearly to his ears. He climbed the stairs. The ship hardly rolled.

This was the last night of the voyage. First-class was having its farewell dance on the wide, spacious afterdeck. Coloured lights and bunting were strung over the dancing space. And all wore evening dress. And all were white except for a small handful isolated at one table. And among all, black-faced and white-coated, rushed the steward boys with their trays, ministering to the revellers' needs. And the black, star-studded dome above was all the roofing the revellers had or needed in the warm tropical night.

Udomo slipped unobtrusively into the dark shadows of a huge vent, far away from the revellers. From there he watched unseen. These were the lords and ladies of Africa today. They thought they would always run Africa. It was their plum and they picked it. That's right, shout "Boy"! The stewards are only black and therefore boys. All blacks are "boys". And those first-class black passengers, they know they're just tolerated. For all their first-class passages these whites think of them as upstage blacks. Taking turns dancing with the two women! Six men and two women. They know they dare not

ask any of the white women to dance. A boatload of civil
servants docking in Africa tomorrow. And would they dance
with, make friends of, the eight Africans travelling with them
in the same class? Of course not! To them the Africans are
the outsiders. Outsiders even in their own homeland.

Look at that woman! She really thinks she's something.
Ag! When I look at you, woman, and think of Lois. . . .

Lois. Yes. Pity about that. And Mabi shutting his door in
my face when I called next day. That hurt. I won't forget that.
Pity about Lois. One never knows with women. If only she'd
let me explain. Funny thing was she frightened me, just looking at me as she did. That damned Jo spoiled everything. I
didn't care a damn about her. But Lois. . . . Wrote but she
wouldn't even answer. Mhendi, too, was angry. But he held it
in. Lanwood understood. He's all right. Not much good except
for writing and speaking. Useful as a figurehead. Nothing
more. But we can use his name. Lois. A man never knows how
much he needs a woman till afterwards. And she was good.
And what she gave she gave. Not like that Mary Feld. God!
How could Lanwood live with a woman who despises him.
He's weak, really. That week I stayed with them was hard.
Wanted to take me to bed when Tom was out. But a man
can't do these things, not to his friend. And she wasn't anything like that Jo Furse. Anyway, she's all right wherever she
is. She'll learn not to play with a man again. But Lois. . . .
You're getting drunk, woman! And you think you're beautiful
and throw your hips about! I wouldn't have any one of you
here for anything! Lois . . . Go on, my friends! Laugh!
Drink! Be happy! The world is yours today! You'll have to
answer to us tomorrow. Tomorrow will come. Go on! Laugh
and drink! Drink and laugh. . . .

He sensed, suddenly, that someone was with him, watching
him. He braced himself and turned.

The short, stocky, white chief steward stood there, lordly
and erect, his hands deep in his pockets.

"Well. . . ." There was a mixture of anger and mockery in the white man's voice.

Udomo came out of the shadows. He stared at the man for a few seconds: saw the superior lordliness in the man's bearing. Then he pushed past the man and went to the stairs.

"Hey, you!" the man called.

Udomo hesitated for a second, then he carried on till he reached the stairs. He put both hands on the rails, paused, turned his head to the man and hissed:

"Go to hell!"

He saw surprise on the man's face. He clattered down the stairs to the dark dinginess of third-class. Down the narrow unlit deck, down another flight of stairs, and then he was in the drabness of the crowded third. No whites here: no lights of many colours here: no cleanliness and stewards. The music from the dance up there came through on an extension-speaker. But there was no room for dancing, no far-flung star-studded dome to invest the night with romance. Down here, the heat of the tropical night was oppressive, stifling.

A woman sat near the entrance, giving her child the breast. The people who had not yet gone to bed sat on the hard wooden benches in the drab dining-room. Some played cards: some talked: others just sat. They had all done their packing, and for them the drab night was unendingly long. They could not dance and drink it away as those upstairs. And the throb of the engines, here, came through more numbingly loud than upstairs.

"How is it up there?" the woman at the door said.

"They dance," Udomo said. "They are dressed up and happy."

He began to move to the dining-room, changed his mind half-way there, veered left and entered the little cabin he shared with three other men. The floor was covered with their baggage. The porthole was wide open but the little cabin was stifling hot. The two men in the top bunks lay naked, only their privates covered with bits of cloth. They talked quietly of home.

"How is it upstairs?" one said to Udomo.

"They dance," he said.

"You went right up?" the second said.

"Yes."

"It must be a sight, man!"

"And you are down here. And it is your land they are going to."

"What else? They have the money."

The first man shook his head.

"And if you had it, would they welcome you? Hey, Mr. Udomo?"

"You know they wouldn't," Udomo said. "Those eight who are up there: they have the money. But I saw them. They sit by themselves. They can't dance with any of the others. The others don't talk to them. It isn't the money, it's the power."

The first man mopped his face with the bit of cloth over his private, then put it back again.

"Me, I don't see how I can be like them. I have no schooling for their ways, and even if I got plenty-plenty money I will still have no schooling for their ways. But it is wrong for them not to let you, Mr. Udomo, be with them. You have schooling for their ways."

The first man said:

"I say with you, Mr. Udomo, all people must be the same."

"That is the thing to fight for," Udomo said.

"You be very angry man," the second said.

"It is good to be angry for freedom," the first said.

Udomo felt his shirt growing wet and beginning to cling to his body. He felt beads of sweat rising on his forehead and upper lip. He got up from his bunk and climbed over the baggage to the door.

"Yes," he said. "It is good to be angry for freedom but it is better to fight for it."

The woman at the entrance looked up as he came.

"You go up top again?"

"Just to the deck. It is too hot here."

"I will come and talk with you when my child sleeps. You are too angry tonight, Mr. Udomo."

He went upstairs and leaned against the rails of the third deck. He stared intently at the darkness, as though to pierce it with his will and see land.

Oh, Mother Africa. . . .

And the lap-lapping of the water was there again, and the hum of the sea, and the steady, vibrant throb of the engines. And the big moon was still up there in the sky: lower now, but still not striking light from the dark water. The stars stood out boldly. The land was in darkness still, but that would pass. That would pass.

Lois could ease my loneliness now. But even she didn't understand. And she loved me truly once.

Oh, Mother Africa. . . .

The woman came up after a while and leaned on the rail beside him.

"Your child sleeps?"

"Yes, Mr. Udomo."

"Why do you all call me Mr. Udomo?"

"You are different to all of us. And you do not speak much. But when you speak we all listen. And we feel the anger that is in you."

"That is no reason to call me mister."

"It is for us. But it is not that I want to speak of. What will you do now you are home? It is a long time that you have been away."

"I went away to learn. Now I will fight for our people."

"How will you fight?"

"Why do you ask?"

"Am I not of your people? Remember I told you I went to England to see for myself how the people who rule us live? I had the money from trading so I thought I would visit for three months and see for myself. I stayed there for one month but only because I could not get a ship back before. You know what happens to black people there, so I wanted to come back very quickly. I went with the feeling of friendship for them . . ." She left it hanging.

The boat made a long, leftward swing that could be traced by the curving line of light foam in its wake.

"I will fight in any way I can," Udomo said. "But first we must start a party. I have friends in England, and there is one already at home. He spoke to the chiefs and elders but they will not help so we will start on our own."

"It will not be easy," the woman said.

"It is freedom we want, not easiness."

"You will need help."

"Only the support of our people. That is the great help."

"Do not forget the women then, Mr. Udomo. . . . When you have started, and when I can see what it is you are doing, come to me and I will speak for you with the women of the market. My name is Selina. Remember it. And do not forget the women."

Udomo turned his head and tried to see her face. It was only a shadow.

"I will not forget," he said.

"I will go back," she said. "You should rest for tomorrow."

"I will stay here a while longer," he said.

She left him as silently as she had come.

Udomo stared out at the darkness that shrouded Africa. Oh, Mother Africa!

2

Udomo sat down and slid his passport across the little card-table.

The black sergeant of police pushed some papers aside and covered the passport with his big hand.

"Name?"

Udomo remained silent till the sergeant looked up. He looked coldly into the sergeant's eyes.

"Why all the whites first?"

The sergeant's eyes went cold and hard.

"You are third-class."

"Then why am I in front of those eight others who are black like me—and you?"

The sergeant sighed and gave him a long, deliberate stare. Then he shifted his eyes to the passport, removed his big hand, and opened it.

"You are Michael Udomo?"

"Yes."

The sergeant consulted some papers. Then he stamped the passport and pushed it back to Udomo.

"Next!"

One of the black first-class passengers took Udomo's place.

Udomo went down to third-class to get his luggage. The woman, Selina, was still there, supervising three porters.

"How is it?" she said.

"We had to wait for all the whites," Udomo said.

"I knew it. That's why I'm still here."

"And it is our country!"

"Calm yourself, Mr. Udomo. It will change."

"Yes, it will change."

Selina turned to one of her porters.

"You will take Mr. Udomo's luggage to the customs house."

Udomo tried to thank her. She waved his thanks aside, strapped the child more firmly to her back, and padded up the stairs to immigration. Udomo became aware of her bare feet. She had discarded her shoes. She was home, and at home she would walk barefooted. He thought: And she could afford first but travelled third. Remember the women, Michael. She'd said that. Remember them.

The porter said:

"All these your things, sah?"

"Yes."

"You go. I bring."

Udomo picked up two small cases and went up. The chief steward stood at the top of the gangway, seeing the passengers off. Most of the white passengers had gone. He smiled as Udomo approached. Udomo stared blankly as he went past and down. He hesitated for a second on the last of the wooden steps, looked at the earth, then he stepped on to African soil. He wished, suddenly, that his feet, like Selina's, were bare. He straightened his back, squared his shoulders. He walked briskly to customs.

Adebhoy had written that he would do his best to come, but if he couldn't he'd send someone. Udomo looked about. And all about people moved in the sun: and the sun was of Africa, and the people of Africa.

He entered the customs shed and heard his name:

"Mr. Udomo! Mr. Udomo, sah! Mr. Udomo!"

"Here!" he called. He felt good now, and sure.

The young man who came to him was long and thin: long-fingered, long-legged: feet like ships in their slender graceful length and they glided over the earth as do ships over water. The youth touched his right temple as he stopped before Udomo.

"Me Samson, sah. Boy for massa Adebhoy."

"Hello, Samson."

"My massa send for get you, sah. Give you this." He fished an envelope from the pocket of his tight khaki shorts. "He say for take taxi to house."

Udomo opened the envelope. There were five one-pound notes, nothing else. He put the money in his pocket.

"Good."

Samson took his two cases and put them on the table for inspection. Selina's porter came in staggering under the weight

of one of Udomo's trunks. Samson went back with the porter to fetch the other one.

Selina appeared just as Udomo was cleared and ready to go.

"Your friends have come?" she said.

"Yes," Udomo smiled.

"You are not so angry now. That is good. Do not forget what I told you."

"I will not forget. And I can pay the porter now. Thank you."

"That is mine," Selina said. "Goodbye, Mr. Udomo. I will wait to hear of the things you do."

"But where will I find you?" Udomo said.

"In the market. Just ask for Selina. Goodbye."

"Goodbye, Selina."

Samson went outside the customs shed, filled his chest with air, flung back his head and yelled at the top of his voice, making it a long-drawn-out singing sound:

"Taxi!"

His face cracked into a huge smile as cars converged on him from all sides. Behind him, Udomo chuckled softly.

"Home-boy!"

Adebhoy opened his arms wide and roared with laughter.

"Welcome home, man! Welcome home!"

Udomo's face lit with happiness. He flung his arms about Adebhoy. Udomo thought: This is my friend, my loyal friend.

After a while they grew calm and sat facing each other. The light of the setting sun streamed in through the window, lighting up the room and making the crowded mid-Victorian furniture look drab and faded. Samson brought in tea.

"Sorry I couldn't make it earlier," Adebhoy said.

"It gave me a chance to sleep," Udomo said. "I didn't sleep last night."

"How is it, man?"

"Now, all right. But I should've starved in London but for

Lanwood. I stayed with them for Christmas. You know about them."

"The woman?"

"Yes."

"Yes, I know."

"It is wrong for a woman to despise a man in that way."

"He's dependent on her."

"Even so. We must get him here as soon as possible. You know she even tried. . . ."

Adebhoy laughed, without humour.

"She tried with all of us, home-boy! All except Mabi. They hated each other from the start."

"You know Mabi shut his door in my face after I left Lois."

"No!"

"He did. . . . I'm sorry about Lois. She was a good woman."

"These things happen, home-boy."

"But it was hell afterwards. If you didn't send the fare when you did I would have been starving and homeless now. The Colonial Office withdrew my grant because I was doing too much of my real work."

"You should've told me all that in your letters."

"You were helping me enough." Udomo smiled sheepishly and looked into his cup. "Tell me: do you hear from Lois?"

"Not since you left."

"And Mabi?"

"No."

There was silence between them for a long while. Udomo finished his tea, turned his head and stared out of the window.

"What about the merchants?"

"We meet them tomorrow night."

"Here?"

Adebhoy laughed.

"No, home-boy. We go to them. They see themselves as the important people. You want to be careful with them."

"Don't worry. And the Council of Chiefs and Elders?"

"They wouldn't see you, home-boy." Adebhoy rose and went to the little desk in the corner of the room. He got some letters and returned to his seat. "As soon as you wrote me I wrote to the Council asking them to hear you. This was their reply." He passed the letter to Udomo.

Udomo read:

"I have to inform you that it is not the policy of this Council to give hearings to any unknown persons simply at their own request. Furthermore, the Council directs me to inform you that there is no record of any family by the name of Udomo ever having held any position of authority either as chief or elder in any of the major tribes of Panafrica. The Council therefore considers the man you write about an ambitious upstart with whom the Council as the traditional representative of the people can have no dealing. Your information of what he did in Europe is of no interest to the Council. . . ."

Udomo looked up.

"Who is this Endura who signs it?"

"Dr. T. T. S. Endura is secretary of the Council and also its most educated and powerful member. He's cousin to the king of the southern people and the African member of the Governor's Council. He and the Governor are great friends; he's much respected in European circles. I went to see him after I got this letter. It was no good. I really tried my best, home-boy."

Udomo read the letter again.

"We will keep it," he said quietly. "It may be useful. Now for our plans. I've been thinking them out all the time on the voyage. . . ."

The sun went down. And suddenly, with no gradual transition, the light of day was replaced by the blackness of tropical night. Mosquitoes emerged from their hiding places. They invaded the room and assaulted the two men with brazen boldness. Samson came in with a spray and a mixture he called keroseneaniza. Udomo and Adebhoy went out on to the veranda. There, the songs of the creatures of the night were loud enough to force them to raise their voices.

Adebhoy passed a phial of tablets to Udomo.

"One twice a day till you're acclimatized."

Udomo went back to outlining his plans.

The moon came up fast, robbed the darkness of some of its inky blackness, grew bigger as it rose, brighter, till the land was bathed in a gentle half-light that made everything soft and beautiful.

Samson called them into supper. They talked while they ate, the oppressive stench of "keroseneaniza" all about them. But the mosquitoes were gone.

They went back to the veranda. The lights of a car turned off the road and bumped towards the house.

"These are the people I've invited to meet you. They're all young and educated and disillusioned with the leadership of the Council. They could be the nucleus."

"How many?"

"There'll be a dozen tonight. They're the best. But there are more. They've come to see you, to see if all I told them about you is true. They'll talk about you to others and so you'll get to be known."

The car came to a halt. Adebhoy went out to meet the people. Two other cars turned off the road and bumped their way towards the house. Inside the house, Samson carted crates of beer and bottles of whisky from the kitchen to the sitting-room. Udomo went into the sitting-room. Samson grinned broadly.

"This party be for you, massa. My massa tell how you be very big man and people come for meet with very big man who is leader of men."

Udomo heard voices on the veranda. He straightened himself, pushed out his chest, thought consciously of his strength. Lois it was who had made him aware of this force within him. Now, for his work, he would make others aware of it. He willed strength into his bearing. This was the beginning of his work. How these people reacted to him could shape the future.

They came in. He smiled and took each hand as Adebhoy introduced them. He spoke to them, quietly, controlledly. And they, who had come to look over Michael Udomo, found him friendly but aloof; sensed, shadowlike, the force the man held prisoner in his body. And when they were all assembled he talked to them of making Africa free and great. And he made them feel they were all shareholders in this great dream. . . .

Adebhoy came back from seeing the last of them off. His eyes glowed.

"You've got them, home-boy! You've got them!"

Udomo smiled wanly. The sustained, two-hour-long effort had worn him out. His eyes drooped heavily.

"I'm tired," he said.

"We'll talk more tomorrow," Adebhoy said. "Come . . . I've given you my mosquito net. I'll get another tomorrow. Sleep well. . . ."

First there is the sea. Then there is the white sand at the edge of the sea. Behind the white sand, on rising land, standing like sentinels against the sea, palm trees are dotted all along the coastal edge. Behind the palms the land rises gently to the crest of a low rolling hill, then falls away into a wide flat-bottomed valley. All this valley is taken up by Queenstown, the capital and first sea-port of Panafrica.

Really, Queenstown is no more than an overgrown African village with an immense European façade. Along the docks it is all European; the cranes and huge storage houses, the immigration and port police offices, and the big buildings of the great Panafrica Company which controls practically all Panafrica's trade and is one of the five biggest monopolies in the world. But just to the left of all this, spilling over the rolling hill and down into the basin of the low valley, is the old

African town, much as it was before the coming of the
Europeans. True, the roads in the centre of the town have
been widened and macadamised. True, Pan-Africa Store, the
Company's immense retail trading concern, is a huge modern
department store, and Greek and Indian merchants have built
modern shops in the main highways. But neither these, nor
the three cinemas, nor the huge cathedral can rob the town
of its essentially African character. Once away from the main
centres, the houses huddle on top of each other any way you
like. Mud and wattle jostle with timber or corrugated iron.
And the people, here, live communally. Doors are always open.
Anyone can always enter. There is no privacy, no need for it.
Here, away from the port and the centre of the city, life goes
on much as it might have done one, two, three thousand years
ago.

And so, two or three thousand years ago, might black
children have played naked outside their houses: so might
the fishermen have sat mending their nets while the sun re-
fined fishy smells, and big black flies swarmed thick over the
nets: and so might a woman have pounded her casava while
the child strapped to her side fed on her long breast, while
another to whom she talked offered fly-riddled food for sale
to passing strangers. Here, the only change as between three
thousand years ago and the present is that the government
had installed an open drainage system. Men and boys use it
as a public lavatory. When pressed they step to the side of the
road and piddle into it. Women use chambers indoors then
come out and empty them into the open drains. But above all,
it is the communal living, the easy, collective, free intimacy
of its citizens, the special nature of its stinking squalor, that
stamps Queenstown as being both older than its name and
the European conquest that gave it that name.

Government buildings—the Governor's Palace, the Secretariat, the offices of the various ministries, police and army
headquarters—are all situated on the side of the valley furthest

from the sea. The homes of the white civil servants are on the slopes of the rising hill behind and above government buildings. The air, here, is cooler in the evenings. These homes have the feel of English county life about them. There are spacious lawns and wonderful flower beds. The rooms are large and cool. Almost, this little area of Africa where the civil servants live is a bit of England transported to the tropics.

On the western edge of the town, almost a community unto themselves, live the new Africans: the black doctors, lawyers, teachers, senior clerks in the civil service and the rich merchants. Their homes are brick-built. In comfort these homes are midway between the crowded squalor of the black town on the one hand, and the spacious luxury of those of the white civil servants on the other. The handful of Assyrian and Indian merchants also live here.

So, first there is the sea; then there is the town called Queenstown. And then, behind that, going away in rolling sweeps of hill and valley, there is the land. And here and there, dotted across the great land, are towns and villages, strips of forest, and great silence. There are no isolated homesteads. All the houses in all the villages and towns are crowded together. It is as though those who live in the houses fear the land and find comfort in crowding together. And the land itself is coldly, impersonally aloof.

And over all this, every day till the rains come, and even then, hangs the sun; harsh, fiercely burning for all the humidity of the air.

Jones, who was in charge of security, tapped on the Chief Secretary's door and went in. The Chief Secretary, Smithers, looked up frowning, then relaxed and pushed some papers aside.

"Take a pew," Smithers said. "Just putting my house in order for our new Governor. Wonder what he'll be like. I don't myself hold with these party Governors."

"They say he was in the service before he went into politics," Jones said.

"He's still a political appointment," Smithers said. "Damn pity that the Progressives should win just as H. E. retires. . . . You're a bit of a Progressive yourself, aren't you?"

"A bit," Jones said. He thought: Pompous ass.

"Not that I mind his party," Smithers said. "Just that I don't like the upsetting of service traditions."

"I suggest we let him show his hand first."

"Oh, I'm not talking about him. I'm thinking what a mess it would be if colonial Governors were changed each time a new party won power at home."

"I hardly think that likely," Jones murmured.

"You don't know these political bods," Smithers said.

"For which give thanks," Jones said. He stuffed his pipe then raised his quiet eyes to Smithers' face. "Look here, Smithers, I don't like this trouble up in the Central Province. It's not like these people to attack the District Commissioner for no reason. Especially the tribal people."

"They've got to learn to pay taxes," Smithers said. "Government can't always foot every bill. They need proper roads, drainage, schools. . . ."

"I know. I'm only concerned about the security angle."

"It will pass. I had a word with Endura this morning. He and one of their chiefs will tour the area and make them see sense."

"All right; but keep me posted."

"Nothing to worry about there. We have these minor eruptions. The D.C. up there's one of my best young chaps."

"Heard anything about Michael Udomo?" Jones said.

"The young firebrand who's just come back?"

"So you have."

"It's not only security that has ears, you know. He's just a firebrand. Endura mentioned him." Smithers surprised Jones by smiling. "Endura tells me the young scamp actually had the nerve to demand a hearing by the Council. Sent the message before he arrived. Which reminds me: that chap Adebhoy is on the government payroll and I want him dismissed from the hospital the moment his playing at politics justifies it. Get someone to keep an eye on him. The service rules must be strictly observed, even by our new middle-class. I shouldn't waste time on Udomo. He'll be a five-day wonder, then he'll come to us for a job."

"I wonder . . ." Jones mused. "That rag he ran in London had quite an influence. Reached even the Council of Nations."

"That was comrade Lanwood's hand," Smithers said. "And we won't let him in! Let him blow as hot as he likes in London."

The hint of a smile flitted across Jones' thin, sallow face.

"I think you and your friend Endura under-estimate Udomo." He chuckled inwardly at Smithers' facial reaction to Endura being called his friend. Really, for all his apparent friendliness, Smithers hated these people. Jones went on: "Saw the latest copy of their *Liberator,* published since Udomo left. New editor is that chap Mhendi who ran that bloody show in Pluralia. It hasn't the punch and fire it had when Udomo edited it. I wouldn't underrate Mr. Udomo. There's a restlessness about the place . . . You can feel it down in the town, and reports from all over the country are the same."

Smithers threw back his head and laughed scornfully. But Jones noticed the absence of laughter in his eyes.

"Trouble with you security blokes is you aren't happy unless you can dig up some real or imaginary plot."

Jones got up.

"You may be right. I overheard one of the most intelligent of my blokes telling another of his meeting Udomo last night. He's drunk with it, and he's no fool. Thought I'd better mention it. But you may be right." He waved his pipe in a vague salute, went out, shut the door behind him and stood listening while he lit his pipe.

His face creased into a smile tinged with malice when he heard Smithers' buzzer summoning his secretary, and, a moment later, Smithers' voice demanding angrily why a copy of the latest *Liberator* was not on his desk.

Jones walked slowly back to his office. Smithers, he decided again, was a pompous, officious ass. Trouble with the whole damned English crowd here was that they knew damn-all of what went on. And they cared less. All they were concerned about was doing the legally prescribed number of hours, then getting back to their bungalow for tennis or cocktail parties. This had become habit. They weren't worthy any more of the empire their forebears had won for them. They'd grown flabby and took it for granted. Young men, now, joined the service because pay and living conditions were better than at home. Faith in their mission had gone out of the whole business. Oh, there were good chaps among them, chaps with a fine loyalty to the service. The tragedy was that there was so little loyalty left for the principles, the ideals that led to the founding of the empire in the first place. Chaps like Smithers didn't believe in the old ideal of serving: they ruled. Native interests were a polite fiction to which they paid lip-service in public only. Privately they scoffed at it. Pity about the whole damn business was that it was still the finest service in the world but it had ceased to believe—really to believe—in the Commonwealth idea. If the Commonwealth idea died it would be . . . Jones shrugged impatiently, as though to free himself of the hold of his own thoughts. He entered his office and pressed the buzzer on his desk. He wondered: Should he ask the chap he'd overheard talking about last night's meeting where Adebhoy lived. No. Might only add to the general whispering. His secretary came in. Nice young chap. Cool and efficient and so politely correct. Did this young fellow ever move among the people, enter their filthy homes, sit down and talk with them? His only contacts were probably with the clerks here and the houseboys at his bungalow who "sah'd" him up and down.

And yet it was wrong to hold it against this youngster. Others set the pattern. He only followed it. Perhaps it was too late in any case. Perhaps the pattern had been going on too long.

Jones became aware of the young man standing there, patiently.

"Sorry. . . . Look, I want you to find out for me—carefully, I don't want any talk about it among the clerks—where Mr. Adebhoy lives. Might be an idea to ring either the police or the hospital."

The young man left. Jones turned his attention to the papers on his desk. The young man returned in less than five minutes with the address written on a slip of paper.

Jones smiled at the young man.

"You're here about six months now, aren't you?"

"Yes, sir."

"Drop the sir. Been out among the people?"

"No—not really."

"I should try. They're wonderfully warm-hearted and friendly. Of course, the bulk of them live in the most awful poverty. But, really, you should try to get to know even that. But there's a middle-class beginning and we will need these people as our friends later on. Things may change quite a bit in the next few years and personal knowledge and friendships could be invaluable then. You know, the pioneers of our service really knew the people among whom they worked. We're a bit cut off today. Think about it, will you . . . ?"

"Yes, sir. Thank you, sir."

Jones went out and down to his car. He wondered whether the young man would take his words seriously or use them to get a laugh from the younger set. He got into the car and drove across town, out to the western end of the rising middle-class. He turned the car off the road and bumped across the sandy track. No real roads here, no drainage even. Oh God! Didn't those political wallahs at the Secretariat realise that it was precisely these people who would most bitterly compare their own surroundings with those on the hill? Perhaps the new Governor would see that.

Samson came to the door in response to his knock.

"Mr. Udomo," Jones said. "Tell him Mr. Jones would like to see him, please."

"Massa Udomo no here now, massa."

"You know where he is?"

"No, massa. Massa Udomo he go for walk after lunchtime chop. He say for get to know town again. He be gone long, long time for town now he get to know again."

"Thank you."

"If massa like he come for house. I bring paper massa write message for massa Udomo. I give message."

"You like Mr. Udomo?"

"He always speak soft-soft. He always say 'Thank you, Samson'. Not even my massa, de doctor, always remember and he be good."

"And Mr. Udomo always does?"

"Always, sah. He big man, massa Udomo. Plenty big man."

"So I hear. Thank you, Samson."

"Maybe massa wait, maybe massa Udomo come soon-soon."

"No, Samson. I will come back again."

Jones drove slowly back to town along the coastal road. The late afternoon sun was at its hottest and even the cooling system of the car was not much help. It was only after he had passed the huge dock buildings that a slight breeze from the sea made the heat more bearable. Instead of turning left and cutting across town to his office, Jones kept along the sea road, feeling relaxed suddenly, and freed, for a spell, of the burden of his duties. And as always, when relaxed, his mind went to the small cemetery at the base of the European settlement. His wife's grave was there. She'd died in their second year of marriage, in her second year out here, a dozen years ago now, of yellow fever when she was two months with child. And now he was tied to this place by that grave of the born and unborn who had been the love of his life. This land, now, was home, had been home since the day that grave was covered, and always would be home now. His roots were buried here.

He drove the car off the road and got out. He walked to the sheltering shade of a palm-tree. Far out to sea, four slim long boats made their way to land across the glasslike water. Their positions suggested that they dragged a full net between them. Then he saw the man sitting under a palm-tree some distance away. His eyes went back to the boats, but something about the man nagged at his brain. He looked again. Of course, a tie. Who else but someone newly arrived from Europe would wear a tie in this heat?

Jones walked quickly from the shade of one tree to the next till he stood under the tree where the man sat, seemingly lost in concentration of the sea. Jones waited a while then coughed.

Udomo looked up. He saw a small, lean-bodied, lean-faced white man. His face was a sallow yellow. His eyes were set deep in his head. He was balding and what remained of his wispy hair was the same yellow colour as his face. His drill shirt was open and the hair on his chest was thick and black. His knees, below his khaki shorts were big and bony. The deep, quiet air the man had showed most clearly in his eyes.

"You are Mr. Udomo?" Jones said.

"Yes."

"My name is Jones. My job here's security. . . ."

The hint of a smile touched Udomo's lips. Jones grinned.

"It always has some effect. But I came really to meet you, to try and see what kind of person you are. Mind if I sit down?"

"It isn't my tree," Udomo said.

Jones sat down beside Udomo, rested his back against the tree.

"'Fraid I only smoke a pipe, but I can offer you tobacco."

"I don't smoke. . . . How did you know I was here?"

"Security isn't that good. I went up to Dr. Adebhoy's but

you weren't there. I drove back and—I don't know—I just felt I needed a little quiet. You know how it is: people get low sometimes: even security blokes like myself. By the way, this isn't a security check or anything like that. I just wanted to meet you after I heard someone talking about you." He lit his pipe then turned his eyes to Udomo's face.

Udomo stared impassively out to sea where the four boats inched their way landwards.

"I've just received the latest issue of the *Liberator*," Jones said quietly. "It lacks your spark and fire. I expect you won't see it as it's banned here. But I'll let you have my copy. If my information is correct you plan to start a paper here."

"Is there any law against that?"

"No. I don't know that you won't do a lot of good. It's my opinion that the Council of Chiefs and Elders and especially old Endura need some shaking up. From what I've seen of your editorial work, you'll do that. These are my personal views. Nothing official about them. I don't think anyone else at the secretariat holds them. They're all for old Endura serving time until he's rewarded with a call to form the first ministry. They're all a little smug up there. Only security knows the restlessness that is abroad."

Udomo turned his head then and stared coldly at the little man beside him.

"What do you want?"

"I told you I just wanted to meet you. Now I've done that. I'd like you to drop in on me sometime if you're so minded. But I'd understand if you're not. I am the head of security, and it would be reasonable for you to think this a trick. I can only assure you that it isn't, and if you give me a chance I'll prove it. Even a policeman has time off and has private friends. We live too much to ourselves up there on the hill. Anyway, I'm in most evenings and if you feel like dropping in for a drink or dinner, you'd be most welcome. I must go now. Glad I met you. I'll send you the *Liberator*: but as it's banned from public circulation I must ask you not to let it get about. I think I'll also send you a copy of the press regulations so that you can see just how much elbow-room you have." Jones rose and knocked out his pipe. "Can I drop you at your home?"

"No thanks."

"There's no public transport as in London, you know."

"I can find my own way," Udomo said.

"Goodbye then, Mr. Udomo. Don't forget my invitation. It's open and for any time."

Udomo watched the little man walk to his car and drive away, an odd, quizzical expression on his face. When the car was out of sight he got up, flung his coat over his arm and crossed the sloping hill to the town.

Udomo met the three merchants that night. After a week of discussions they each agreed to put five hundred pounds into starting a paper. They made many conditions.

3

Udomo stared at the proof sheet of tomorrow's front page of the *Queenstown Post*. The big black headline said:

SUPPORT THE STRIKERS!

His office was a filthy, threadbare little room on the first floor of an ancient, rotting building. The bare floorboards were black with dirt. The one little window had a layer of dirt that rendered the panes opaque. A hole in one pane was stuffed with paper, turned a dark yellow with time and dirt. Apart from his desk and chair, two benches were ranged along two walls. An ancient typewriter stood on a corner of the equally ancient, unvarnished, paper-littered desk.

Udomo stared discontentedly at the headline.

"After six months!" His voice was bitter. Those damned merchants were always on his back, controlling, inhibiting.

This could be the moment, and they were frightened. "I'm not here to play their game!" he snapped out aloud.

One of his two assistants poked his head round the door. "You called?"

"No!" Udomo snapped.

The man withdrew to the veranda which was their office.

"I must break free!" Udomo said.

But he was under their thumb. Without their money there could be no paper. Already they'd been in today to tell him he must stop supporting the strike. The primitive printing plant, this building, the paper, were all theirs.

For six months now he'd been sweating at this, and what was there to show for it? Oh, he was known all right, respected all right. But hell! It wasn't respect he was after. And those damned intellectuals were no better than the merchants. With you as long as they didn't have to put their hands in their pockets. The moment he and Adebhoy had suggested they pool their money and buy out the merchants they'd stopped coming. They'd forgotten their enthusiasm for a new party to get rid of the old gang. Damn them! Damn them!

He leaned forward suddenly, grabbed his red pencil and scored an angry line across the headline. To hell with them and their money! He'd show those damned merchants they couldn't treat him like a stooge! He rose and stalked to the door.

"Hold everything," he told his two sleepy assistants on the veranda. "We'll probably work late tonight. Tell the printer not to set up any more and to stand by. And you two as well. I'll be back as soon as possible."

He clattered down the dangerously rickety stairs, out of the filthy yard that reeked of piddle, and into the equally dirty street. Heat waves from the parched earth struck his face. He felt breathless suddenly. He slowed his pace. He walked in the direction of the big open market. The late afternoon sun beat down fiercely.

"Hiya, Mr. Udomo, sah! Taxi?" The driver brought his little car to a crawl. He poked out his head and grinned broadly.

"No money." Udomo grinned back.

"For you I give ride for free, sah. You our man."

"I no go far, man," Udomo said.

"Why walk when there be ride for free?"

Udomo went round the crawling car and got in beside the driver. Families, whole clans sometimes, often pooled their savings to buy a young man a car and so set him up in business. And the town was littered with "taxis".

"Where you go, sah?"

"For market."

"Good. I take you. Me, I read your paper. All taxi boys read your paper. All say only your paper write for true. You write more about strike for docks? We like way you beat white man when you tell how he make money from we. All people like that."

"Listen," Udomo said. "I want to write more of the strike. I want to tell more of the truth. But you know I got no money. Money for the paper is given by the merchants but now they frighten because I write about strike. Today they tell me not to write any more about strike. They say they take paper from me if I write about strike. You tell your friends that. Tell them Udomo want to write about strike but merchants want to stop. Tell everybody that. Tell everybody. Say maybe government arrest Udomo because he write about strike. But merchants frighten for their money. Merchants don't care about freedom of our people."

"Those merchants wicked men!" The driver was indignant.

Yes, Udomo thought, tell everybody, my friend.

The car pulled up outside the market. Udomo got out.

"Thank you, my friend, and don't forget what I tell you. Maybe time for fighting is near now."

"I tell everybody," the driver said and waved.

The market was old, timeless Africa; loud, crowded and free. Here, a man sat making sandals from old discarded motor-car tyres; there, another worked at an old sewing machine, making a nightgown-like affair while the buyer waited; a little further on an old goldsmith worked at his dying art, but using, now, copper filings instead of gold to fashion the lovely trinkets women wear the world over; elsewhere a woman sold country cloth fashioned with such fine art that only Africans think of it as a garment of utility. Trade was slow and loud everywhere. This was as much a social as a shopping centre. For excuse to spend the day at the market a woman would walk all the way from her village to town with half a dozen eggs. She would spread them on a little bit of ground for which she paid rent. And through the day she would squat on the ground and talk to others who came for the same reason. She would refuse to sell her wares till it was time to leave. They were the excuse for her being there. There were many like that. But there were many others for whom trade was an earnest business. But, whether earnest or as an excuse, the traders were all boisterously free, loud-mouthed and happy. And the laughter of the market was a laughter found nowhere else in all the world. . . .

Udomo stopped at a stall. The woman looked a fixture here.

"Where will I find Selina, please?"

The woman looked him up and down. She flung back her head and shouted:

"Someone wants Selina!"

The noise all but drowned her yelling. She turned to someone else. She had done her duty by this man and now lost all interest in him. Udomo grinned and moved on to the next stall.

"Where will I find Selina, please?"

This woman was in animated conversation with a customer. She waved him in the direction of the heart of the market without interrupting her flow of words.

Udomo fought his way through the mass of milling people. The din was terrible. The closeness of many people in a confined space added to the heat of the day, made it oppressive. Towards the centre the traders were bigger, their wares more varied, more costly. Machines and furniture were on display here instead of bits of food. Udomo stopped beside a lanky young man at a huge, storelike affair that seemed to sell everything under the sun.

"Where can I find Selina?" He did not have to shout so loudly here. The centre of the market was a pool of comparative tranquillity.

The young man looked him up and down.

"Who wants her?"

"I do. Where can I find her? She said all I had to do was ask for her."

"You know her?"

"Yes! Now will you tell me where she is?"

"Who are you?"

Udomo restrained his impatience.

"What is it to you! I'm Udomo and I want to see Selina."

Udomo started to move to the next stall. The young man changed in an instant.

"Mr. Udomo! Wait please, sah! Wait one minute!"

The young man disappeared behind a mountain of crates. Seems to know me, Udomo thought. A minute or two more can't make much difference. Not as easy to find Selina as she made out it would be.

The young man returned. Behind him came Selina.

"Selina!" Udomo said.

He'd forgotten how tall and impassive she was. Her quiet stare reminded him of the long weeks in the dingy third-class on the boat.

She said:

"I thought you had forgotten me, Mr. Udomo."

Her eyes travelled slowly down him, from head to feet. She

remembered how well pressed his clothes had always been on board ship. Even the jacket he now wore had once been well pressed. She'd seen it on the boat. Now it was creased. The lapels curled limply. His collar was a dirty grey. On the ship it had always been spotlessly white. And that tie had once been broad and flat. Now it was spotted with dirt and rolled into almost stringlike roundness. There were no creases in the trouser-legs, and they were baggy and worn at the knees. The shoes had very little heel left. The leather on the left one had split and only the sock prevented his little toe showing.

Her eyes went back to his face. He'd gone thin. His cheek-bones and jawline stood out more than on the boat.

Udomo grinned. Their eyes met and she knew he had read her thoughts. He made a slight movement with his left shoulder. She knew then that she'd been wrong. He hadn't really changed. Shirts and jackets and trousers and shoes didn't really matter very much. The thing in his eyes was still there as on that ship. He was not here because he was hard up.

"Come," she said.

The young man stepped aside. Udomo followed Selina behind the crates. The goods had been arranged so that they walled off a space the size and shape of a small room. The bare ground had been covered with a carpet. There were chairs, a table, and a narrow canvas bed on which Selina's child slept.

"This is like a room," Udomo said.

"It is a room," she said. "I spend much time here."

Udomo looked up at the clear bright sky.

"We put up a roof of canvas very quickly," she said.

"You sleep here sometimes," he said.

"Sometimes. . . . Sit down, Mr. Udomo."

Udomo sat facing her. She folded her hands in her lap and waited.

"You looked at me just now," he made a gesture taking in

his person, "and you thought 'He has changed'. Things have not been easy, as you see from my clothes and the hole in my shoe. It is not that I came to talk about. But if you are like some merchants I know and only talk to people who have money, then I'd better go. I came to you because on the ship you said I should come when I was ready to do things. Have you forgotten that? Shall I go?"

"I have not forgotten. Speak."

"Since I came back I have run a paper——"

"I know that part. My child reads it to me every day. I think to myself: Yes, he tells the truth. But it is the truth we know. He does not tell us what to do. So the child reads every day and I wait."

"To run that paper I had to get money from three merchants."

"I know that too."

"And that these merchants sit on me all the time? Did you know that?"

"No."

"Well, they do. First it was to protect their money. Then, later, it was for their money and also because they feared to offend the Council of Chiefs and Elders and the government. Now they see the paper as something they can use for bargaining with Endura. They say to him 'We will keep Udomo quiet if you will do so-and-so for us'. They have just seen what a good tool a paper can be. . . ."

"You showed them."

"I thought they were honest. I knew they were out for themselves only. But I still thought they were honest."

"Can't you leave them?"

"I need a paper for my work. Also, there is the contract I signed with them. It is for a year."

"So for a year you must be a tool in their interests."

"That is what I came to talk to you about."

"I'm listening."

She rose, pumped up the pressure stove, lit it and put a kettle on.

"This strike at the docks," he said slowly. "You saw what I wrote about that?"

"What you wrote the first day was best. You told all the truth then."

Udomo's lips curved in a bitter smile.

"Yes. They visited me that day. Endura had been to see them. He had warned them the government would close down the paper."

"So next day you were a little softer."

"So next day I was a little softer. But this strike could be the start of things. Only, I would need help, for I would go to jail, and I don't want to go to jail for nothing. That is why I came to you."

Selina jerked to a stop in the act of reaching for a cup. She turned to Udomo. The kettle started boiling. The child woke and yelled. She stared at Udomo for a long while, then she turned and went to the camp bed. While she reached for the child, one hand undid the top of her dress. She lifted the child. Its hungry mouth reached for the hanging breast. The child's crying died in mid-note as its mouth found the breast.

Selina turned and Udomo saw a smile on her lips. It was the first time he had seen her smile.

"Tell me," she said. She made the tea, poured it and brought him a cup. And all the while the child sucked away at her breast.

Udomo straightened his back. And now there was the hint of a smile about his lips too.

"When I leave you, I will go back to the paper. I will sit down at my desk and I will write a call to our people to rise against the foreigners and demand the freedom to rule themselves. I will say that the Council of Chiefs and Elders and Dr. Endura are the tools of the British. I will say that the time has come for us to fight and to go on fighting until we and our land are free of the rule of white foreigners. Then we will print the paper. It will be all over the front page. And to-morrow all the people will read it."

"And they will arrest you."

"Yes."

"What then?"

"Then you and my friend Adebhoy will rally the people. The leaders of the dock strike will join you. I have spoken to them."

"And shall we then collect money to pay your fine?"

"No!" Udomo shouted.

Selina chuckled.

"There is no need to be angry, Mr. Udomo."

"No matter what happens, you are not to pay any fine. I must stay in jail and serve my time. Your duty will be to keep up the anger of the people and to build up a party that would lead them to freedom. Don't you see, Selina, in jail I'll be the rallying point for our people. Are you with me?"

Selina rose then and went to him, holding the child care-lessly. Her eyes were burning bright. She made a strange little dancing bow before him. Then she took his right hand and pressed it to her lips.

"Would you do this for your people and still ask if I am with you?"

He rose. He felt all the strength of earth rise in him, felt himself grow.

"I will die for my people!"

"They want you to live and free them, Udomo! Go and write! I have many things to do now, many people to talk with. You should have come earlier."

"The plan was only born in my mind a little while ago. I came straight to you."

"All right. There is much we must plan before they take you tomorrow. I will send a car to take you to my house when your work is done."

"It might be late, after midnight, before I am done. It is an important thing I must write."

"That is of no moment. We will be awake all this night to think and plan for tomorrow, and for all the other tomorrows. Your friend the doctor, he's a good man? A man who can plan?"

"You will see that when you meet him."

"Good. I will send the car for him. And we will talk and plan till your coming. We have not much time and there is much to do. There will be food and rest at my house when it is done. Go now, Udomo."

Selina followed Udomo out. The babel of the market hit them. Udomo had forgotten he was in the centre of the market. Now it was all about him. Odd that that place should have cut off the noise so effectively. Selina gave the young man a list of names of people she wanted at her house that night. Then she turned to Udomo.

"Do you need money, Udomo?"

"No." He set off briskly, pushing his way through the crowds.

"There will be a feast for you tonight!" Selina shouted above the din.

His two assistants were droopily reading copy.

"Anybody come?" Udomo's new briskness shook them awake.

"One of the directors has been," the senior said.

"Well?"

"He went into your office and read the front-page proof. We told him you didn't like that but he said he owned the paper." The man paused expectantly. Udomo didn't explode, so he went on: "He said he'd made some changes and for you to let him know if you object to any of them before printing the paper. He said he'd wait at his office till five o'clock."

"Nearly that now," Udomo said. "You'd better run along

and tell our director everything is in order. I will run it exactly as he wants. Go on, man! What are you gaping at? We mustn't disappoint our directors. They pay our wages."

"But Mr. Udomo, sir!"

"And see that you are back as soon as possible. We've got great work on hand!"

The senior assistant clattered unwillingly down the stairs.

"I don't want to be disturbed by anybody—*anybody*."

He went into his office, cleared his desk with one sweep of the arm, then pulled the typewriter to him. He realised he had swept his paper on to the floor and grinned. He went on his knees and collected typing paper. He rose, slipped it into the old machine, and began to tap. The words came out hesitantly at first:

"A CALL TO THE PEOPLE! RISE AND BE FREE!

"People of Panafrica! This is a call to you to rise and free yourselves. This is a call to battle! Down at the docks today our brothers are striking. That is only a beginning. They are striking because they are tired of receiving the wages of slaves! Because . . ."

He wrote steadily for a long time. Then he closed his eyes and leaned back in his chair till the drunkenness caused by the words he had written passed. It was done now. There was no going back now. After a while he opened his eyes. He read through what he had written. He changed a line here, deleted a word there, altered a sentence. Yes. Yes, there was no other way. There was very little education among the people so he had to speak in slogans. After this it was up to the others: to Adebhoy and Selina and the dockers. But what if it didn't come off and he rotted in jail for years with no one caring? No! . . . He rose, unlocked his door and called in his assistants.

"You saw him?"

"Yes," the senior said.

"What did he say?"

"He was happy. He said you were learning sense at last. He laughed and said there had been no need for him to tell the printer not to accept any violent copy from you."

"Good. Now read this." He pushed what he had written to them.

They read, standing side-by-side, leaning over his desk. When they looked up he relaxed. Their faces told him all he wanted to know about the impact of the piece.

"My God!" the senior gasped.

"Oh man! Oh man!" the other said. He yelled suddenly: "FREEDOM!"

"Come on, we'll set that up."

"But they'll arrest you," the senior said.

"I know." Udomo grinned. He was on the stage already, and he knew it. "We'll print as many copies as we have paper for. Use up all the paper. I won't need any after tonight. I think we'd better each take some copies with us. They'll want to confiscate it tomorrow."

"Yessir!" the second assistant said, eyes shining.

"But the printer," the first assistant said. "He won't set this up. I know he won't set this up! He'll look at this and then run to tell those directors or the police. He's scared for his licence and his job."

"And you?" Udomo said quietly.

"You know I'm your man."

"Good. You'll be editor of our paper one day. It'll be a real paper."

"But what of the printer?"

"That one likes the bottle," the second said.

"Can the boy who helps him set up?"

"The boy does all the real work," the first said.

"Will he do this if the old man's gone?"

"You his hero, sir," the second assistant said quickly. "He'll do anything you ask."

"But how'll we get rid of the old man?" the first said.

"You know Selina at the market?"

"Everybody knows Selina. She's a big trading woman. Rich, too."

"Go to her. Say I sent you and explain our problem with the old man. Tell her he likes the bottle."

"That all?"

"Yes. No. Tell her we'll need some money for taxis; and addresses where copies of the paper can be hidden from the police. Go now before she leaves."

There was no unwillingness about the chief assistant this time. He came back very quickly. From his pocket he pulled a thick roll of money.

"Selina says give her fifteen minutes and the old man will be gone. She came back with me and gave me a ride in her taxi. She said she would wait till I came up, then she would go in to the old man."

Udomo bounded to the door. He was just in time to see Selina enter the shed downstairs. After a while Selina and the old man came out together. They stood talking, then the old man came to the stairs.

"You boys had better be at your desk," Udomo snapped.

He rushed into his office. He pocketed the copy he had written. When the old man knocked and came in he was busy on the proof sheet.

"Mr. Udomo! I must protest at your delay in sending copy down. You know it is late?"

"I'm so sorry," Udomo said mildly. "One of the directors made some changes which I'm just adding."

"I knew that an hour ago!"

"Sorry, Mr. Townsend. You know how it is. I had a tip the strike might be settled. . . ."

"All rumours. Those fools have no sense. You know I don't hold with your supporting them. . . ."

"That's over now, Mr. Townsend, I assure you."

"Time you learnt some sense. But what I came to tell you is that I've got to see a client on an important printing job. You know your paper doesn't support the press. The boy can handle the copy. I'll try to be back later."

"There's no need to disturb your rest. I'll send one of my boys down to help him."

"All right. But no nonsense, mind you."

Udomo spread his hands deprecatingly.

"Good night, then. I'm glad you've seen sense about this strike."

"Good night, Mr. Townsend."

Damn these creoles with their superior airs, Udomo thought; but without anger.

The first assistant poked his head round the door.

"They've gone! She's taken him away!"

Udomo got up and moved briskly.

"Come on! We've work to do." They clattered down the rickety stairs. "Got the addresses?"

"She said to bring the papers to her place in a taxi."

"Good." He led the way into the printing shed. "Lock it behind you."

He beamed at the young black boy who came to him.

"I've got a big job for you, son. When you're an old man you'll tell your grandchildren about this! Hungry?"

"Yes, sah." The boy grinned.

Udomo took a pound note from the wad Selina had sent. He gave it to his second assistant.

"Get us some food. We'll need it. Lock the door behind him." He took off his jacket and rolled up his sleeves, unmindful, now, of the rents in his shirt. He gave the boy his copy. "Show us how to print and we'll do it while you set this up."

"Yes, sah," the boy said. It was a great game to him.

It was nearly two in the morning when the taxi stopped outside Selina's house on the western edge of the town. Hers was one of the few houses in the area with electric light. All the rooms were ablaze with it.

"We are here, sah," the taximan said.

The noise from the house reached Udomo and, above it, a voice:

"He has come!"

Adebhoy and Selina led the procession that came to meet him. Suddenly, there were people all about him. Hands took his and shook them.

"It is done?" Selina said.

"It is done," he said. He handed the copy he held to Adebhoy. "There are ten thousand copies in the taxi, Selina."

"We will take care of that," Selina said. "Your part is done."

"You must be tired," Adebhoy said.

"I'll have time to rest later."

"Come," Selina said. "You will first eat, Udomo. While you eat the doctor will read this to us, this call to our people. Come."

The big room was stacked with liquor. There were about twenty people. They were all sober, had drunk only moderately. This cheered Udomo. These were serious people. He found himself alone with Adebhoy for a few seconds.

"How is it?" he asked.

Adebhoy beamed happily.

"They're wonderful! They'll go all the way! They'll not let us down! That Selina, man!" He roared with happy laughter. "And we've made many plans."

Selina brought her husband and elder girl to Udomo. The man was short, fat and sleepy. He smiled amiably. The girl was a strapping twelve. Selina introduced her husband, then ordered him to go and see to the papers in the taxi and pay the taximan.

"And you are the one who reads to your mother," Udomo said to the girl.

The child hung her head shyly.

"She is the one," Selina said. "Now she has prepared your food and will see to you. Take him away and feed him well, child. He is the great blade of our land. He must be sharp. You come and read to us now, Doctor."

Udomo followed the girl into a small room that led off the big one.

"Leave the door open," he told the girl. "I want to hear."

The people ranged themselves about the big room. Adebhoy stood in the centre and read what Udomo had written. As he read, his voice gained power and passion, echoed the feelings that had stirred Udomo while he had written.

Udomo stopped eating, gave all his attention to Adebhoy's reading. Tomorrow thousands, maybe hundreds of thousands, would read or hear those words. They would creep through the land like fire, like the talking drums of old. Would they awake the people? Would they rouse them?

Adebhoy stopped reading. There was a long spell of silence. Then one voice, charged with passion, broke the silence.

"FREEDOM!"

Others took it up. And it was a mighty roar that shook the house.

Udomo leaned back and closed his eyes. His body tingled all over. His heart pounded. Then he sighed softly and opened his eyes. This was it, then; it was right. This *was* the moment and he had taken it well.

"But the battle is still ahead," he whispered to himself.

They all spoke now and Selina had to prevent them from rushing into the little room and falling on him.

"He's hungry and tired!" she roared. "He will eat! Then he will rest for an hour, and no one will disturb him. No one! After that he will come here and we will tell him our plans. And then he must go to wait for those who will come for him, and our work will begin. To work! He wants victory, not cheering! Heh, Doctor?"

Fine, Udomo thought, fine. Great woman, Selina. Let her

manage. Adebhoy would see that she manages well. Remind
Adebhoy to get a full report to the Group in London. They'd
have to spread it about, organise demonstrations and questions in the Commons, get it to the Council of Nations. My
God. Oh, my God. Is this how those others who made revolutions in the past felt? Those men who are history now, did
they feel like this? Like being carried along on a fast-flowing
river? And yet calm? And were they as sure of success, too?
Must have been, otherwise they wouldn't have started. They
won't let me down. They won't! Spread through the land like
a fire and rouse them to action. Action, my people! You must
think calmly, man. The excitement's for the others. Yours is
responsibility. It could go wrong. Think about that. No. It
won't go wrong! It can't. It must not! IT WILL NOT! If
only all the Group were here now. Even Mabi. But they'll
come. Yes, they'll come. I'll send for them and they'll come.
And Tom will be free of that woman who feeds and clothes
and despises him. And Mhendi will plan for his land. Yes!
We'll do it!

Selina came in to him. The girl left.

"You have eaten?"

"Very well, Selina." He remembered the wad of notes in
his pocket. He took them out and held them to her. "I've used
all we needed."

"Keep them."

"No. I've used what I needed. This is yours."

"What is mine is also yours now, Udomo."

"Take the money!"

Selina grinned.

"No need for anger. I'll take it." She took the money. "Now
come."

"I'm not tired."

"Come, Udomo."

He rose and followed her through the house to a room at
the back.

"This is the room. I will come myself and knock for you in an hour. There is a key on the inside. Use it. But no one will disturb you. There is another door. You will understand the use for that. Now go in."

Udomo opened the door, stepped in, then turned quickly back to Selina.

"What is this?"

There was a touch of tenderness in Selina's face now.

"She's for your hour of rest, Udomo. There are no women in prison. Look at her. She's young and beautiful. She's untouched but she has been trained in our ways. She will comfort you in this hour."

"But Selina, who is she? I——"

"Are you prisoner to the ways of the whites? She is your land. She's for you. You are a man and she's a woman. Is that not enough? Is that not how it has always been with us? Then go to her and rest. One promise only you must give me. It is this. If the thing we dream of comes you will put no white woman over us, you will take no white woman for wife. That is the only promise I ask."

Yes, Udomo thought, yes.

"I promise," he said solemnly.

"Now go in. None of the others know. Be happy."

The girl turned as he entered. And she was beautiful. Her eyes welcomed him. They were dark eyes that touched his face and slid away.

"Come here," he said.

She came and stood in front of him, head down. He saw that she had nothing on under the fine cloth that covered her body.

"What is your name?"

"They call me Nancy," she whispered.

"Look at me, Nancy."

She raised her head. The smell of scented soap came from her body.

Dark eyes, black as the African night. Not light and clear as those of Lois. Lois . . . Why was she always at the back of his mind? He never thought of her but she was always there.

"There is too much light," he said.

Nancy leaned sideways and flicked off the light. Then she felt for his hand.

"Come," she whispered, pulling him across the dark room. Not clear as those of Lois. . . .

Afterwards it seemed that it had been Lois: a new Lois with new skills learnt in the African bush where women had learned these skills through the centuries. He knew it was an illusion. He clung to the illusion till he could do so no more. Then he relaxed. And then his mind went back to the Lois he had known in her mountain cottage in another land. And he preferred her, the old one, to this new one. The old had used the skill of the heart only: this new one used the skill of art only.

"Were you pleased?" Nancy whispered.

He put his hand to her cheek but said nothing.

Lois. . . .

TWO

I

The Governor's aide opened the door and announced:

"His Excellency."

Jones and Smithers rose. The Governor, Lord Rosslee, walked briskly into the room and sank into his chair.

"Gentlemen. . . ."

"Sir," the two men said, almost in unison.

"Sit down, please. I asked you here because I don't like this new development. I wanted your views before the Executive Council meeting."

"You've seen the paper?" Smithers asked.

"Just read it. Damned explosive stuff if it gets a hold. The point is, will it?"

Smithers said:

"Police are out in force now, confiscating all the copies they can lay their hands on. We'll keep its circulation confined to the town and hunt down all the copies."

"Do we know how many copies are about?" Rosslee asked.

"I spoke to one of the owners. The usual edition is about three thousand."

"But this edition wasn't usual," Jones said quietly. "I went down to the press this morning. Three weeks' stock of newsprint had been used up last night. Perhaps more; the old printer wasn't sure."

"What did he have to say for himself?"

"He's not implicated at all, sir. He had to go out to see about a piece of job printing. Udomo seized his opportunity while the old man was out."

"What about the owners?"

"I'm sure they're not implicated," Smithers said.

"For all we know, then, there may be tens of thousands of copies of this paper hidden away somewhere in the town?"

"I'm afraid so," Jones said.

"I doubt it myself," Smithers said.

The Governor said: "The important thing is, where do we go from here? What is the mood of the town? Is this thing getting a hold? And this is the question that worries me: is there some organisation behind Udomo?"

The Governor looked first at Smithers, then at Jones. He took out his cigarette-case and held it to them. Smithers took one. Jones reached for his pipe.

Smithers cleared his throat. Jones thought: Pompous ass. He saw a glint in the Governor's eye and looked away quickly.

"This is a storm in a tea-cup," Smithers said firmly. "Udomo is nothing more than a firebrand. He and his two dupes are under lock and key where they can cool their heels for a spell. The police will soon gather up all this foul rubbish and that will be the end of it. There'll be a seven-day wonder; no more. I'm an old hand, sir. I've seen this sort of thing before."

"You don't think, then, that there's any kind of organisation behind Udomo?"

"No, sir. The sooner we bring Udomo to trial and get the matter out of the way, the sooner will things settle down again. These people respect firmness. I'm certain all the fuss would be over in a week if we handle this Udomo affair firmly. I know the Council of Chiefs and Elders will back whatever action Government takes in this matter. Endura will tell you so himself at this afternoon's meeting."

"Will the people follow Endura?"

"He's the shrewdest and most respected politician in the colony. I would suggest that we bring Udomo to trial quickly, tomorrow or the day after; and that we deal firmly and sternly and swiftly with any unlawful acts of violence and looting. That will bring them to their senses. They'll forget Udomo quickly enough."

"In short," Rosslee murmured, "you advocate a show of force."

"In this case, yes, sir."

"D'you think it will work, Jones?"

Smithers flushed. The fingers that held the cigarette trembled.

"It might," Jones said.

Something in his voice made both the Chief Secretary and the Governor stare at him. Jones stuffed his pipe as though unaware of their stares.

The Governor looked at his watch and rose.

"Thank you, gentlemen. I now have something on which to base my report. Stay for tea?"

"Regret I can't, sir," Smithers said. "A couple of my up-country men are waiting for me now."

"I hope you can, Jones."

"Thank you, sir," Jones murmured.

"Then I'll be off," Smithers said. "Good morning, sir."

"Good morning, Smithers. And thanks for all your help."

"That's what we are here for, sir."

Smithers left.

Rosslee laughed aloud suddenly.

"In other words, my dear Jones, Governors come and Governors go, but Chief Secretaries are on the permanent list and really run the show. . . . Our Chief Secretary doesn't really like me, Jones. But the first rule of the Governors' Manual says: 'It is the duty of all good Governors to be on the best of terms with all their staff; this makes for team spirit.'"

"Does it really?" Jones was genuinely curious.

Rosslee roared with laughter. Jones thought: I like him.

"Of course not. There's no such thing as a Governors' Manual. But there ought to be, and that ought to be the first rule. . . . Come, let's go up to my private quarters. Not as austere as all this polished glory. I always feel out of place here, like an intruder. . . . Martin!"

The aide came in.

"Relax," Rosslee said. "Look, Mr. Jones and I will have tea up in my quarters. And His Excellency is not available to any callers for an hour. Awful lot of homework to do. Up we go, Jones."

Upstairs, part of the gubernatorial private apartments had been turned into a comfortable, untidy, bachelor's flat. They sat in the severely masculine sitting-room. A black boy in white uniform brought in tea. The Governor made a point of thanking him. This man has the right idea, Jones thought.

"Well now, Jones, I really wanted to talk to you and I'm glad Smithers couldn't stay. He sees this through the old conventional eyes of traditional Service response to such situations."

"I shouldn't underestimate Smithers, sir. He may be pompous and conventional in his approach but I would say he's one of the really outstanding men in the Service today."

"Believe me, I'm not underestimating him, Jones. But I think you put your finger on the problem when you use the word 'conventional'. Will Smithers' conventional remedies work in this case? Is it just a storm in a tea-cup, a seven-day wonder, as he thinks?

"Don't answer yet. Let me tell you the way I see the whole general problem of empire today. As I see it, there is a mood abroad in the world today. The essence of this mood is a deep-seated revulsion against the idea of one people ruling another, no matter how well, no matter how benevolently. It is like a charged cloud floating about the earth and infecting all people in all lands. It creates this urge, this desire, this *need* in people to manage their own affairs, no matter how badly. D'you see what I'm getting at? Is it here?"

"Yes. And it is here."

"You don't think I'm mad, man? For heaven's sake tell me if you think me up the pole. Smithers would think I am but would be too polite to say so."

Jones smiled. His sallow face took on a boyish attractiveness.

"No, sir. I don't think you mad. I once tried to tell Smithers what you've just said, but I couldn't find the words. It's easier to think it than express it. And they call us Shakespeare's people! Anyway, I'm convinced you are dead right. I've been sensing this for an awful long time now. There's a growing restlessness among the people. It's like some sickness of the mind. Decent chaps I've known for a long time, chaps I've joked with, suddenly turn offended and aggressive about the most harmless remark. There's a new touchiness about them. . . ."

"Yes," Rosslee said thoughtfully.

"You ought to go down into the town," Jones said. "I felt it particularly strongly this morning."

"Explosive?"

"More like a thunder-cloud."

"And into this steps friend Udomo. Would you say he's cause or effect?"

"Neither, sir. I would say it's independent of him."

"But he can use and direct it."

"Yes, sir."

"We shouldn't have locked him up, you know, Jones."

"There's the law, sir. I sent him the press regulations myself."

"So you know him?"

"What I heard of him made me want to meet him. Met him on the beach the day you arrived."

"What did you make of him?"

"Funny thing is I liked him straightaway. He was very aloof. Made it coldly clear that he didn't want any part of me. Nothing rude, but quite clear." Jones smiled ruefully.

"Yes, there's something about our Mr. Udomo."

"Knew him in London, sir?"

"Yes. I met him first at the flat of a very charming woman on the bohemian artistic fringe. Heard later that she'd become his mistress, but I doubted it. She wasn't that kind of woman. Anyway, that's just idle gossip. Met him later at one of our conferences." Rosslee grinned. "You know, it's the fact that I'm a Progressive that sticks in Smithers' gullet."

"Nothing personal, sir. He's concerned with the principle."

"Of course he is. You really don't have to defend him so hard, man."

"Sorry, sir."

"Believe me, I'm not unmindful of the virtues of Smithers. Anyway, Udomo certainly made an impression on me then. A sort of smouldering fury. And the speech he made shook everybody to the core. Much as this thing in his paper. What are we going to do about him? If only he weren't so damned passionately sincere and dedicated . . ."

There was a long spell of silence in the room then. Jones sat sucking at his pipe. The room was cool. The blinding glare of daylight was subdued here. Must be the thick stone slabs with which this palace was built, Jones mused. Something to be said for being Governor in this furnace. And a damn fine one this chap seems.

Rosslee rose and went to the window. He stared out.

"Look, Jones. I want to try something. We're out of touch with the educated Africans here. I'd say Endura's Council is out of touch too. I'd say their hold, such as it is, is now largely confined to the remoter tribal areas of the bush. I want us to try and make contact with these town Africans. I want a list of them. His Excellency will throw a party to which they will all be invited. And no formal dressing up. What d'you think of the idea?"

"Excellent, sir."

Rosslee swung about and looked closely at Jones.

"You mean that?"

"It's the kind of thing I've tried to get going for a while now," Jones murmured. "I even tried it with Udomo."

"But they wouldn't play?"

"Perhaps it's because I'm security, sir. Can't blame them, really. Our people at home are touchy about the police. They'd be more so about M.I.5."

"Yes. Can you get me that list? I want the invitations to go out tomorrow."

"Right, sir."

"Another thing. D'you think it necessary that it should be known that H.E. would like fraternisation all round?"

"It certainly would carry weight, sir."

"Now for the touchiest point of all. Remember the first rule in my imaginary Governors' Manual. How do I get Smithers' approval?"

Jones chewed his pipe for a while. Then he looked up with twinkling eyes.

"His Excellency could give a private dinner party to which only heads of departments and certain business V.I.P.s are invited. The purpose would be for the Governor to express his appreciation of the way in which his Chief Secretary has steered him clear of the pitfalls in the way of those taking on a new job."

"Wonderful! I can then take him aside at some point and broach the subject. Excellent, Jones. I'd better make it to-night."

"It'll be a smack in the eye for me," Jones smiled

"You can take it! Now about Udomo: he's more danger to us in prison than out. You see that, don't you?"

"Yes. But there's nothing we can do at the moment. The due process of law must take its course."

"Suppose so. But we can't play this according to the book! We want to go along with this thing, guide it into creative channels. It'll smash us and the colony if we try to stand in its way. Wish to heaven they hadn't locked him up!"

"Smithers' way might work, sir. I hope so, anyway."

"So do I, Jones, so do I. But I fear it won't."

"I'm with you there, sir."

"Keep a watch on this thing and keep me posted. And if you get any ideas shoot them to me. I'm depending on you."

"Yes, sir," Jones said. He rose. "Thanks for the tea."

"Come again," the Governor said. "I'll drop in on you one evening, incognito, if I may."

"Do."

"The damn thing about empire, Jones, is that we sit on our fannies until something hits us in the face. And yet, could it ever be otherwise?"

"Good morning, sir," Jones said.

"Good morning, Jones. And you might drop the 'sir' in private."

Jones went down and out of the Governor's palace. Quite a chap, this Rosslee, he thought, quite a chap.

The policeman at the gate saluted.

2

The town, on the surface, lay quiet under the burning sun. All the ships lay idle in the harbour. The normally busy port was silent. Even the noonday sun seemed fixed overhead, as though it, too, was on strike.

Down near the fishermen's boats, two men walked. They were deep in conversation.

"They say nothing the white man does can stop this. They say Udomo is too strong and even the prison cannot stop his spirit."

"Did you see the soldiers?"

"Ai, man! They would frighten us as you frighten children. But you will see. They will take the papers and take the papers but there will be more. They say Udomo has more of the papers than they can take. They say even now the papers are being sent all over the country so that all can see them."

"But will he make us free, this Udomo?"

"They say that if we stand with him there is nothing he cannot do. They say one day he will speak to us and we will see that."

"Have you seen the paper?"

"I had it read to me."

"What does it say?"

"You want to know?"

"I am asking."

"You can hear it for yourself. But you must swear an oath to keep it quiet."

"I'll keep it quiet."

"Even if the police came to you?"

"Even then."

"All right. But when you have heard Udomo's words you must find another person whom you trust and send him so that he, too, can hear the words. So the words will go to all the people. You know Josiah the cripple?"

"Yes."

"Go to his house."

"Will I find——"

"Go to his house and see what you will find. Say I sent you. Go now."

The one man left. The other walked among the fishermen at their nets till he came to another whom he knew well, whom he trusted.

"Well, man! What do you think of this Udomo business?"

"From what I hear he speaks for us, brother, even from prison."

"I have heard his words. Would you like to hear them?"

"Would I like to hear them! Why, man, I got a paper this morning, meaning to keep it until my child came from school and read it to me. But those police dogs took it from me! Took it and warned me!"

"Not so loud, brother. You can hear those words if you want to, all of them."

"How?"

"Listen——"

All over the town men and women slipped into dingy little rooms in obscure places. Someone met them at the door and made them take an oath of secrecy. Then they went into the room. There, someone read Udomo's words to them. Usually, there were only three people at a time. But as the day wore on the figure had first to be doubled, then trebled. After each reading the people were invited to join Udomo's party, the Africa Freedom Party. By the late afternoon more than ten thousand people had joined the new party. Each paid one shilling membership fee.

And all over the town the quiet reading circles took place. And the police were everywhere, going about in twos and threes, hunting out the offending issue of the *Queenstown Post*.

But there were no incidents of any kind.

* * *

At the market, the men driving the gay, ramshackle, private transport trucks from one end of the land to the other, all called on Selina before setting out. Each left her place with a hundred copies of the offending paper. One or two of the trucks were stopped at the town boundary. A copy of the paper was found on a passenger, usually a woman, here and there. But the main supplies were missed and the trucks went on their way.

People dropped in on Selina. They talked quietly with her for a little while and then went away.

Dr. Endura walked into Smithers' office and took a seat.

"Hello," Smithers said, and looked at his watch. "We've a few minutes before the meeting starts. I saw the Governor this morning. He's worried about this Udomo business." Smithers studied his caller carefully. He'd never quite made up his mind about this chap Endura. These black aristocrats were deep.

There was the hint of a smile on Endura's lips; the glint of laughter in his eyes. He was a big man, well over six feet, and heavily built. He carried his bulk with easy grace. He radiated an air of superiority.

"Don't tell me our good Governor is frightened of a little rabble-rouser." He smiled mockingly. Then he chuckled deep in his throat.

"This is serious!" Smithers snapped. This damn chap could always ruffle him with his la-di-da voice and Oxford accent. A Doctor of Philosophy who worshipped at the shrines of his ancestors.

"But I'm not joking, my dear chap. I'm deadly serious, and disturbed. My education was based on the proposition that the English were never frightened. Think of the way you won your empire. Surely it wasn't by getting frightened every time some rabble-rouser got up and shouted semi-literate slogans! Don't undermine my respect for the bulldog breed."

Smithers controlled his mounting rage. Endura saw this and laughed, rocking his big body gently.

"We'd better go over to the meeting if you're going to treat this as a joke. Perhaps His Excellency will see the point."

"Come now, Smithers——"

Damn your impertinence! Smithers thought.

Endura went on:

"Government is the art of ruling. Good government is the art of ruling well, so that the ruled accepts it. A firm, confident—in other words a good—government would know how to deal with Udomo instead of running around in circles."

"I suppose you would know how to deal with Udomo."

"We've dealt with people like him before you came on the scene. At least, our forebears did."

"By poison or murder, I suppose."

"Oh, Smithers! You know better than I do that governments can't murder. They can only punish offenders. When they are too weak to do that they ought to give way. In fact, they generally do give way, if they are wise."

"What are you driving at?"

The smile passed from Endura's lips, the mocking note from his voice.

"It's really very simple, you know. I think the time has come for you to put the reins of government in our hands——"

"What! You——"

"Drop the indignation, Smithers. We're both old hands at this, so let's face the facts calmly. We both know that we didn't welcome you here out of any love. You conquered us. We submitted to superior might. You could rule while we respected your superior might. But things are changing now. Your power is waning and the tide of world affairs flows strongly against colonial powers, so strongly that you are losing confidence in your divine mission. So your governors grow indecisive and peoples rise against you, led by hotheads like Udomo. What is the answer to this?" He paused. The smile returned to his lips but did not reach his eyes.

"You tell me," Smithers said coldly.

"I will. I've been waiting for this situation for a very long time. Now it has arisen. The way out is to revise the constitutional position so that power is transferred to us. Only we can restore the people to the calm Udomo has disturbed. Of course, you know, Smithers, we'll need you for a very long time to come. You have the know-how and the best and cleanest Service in the world and we would be fools to get rid of that. We shall probably need you for at least half a century, if not longer. But we, the traditional rulers, are the only people who can now restore order without having to resort to violence. In fact, I doubt if even violence on the part of the police or the military can permanently restore the situation now."

"You are bargaining for power!" Smithers exploded.

"Yes, of course. If you don't like it, consider the alternative. And remember, politics is the art of the possible; for sensible men, that is. Our friend Udomo would have no compunction about setting the whole land on fire. You and I have this in common. We both want law and order restored to the land as soon as possible."

"But you yourself told me only this morning that a show of firmness would restore the situation!"

"I had underrated the basic restlessness of the people." He laughed softly.

"This is blackmail!"

"Is it? All right, drop it then."

Smithers leaned back in his chair and stared at a corner of his room for a long time.

Think carefully, Mr. Chief Secretary, Endura thought. The thought gave him great satisfaction.

At last Smithers looked at him.

"I suppose you want to put this up to the meeting?"

"If you don't object. I had hoped that you would put it up but——"

"Time we went," Smithers said roughly.

Endura stood aside at the door. Smithers passed and led the way to the chamber where the Executive Council was to meet.

Towards sundown the police got their first inkling of the readings. A zealous black inspector of police took it on his own shoulders to lead a number of raids and make a number of arrests. It threw his white superiors into a dither when they discovered this.

After the arrests two black lawyers called on Selina. One told her:

"The press regulations say nothing about people reading these papers. These people are falsely arrested. We are prepared to defend them for you, for the party."

"So you know about the party?"

"Everybody knows. We want to join."

"Come to my house tonight. We will hear what Dr. Adebhoy says. He is second to Udomo. He speaks for Udomo till Udomo can speak for himself."

Jones said:

"How did this get through?"

"That telegraphist is one of them, sir," the black security officer said.

"Them?" Jones said.

The security man shrugged helplessly. Jones read the cablegram again.

LANWOOD 36 REGENCY MEWS LONDON
URGENT UDOMO IMPRISONED PRESS REGULATION 11(C) STOP
COUNTRY STATE UNREST PUBLICISE

ADEBHOY.

"All right," Jones said.

The security man left. Jones went briskly along the corridor to Smithers' office. He entered without knocking and flung the cablegram on Smithers' desk. Smithers dismissed an assistant, then read it.

"Has it gone?"

"Yes."

Smithers picked up his phone:

"Get me the hospital! . . . It'll be all over the home press tomorrow. And there are always enough fools in Parliament to kick up a fuss. . . . Hello. Yes . . . Smithers. Look, you've got a chap, Adebhoy. . . . Yes. Well, I want him dismissed on the spot, no matter how good he is. . . . No, he's still un-established. Yes. I'll take full responsibility. . . . The usual thing, prejudicial conduct. He's involved in this Udomo busi-ness. . . ."

"He's behind this new party," Jones said.

"Jones just said he's behind the new party. No. . . . No. . . . Yes, it's beginning to feel ugly. Had a call through from one of my chaps upcountry. Those damn papers are everywhere. . . . Right." He rang off. He looked at Jones. "Anything more come up?"

"There are rumours about a meeting tonight."

"What about these reading circles?"

"That's a bit of a mess, you know. Their lawyers are going to have a great time. Legally we've not proclaimed an emer-gency and our inspector acted as though we had."

"Can't be helped now," Smithers said. "We'll have to pro-claim one if this goes on."

"Trouble is nothing's happened," Jones said, then he added, "Yet."

"That's the damnable part! What have we got on this woman Selina?"

"One of the biggest and most influential mammy-merchants. Deals in everything. No one knows how rich she is. Deals in cash even when it runs into thousands. Proud and aloof, especially where Europeans are concerned. More so since her return from England. She travelled back on the same boat as Udomo. It's reasonable to assume she fell under his spell then."

"Why did she go to England?"

"That no one knows. My information is that she went out intending to stay for three months but was back at the shipping office within a week of her arrival. Created quite a scene when they told her they couldn't give her a passage back before the three months were up. In the end they had to put back another African's passage to make room for her. Seems she got the London office of the Pan-Africa Company to pull all the strings they had. She's one of their biggest individual customers. Interesting thing is that she was quite friendly with their people here until she went to England. Used to have them in for drinks sometimes. You know, the usual sort of thing. But all that's ended since she came back. The Pan-Africa chap here told me she told him bluntly she would only get from them what she couldn't get elsewhere in future and that she would drop them as soon as others could supply her needs. Indian importers are doing quite a trade with her in Japanese goods. And all since she came back."

"But why? Why did she go in the first place? And why this anti-British thing now?"

"I can hazard a good guess at your last question, Smithers. Selina is completely illiterate, basically completely tribal still. We tell them here that they're all British. Can't you see her going there as someone going to the mother country of this empire we've told them so much about? Then think of all the colour incidents that could hit a tribal mammy walking in London with her *toto* on her back. We haven't told our own people as much about the empire and commonwealth as we've told even the most illiterate of these people. We too often forget that we are dealing with a proud people."

"You know," Smithers said quietly, "I'm beginning to think I don't understand these people at all, Jones. Take Endura.

I've known him all these years, and then suddenly, today, I saw him in a new light. He wasn't at all the man I'd always thought. . . ." Smithers told Jones of his conversation with Endura.

A sudden wave of compassion swept over Jones. Smithers was so desperately, so fallibly human suddenly. He had believed in Endura in an odd sort of way. For all his private jeering at Endura's accent and worshipping at the shrines of his ancestor, he had believed there was a common body of ideals they shared that would make Endura see and appreciate the positive achievements of British rule. He had looked on Endura as the new type of African, consciously and appreciatively learning the art of Western civilised government from his British mentors. And then Endura had come with his blackmailing idea. . . .

"Ours is a hard and thankless chore," Jones said tenderly. He hesitated a while then added, "Yours rather more than that of most of us."

He rose and left quickly.

Well I'm damned, Smithers thought. Am I wrong about everybody? But he felt better, much better. Loyalty in difficult times: that's the thing these people still had to learn. And they'd have to learn it from us. Jones . . .

The Africa Freedom Party was officially launched that night. A hundred thousand people gathered on a strip of land on the northern outskirts of the town. In the darkness, under the new African moon, Adebhoy announced the programme of the new party. It was: Freedom.

Selina offered them Udomo as leader, chairman and president of the party for the rest of his life. Then she led them in a pledge of loyalty to Udomo and the new party. Suddenly, in all parts of the great gathering, flaming torches sprang alight. Tall young men held them high overhead.

"We, the people of Panafrica——" Selina said.

"We, the people of Panafrica——" the great throng echoed.
"Swear undying loyalty to the Africa Freedom Party——"
"Swear undying loyalty to the Africa Freedom Party——"
"And to its great and beloved leader——"
"And to its great and beloved leader——".
"UDOMO!"
"UDOMO!"
"We will follow him——"
"We will follow him——"
"To FREEDOM!"
"To FREEDOM!"
Then an old, old man stepped to the improvised loudspeaker
system and prayed in a whispering voice for their ancestors to
be with them in this great enterprise.

The Chief Secretary and the head of security sat in a car
on the edge of the vast gathering. No one paid them, or the
scores of police about, any attention.

"I wouldn't have believed it!" Smithers said. "I can't, even
now. This is like going back into the past. As though we have
never been here!"

"Or into the future. It's probably a bit of both," Jones said.
"I'm afraid events have robbed our best intentions of any
value. We've lost the initiative to Udomo."

"Damn him!" Smithers exploded.

"He's only the spark," Jones said. "The situation was waiting for him. But there's an element of greatness, I think
you'll agree, in recognising the situation and using it. It needs
boldness and daring at the level of greatness."

"Are you mad!" Smithers exploded. "Greatness indeed!"

Jones smiled in the dark. "Well, we'd better go. There's
work to do this night. We must go with the current now and
try to help guide the ship past the rocks ahead. That is not
going to be easy. . . . Go on, driver."

*　　*　　*

The prison stood on the hill above the Governor's Palace. Inside the prison, in a small cell, Udomo gripped the bars till his knuckles hurt. He stared out at the hundreds of flickering flames. The lawyer stood behind him.

"They are saying the oath now," the lawyer said.

"A hundred thousand, you say?" Udomo's voice choked. He didn't turn.

"More," the lawyer said. "And it's happening in other places too."

Udomo stayed there, on tiptoe, clinging to the bars, till the flames went out. Then he shut his eyes. O Mother Africa! O Mother Africa! His eyes filled with tears. The tears ran down his cheeks. He released the bars, turned and faced the lawyer.

"Go now, my friend. Tell them I wept."

"But we've got to prepare your case. It comes up tomorrow."

Udomo smiled through his tears, a smile lit with sunshine.

"Don't you understand what's happened, man! The case isn't anything now. We can see to that any time: tomorrow. Any time. Go! . . . Go to the people and tell them I wept. Say: 'Udomo stood at his prison window and held the bars and looked out. And then he saw the flames and knew they were taking the oath. And then Udomo wept.' Tell them that. Go now, man!"

The lawyer left. Udomo went and sat on his hard prison bed, smiling through his tears. There was a new brightness in his eyes.

This little cell, this prison, was the gateway to freedom.

I've unlocked the door, Mother Africa! I've unlocked the door!

MHENDI
LANWOOD
MABI

ONE

I

"My God!" Lanwood exclaimed.

"Quite a reception committee," Mhendi said.

A huge, silent crowd watched the boat being made fast. Behind them, at the side of the customs shed, the Africa Freedom Party van's loudspeaker blared out:

"Our party welcomes you, Lanwood! Our party welcomes you, Mhendi!

"Africa welcomes her two great sons! Long live Africa's freedom!

"Long live the Africa Freedom Party! Long live our leader, Udomo!

"Welcome, Lanwood! Welcome, Mhendi!"

There was a pause, then the voice in the van repeated it again.

Now, the gangplank was being put into position. The crowd surged forward slightly. The white passengers stood aside. Lanwood's eyes shone. His dark face glowed. He touched Mhendi's arm.

"My God!" he murmured.

"Go on," Mhendi whispered.

Lanwood led the way down. Mhendi followed.

The voice in the van yelled:

"There they are!"

A great shout rose from the people. The man in the van put on a gramophone record. Gay dance music with an undercurrent of drumbeats pervaded the air. Women put their hands to their mouths and ululated on a high-pitched note. The great crowd jigged to the rhythm of the music.

Near the bottom of the gangway Lanwood paused and looked back at Mhendi. There were tears in his eyes now. He searched his pockets frantically for a handkerchief.

"Go on," Mhendi urged gently.

Lanwood turned, and the people saw his tears. As he reached the bottom of the gangplank one of the women pushed past the harbour police, pulled Lanwood down to her own level, and kissed the tears away. Another great roar rose from the people. The loudspeaker roared:

"With Udomo they planned our freedom! Welcome!"

A big car, painted the same black and red as the van, came to a stop behind the crowd. The music stopped. A new cry went up:

"Udomo! Udomo and Adebhoy have come! Udomo and Adebhoy! Udomo!"

A hush fell on the crowd as Udomo got out of the car, followed by Adebhoy. They both wore cloth, tied at the shoulders like Roman togas. People made way for them, made a little passage that led to the foot of the gangplank. Udomo hurried forward, his face lit by a huge smile, his eyes glowing.

"Welcome, Tom, Mhendi! Welcome!"

183

"Mike . . ." Lanwood's voice faltered.

"Welcome, brothers!" Adebhoy roared with happy laughter.

Udomo flung one arm about Lanwood, the other about Mhendi.

"Hold it, sir!" There was a flash and pop.

"What a reception!" Mhendi said.

"You've seen nothing yet!" Adebhoy said. "You wait!"

"Had a good journey?" Udomo said.

"Treated us like kings," Lanwood said. "How are you, Mike? It's a long time. God!"

"Good." Udomo looked briefly up at the ship. "When I came over they treated me like dirt. Glad they've learned their lesson."

Lanwood pushed out his chest.

"They tried to fraternise on board but we cut them dead. They're all two-faced."

Udomo nodded absently. Mhendi watched him closely. He's changed, Mhendi thought; but how?

"They'll be waiting," Adebhoy said.

"Yes," Udomo said. "Come." He led the way to the big car. "Wave before you get in. The people will like that."

Three black photographers wanted pictures so they all posed beside the car. The man in the van turned on the music. Udomo waved to the crowd. The ululating of the women started up again. Lanwood and Mhendi waved and followed Udomo into the car. There was a great new roar as the car turned and moved off.

Up on board ship one of the new white men just sent out by the Pan-Africa Company said to the man who had come to meet him:

"Thank goodness for that! Now we can get on with the business of disembarking. What a circus!"

"Shouldn't make remarks like that around here," his companion said quietly. "Not even in front of your servants."

"I didn't mean anything," the new man protested.

"I know, old boy. But *they* wouldn't see it like that. It's awfully tricky. They're touchy as hell. We all have to watch our step if we are to go on trading here. You know they burned down a couple of our warehouses in the early days of the change. That cost us a packet. The rule is: Bend over backwards to be polite to everybody, but especially to the big boys. And, above all, don't enter into any political discussion. This is *their* show now. We're only here as traders. Forget all you've heard about Africa and Africans, or you'll come a cropper—in this part of Africa, at least."

"I see . . ." the new man said dubiously.

"The old days are over," the old hand said with a tinge of regret. "Come on, old boy."

The car sped through the town. Here and there houses were decorated with bits of faded bunting; here and there the red-and-black flag of the Africa Freedom Party hung drably in the morning sun, "Red as the blood of the people, black as the land of their birth". And wherever the car passed, people came out to wave and shout their greetings.

Lanwood was quite overcome. He sat holding Udomo's hand, repeating at intervals:

"My God, Mike! My God, what an achievement! What a welcome!"

Adebhoy sat with his arm about Mhendi's shoulders.

Udomo leaned forward and put his free hand on Mhendi's knee.

"Well, brother, what do you think of us?"

"It makes me restless for our own fight," Mhendi said. "I began to despair of hearing from you after you'd been in power a year and there was no call. I thought you'd forgotten."

"I could hardly believe it when your cable came," Lanwood said.

"It's nearly two years now," Mhendi said.

"These things take time," Udomo said. "We had to fight to get you in."

"Much is still in their hands," Adebhoy said. "But we'll get it."

"You know how smart they are," Udomo said. "We have to go carefully."

"Nothing can hold us now!" Lanwood snapped, his black face flushed.

Again, Mhendi sensed Udomo withdrawing as he had done at the docks.

"Our plans for me still stand?" he asked quietly.

"We'll talk later," Udomo said. "The thing is: you are here now."

"Yes," Mhendi said. "I'm back in Africa at last."

Udomo leaned forward suddenly and gripped Mhendi's arm.

"Don't worry, brother . . ." The old feeling of the London days was back in his voice.

Mhendi relaxed and smiled.

The car swept over the crest of a low hill.

"Look!" Adebhoy said.

They were on the western outskirts of the town now, and ahead of them thousands of people milled around a raised platform, unmindful of the heat of the morning sun. Music blared from loudspeakers dotted all over the huge square.

"That's Freedom Square," Udomo said.

"That's where the party was founded," Adebhoy said. "That's where we all took the oath on the day Udomo went to prison. That's why we call it Freedom Square. One day the party headquarters will be built there. All our great decisions are given to the people there."

A great roar rose from the crowd as they saw the car. Hundreds rushed forward to meet it.

"I must write the history of this bloodless revolution!" Lanwood exclaimed.

The car came to a stop. Udomo led the way to the platform. He moved among the people with easy freedom. From time to time a man or woman stopped him. He listened carefully to what they said. Occasionally he brought a pad and pencil from the folds of his toga and noted down what they said. When they neared the platform an old woman shouted:

"Udomo! Udomo! I'm not strong enough to get near you, so make quiet."

Udomo raised his arms.

"Quiet!"

There was quiet.

"I hear you do not sleep much," the old woman called. "It is a thing I want to know about. How much do you sleep?"

"I am strong, mother," Udomo said. "I sleep enough."

"That is no answer. Tell us the number of hours."

"But I don't know the number of hours. Some nights I sleep more than others."

"They say some nights you do not go to sleep until it is nearly daylight, and then at daylight you get up and go to that office of yours. Is it so?"

"Only when I have much work to do."

"And you have much work all the time? Yes?"

Udomo turned grinning to the crowd and flung up his hands.

"My mother traps me with clever words."

The crowd roared their approval.

"It is because we need your strength," the old woman called. "So you must take care of it. It belongs to Africa."

"I promise you I will take care of it."

"Then sleep enough and let others do some of your work. We need your brain to think for us."

"There is wisdom in your words, mother," Udomo called. "I promise to take care."

He led the way onto the platform. Selina and the other party stalwarts were there already. Udomo went to the microphone. The great crowd became silent. He spoke quietly, as though talking privately to each person.

"You remember I told you at meetings here, and also in our paper, about the people who were with me as I dreamed of the freedom we have now won. You know Adebhoy. He has been among you all the time. He and Selina built our party while I was in that place." He pointed to the prison on top of the hill. "But while Adebhoy and Selina and all you others fought here, these people about whom I have told you, about whom I have written for you in our paper, these brothers of mine, fought for us in a foreign and cold country with the weapon of their words and their writings. You have seen the words they have written in our paper. Now they are here in person. It has taken us a long time to get them here. We have not yet got all the freedom we want. Others still control many things in our land. There is an animal called immigration and they control that. In the past this animal has meant that it is easier for white people to move about our country, about all Africa, than it is for the people born in Africa. Remember, I told you how it was when I came home? Selina and I had to wait for all the white people to get off before we could. That was all part of this animal called immigration. But today my brothers who, as you can see, are black, got off the ship first. So you see, we are taming this animal and before so long it will come into our hands and we will control it as a man controls his dog. It is in this way that we shall get all the things that make up freedom into our hands. We will get them quietly and firmly, if we can. But if anybody tries to resist us we will use other methods, won't we?"

A thunderous, deep-throated "Yes" rose to the skies.

"Well, they wanted to keep out my brothers, but I was firm. Now my brothers are here. We will know how to be firm when firmness is needed.

"Now, my friends, you've all heard about that place called Pluralia where five million whites are the lords and masters over forty millions of our fellow Africans. Today, our people there have no rights. I am now speaking as an African nationalist, as the leader of your party. I cannot yet speak like this for the government of this country. You understand that. As the leader of your party, I say our people there have no rights. They have fought for their rights and they have been ruthlessly crushed. But they will rise again. And one day they will be free. Here, then, is my brother, David Mhendi, leader of our oppressed brothers in Pluralia. Greet him; welcome him so that those whites of Pluralia should know how you feel!"

Udomo brought Mhendi to the microphone. The crowd raised their voices.

"Don't make a speech," Udomo whispered. "I'll explain later."

"I'm very happy to be here," Mhendi said. "Very happy to be back in Africa again. Thank you for your welcome." He went back to his seat.

Udomo slipped his arm through Lanwood's and led him to the microphone.

"Don't make a speech, Tom. I'll explain later." He spoke into the microphone: "And here is my friend, one of our greatest political teachers, Tom Lanwood. You all know his name. You've all read his words. He has given our generation the words of freedom. Welcome him!"

Again, a great roar went up from the crowd.

"My friends!" Lanwood began. "African brothers and sisters! This is the proudest day of all my life! This is the reward for all the years of struggle and suffering." His voice gathered strength. "This is also the proud beginning of the great forward march of the African peoples, all over the continent, including Pluralia, to their ultimate freedom from imperialist and capitalist exploitation . . ."

Udomo tugged firmly at his sleeve. Lanwood paused. Udomo took over the microphone.

"Now you have met my brothers. You will meet them again.

189

There will be time for that later; time for talking and playing, for they will need playing after their years among the cold people of cold countries. Show them our warmth! Remember, they are my guests, my brothers, so that they are yours too.

"Now one last thing. You remember I told you about our great need for education if our people are to take over the running of all our services. We will need experts in all departments of life before we can make Africanisation real. This means training. Well, two thousand men and women are going abroad this year for this kind of training. And we are now working on a Bill to make education free and compulsory for every child in our land. This is planning for the future. It will all cost money. The Council of Nations is sending a delegation to study our needs in the next few weeks. I will tell them of our needs. But we must not depend on others. We must pay our own way. When all has been worked out, I will come and tell you as I always do." He raised his hand in the party salute.

Tumultuous cheering broke out.

Music struck up again and blared forth through the loudspeakers. Scores of people jumped on the platform to shake Mhendi and Lanwood by the hand. People started drifting down to the town in small, laughing, talking clusters. Party girls in their black-and-red uniforms did a brisk trade selling red-and-black rosettes. One pretty girl pinned extra large rosettes to the lapels of the two honoured guests. And through it all, Udomo stood a little aside, watching everything.

Mhendi thought: There are no flags in his eyes now, they're all about him; and how it's relaxed him, how he's grown! Mhendi watched closely as the tall, barefooted woman, Selina, went and talked to Udomo. She's a key person, Mhendi decided. Udomo beckoned him. He went over. Lanwood was having a high time. Party youths were clustered about him and he was autographing slips of paper and answering their questions, a fatherly beam on his face all the time.

"Selina will take care of you," Udomo said. "We have to go to the secretariat. If you want anything, just ask. See you to-night. Sorry we can't stay with you but there's a lot to do."

"I understand," Mhendi said.

Adebhoy pushed his way to Lanwood and told him they had to go off. Lanwood replied absently. Then Udomo and Adebhoy went off. With their going, the crowds dispersed more rapidly. Only Lanwood still held a firm grip on his audience. He was getting worked up now; he waved his arms as he held forth. Mhendi saw the cold detachment with which Selina watched Lanwood's performance. I'd better warn Tom, he decided; he's going on as though he's still in England. He's been away from Africa too long. He's lost touch and could mess up things for himself.

"Your welcome has filled my heart," Mendhi said to Selina. "I have no words to tell you of the fullness of my heart."

A smile flickered across the woman's cold, austere face. She patted his sleeve with her long, thin, black fingers.

"The welcome is from our hearts, my friend. Not all know why you are here, but I do. Our fight is the same. Do not feel a stranger. We will talk later, you and I, of the things you dream of. . . . Your friend . . ." The friendliness went from her voice. "He likes to talk. When he has done we will go to my house where you will eat and rest."

"I will call him."

"Let him finish."

"He gets excited. He may go on."

"I know he is of our country. But he has been away a long time?"

"Thirty years."

"And he has been over there all the time?"

"Yes."

"I see. . . . Though he's black his ways are like theirs. Yes. . . ."

"I'll call him. It is the excitement of the welcome."

191

Mhendi walked to the other end of the platform. He pushed his way through the crowd of young people.

"Tom! You must stop now, man! Come; Selina's waiting."

"I'll be with you in a minute."

"Now, Tom!"

"Can't leave these young people in the air, man! Tell you I'll be with you in a minute."

"For heaven's sake, Tom! Think where you are!"

"You go, sah," one of the young people said. "Selina is important."

"All right." Lanwood stifled his impatience with obvious effort. "But we must meet again. I didn't come back to make the social round but to work for the revolution. You young people are the future of the revolution. You must understand the world in which you live. We'll set up study and discussion groups. We'll . . ."

"Come on, Tom!"

An angry glint showed in Lanwood's eyes. The young people drifted off.

"Goodbye, sah!"

"See you again, sah."

Selina came over.

"The car waits."

"Sorry we kept you," Mhendi said.

"It is nothing."

"Those young people are wonderful!" Lanwood said. "It is great to be alive in these days, in the days of our revolution. Heh, Selina?"

Oh God, Mhendi thought.

"Come," Selina said.

Like Udomo's, her car was painted the party colours and flew a red-and-black standard; like Udomo's driver, hers was dressed in a red-and-black uniform. They drove away to the cheers of the remaining people. Two cars carrying members of the party executive followed.

A feast awaited them at Selina's. All the important party members were there. The Assembly was in recess so most of the party's Assemblymen were there too. Feasting, talking and drinking went on all through the day. In the late afternoon troupes of dancers and singers came to perform outside Selina's house. Then Selina led them to separate rooms to rest till Udomo's return in the evening. First, she took Lanwood and ushered him into an empty room. Then she led Mhendi to the room where she had taken Udomo the night before he went to prison. Mhendi was slightly tight and very happy. They walked arm-in-arm.

"For you, there is someone to make your sleep more restful," Selina said. "You are of us so there is no need to explain."

"And my friend?"

"That one is white for all his black skin. He would not understand."

"You are wrong, Selina dear; you are wrong. It is only that he has been there too long. He will forget their ways and come back to ours."

"It is you who are wrong, Mhendi. All day I have watched him. And it was like watching a white man with a black skin. He is too old to change. As you say he stayed away too long. He will never come back to us. He is lost to us."

"Be kind to him, Selina. In his heart he is one of us, for all his funny ways. Be kind to him. He's an old man now, and he needs the help of Africa."

"Did he have a white woman over there, all these years?"

"We all did."

"That is not what I mean. You and Udomo and Adebhoy had them to sleep with, but always your hearts were in Africa. How long did he have his woman?"

"You must be kind to him, Selina; or his life will be empty."

"How long, Mhendi?"

"Twenty years, my sister."

"You see——"

"But he left her to come home."

"Too late, I fear. But we will see."

"Give him time. Time to settle down and you will see. And please, be kind to him. I beg you."

"For your sake and for Udomo's I will try. But I fear it is too late. And I am not the only one. Still . . . We'll see. . . . How long will you keep the girl waiting?"

Mhendi swayed slightly.

"Is she beautiful, sister?"

Selina faced him squarely. A new tenderness showed in her eyes.

"Mhendi, listen carefully. Two years ago—maybe longer— they shot your wife over there in that place called Pluralia. I saw the picture of your wife. Go in. The one in there is like her. I found her especially for you. She will be your wife if you want it so, for you are of the blood of Africa. Now go, my brother, and rest well."

"So you know of her," Mhendi said quietly.

"I know. . . . Now go in and ease your pain and loneliness. You are no stranger here."

"Selina. . . ." He took her long, thin, black hand in his own. "It has not been easy." His eyes turned sombre.

"I know, Mhendi," she said tenderly. "I know."

She left him then. He stood at the door for a while, then he opened it and went in. The woman sat on the bed, hands in her lap, waiting. Mhendi stopped and stared at her. I'm drunk, he thought. A small round face and big, dark, quiet eyes. That's what the other one looked like; the one he had never really got to know; the one they killed; his wife. And here was the image of her in another woman, in another land. . . . The woman rose and looked at him.

"What are you called?" he asked quietly.

"Maria," she said.

"Sit, child." He went and sat beside her on the bed. The face and form of his dead wife, a little older perhaps than when he

194

had last seen her. But perhaps she would have looked just like this had she lived and had he seen her again. He felt her grow restless under his close scrutiny, so he turned his eyes away. "How old are you?"

"Twenty-six."

"And without a man?"

Her lips curved in a smile, and it was just like that other's.

"I had a man but he died. He had no brothers to take me so I went back to my mother's house."

"And did you——" He was going to say "love him" but changed it to: "Have any children?"

"A boy," she said. "He is with my mother."

"Where?" I must sober up. I must.

"My home is in the north, near the great lake."

"And why are you here?"

"Selina sent for me. She passed my home a year ago and stayed in my mother's house for one night. Then, two weeks ago, she sent a message and money to bring me here."

"To wait for me?"

"To wait for you. She showed me the picture of your wife, who was like me, and she told me of what happened to you and how your wife was killed."

"And you were willing to come here and wait for me?"

"Not at first, for I did not know you and you are not of our land. But I have watched you all day. Now I am here."

"Why?"

She lowered her head and turned it from him.

"I have watched you all day, and you are one of us, though not of our land. And I have seen the loneliness that is in you. It is in your voice now, when you speak. . . ."

He put his hand on her neck.

"I have been lonely, my child."

"Come then," she murmured and turned to him.

He gathered her in his arms. And it was the dead one come

alive; only, grown older, stronger, more assured, more subtly passionate in her responses.

Afterwards, as she lay in his arms, he said:

"You have much skill. Where did you learn it?"

"Are not the women in your land taught? I was; at our schools for young girls."

"They are: but they have not your skill."

"Perhaps they are cut. That dulls the feeling. We are not."

"Yes, they are circumcised in my land. I thought perhaps you learn it from other men."

She turned her head and looked into his eyes.

"There have been no others since my man died."

"And if I want you to stay with me always?" He touched her face.

"Then I am yours. There is great tenderness in you."

"And you will love me?"

"You can teach me, for I want to, Mhendi. Now sleep. . . ."

She put her hand on his body and caressed him gently till he fell asleep. Then, quietly, she got out of bed, dressed, and went in search of Selina.

"What is it? Why are you not with Mhendi? Have you displeased him?"

"He is well pleased, Selina. He sleeps."

"Then what is it, child? Why are you here instead of with him?"

"There is a bond between us. It came suddenly. Now I fear it may not be what you planned. It may be that you have other plans."

"You are anxious about a stranger you have only met to-day."

"He is no stranger to me now. I have felt the things in his heart."

"So soon?"

"So soon. He has great tenderness."

"And you fear that I may not want you tied to him?"

196

"Or him to me."

Selina's face softened.

"Fear not, my child. I told him he can have you for wife
if you are agreed. Comfort him well that he may serve Africa
well. Go to your man. You must not believe those who tell
you Selina is hard and scheming. It is only with the enemies
of our land, of Africa, that it is so. Go to your man so that
he does not wake alone in a strange bed. We will arrange
things."

Maria went back. Mhendi was still asleep. His face, in sleep,
was tranquil. She sat on the bed and watched him.

2

"Now we can talk."

Udomo leaned his head against the chair rest. It was close
on midnight and they were in the sitting-room of the fine new
house the party had built for him.

"What a day!" Lanwood said happily.

Adebhoy turned from the window and chuckled softly.

"Tell us," Mhendi said. "You've lived through it. Tell us
the things the papers didn't report."

"How I wished I were here at the time!" Lanwood said.

"You were more useful where you were," Adebhoy said.
"Udomo was more useful in prison than out."

"See!" Udomo grinned. "I'm just a figurehead. Adebhoy
and Selina built the party. They have the real power. Heh,
Ade?"

Udomo's eyes twinkled, but Mhendi sensed an undercurrent
of seriousness.

Adebhoy's chuckle turned into a roar of laughter. He strode
across the room to the liquor table, replenished his glass and
brought the whisky bottle to Mhendi. Udomo touched his
glass of sherry to his lips, then put it down.

"They call him the joker, now," Adebhoy said.

"See . . . They even mock me to my face. Udomo the joker."

"Come on, boys. Tell us."

"Tell them," Udomo said.

Adebhoy sat on the arm of Udomo's chair.

"He jokes about it now but he knows it couldn't have started without his call to the people. . . ."

"What an historic document!" Lanwood said. "I'm going to have a photostat reproduced in my book."

"Go on," Mhendi urged.

Udomo tilted his head and looked up at Adebhoy. A private, enigmatic little smile played on his lips.

"You know they tried to confiscate the paper the day it came out. Well, they *tried,* but we smuggled it out under their noses. In less than twelve hours Selina had an efficient smuggling organisation going. Also, we set up reading circles so that as many people as possible could hear the call. It became the duty of every person who could read—man, woman or child—to read the call to at least a dozen others who could not. That's why the party paper is now called *The Call.* All that we did on the day he was arrested. That night we launched the party. Next morning we printed the leaflet about him weeping. That really stirred the people. You know all about the trial. It was then that reporters from all over the world started flocking in. It was the speech he made at the trial calling for a general strike that stopped everything and really finished them. No one went to work next day.

"They declared an emergency then. They banned the party and all gatherings. . . ."

"And all the time, all the three months, I lay uselessly in prison," Udomo said mockingly.

"But the party went underground and carried on. And then Rosslee played his last card. He issued the draft of his new constitution and promised that it would come into operation within a month of the people returning to work. The govern-

ment and the Council of Chiefs and Elders really thought
they could by-pass the party in this way and so destroy our
influence."

"They nearly did," Udomo said quietly. "Although there
was an emergency forbidding public meetings, the government allowed Endura to stump the country telling the people
the new constitution was his idea. For a time it seemed the
people would accept his lead."

Adebhoy took it up again:

"But then Selina and the women went to work. They left
their work and wandered from village to village, from town
to town, talking to the people. They didn't hold public meetings. They went from house to house and talked to the people
in their homes. The tide turned and resistance stiffened again."
Suddenly, Adebhoy's laughter filled the room. "I tell you,
Tom, Endura turned up at one village after Selina and her
women had been there. The people of the village turned on
him and he and his chiefs had to run for their lives! After
that they were chased from village after village!"

"Served the dirty rats right!" Lanwood snapped.

Adebhoy refilled his glass.

"That's all, really. The country was paralysed till Udomo
came out——"

"So I got remission for 'good conduct' and served only three
of my five months." Udomo chuckled softly.

"They had at last realised the people wouldn't do a thing
till he gave them the word. . . . You're thrilled by your reception today. Well, if you'd been here on the day he came
out you would have seen something. Man! Emergency just
didn't mean a thing that day! People flocked in from all over
the country and the government had the sense to let them be.
Udomo studied the constitution and recommended to the
party that we give it a trial. The party told the people to go
back to work. And because the party directive was signed by
Udomo, they went back. Elections were held two months later.

We won fifty-one out of the sixty seats and Rosslee had no option but to call Udomo in to form a government. Right, home-boy?"

"The first African revolution to succeed," Lanwood mused. "And a bloodless one. Man! You boys have really done a great job!"

"Don't forget the women," Udomo said.

"And how is it now?" Mhendi said. "Do these fellow co-operate?"

"They've no choice!" Lanwood snapped.

"Those who couldn't left," Udomo murmured. "Smithers, the former Chief Secretary, couldn't, so he's gone. His successor, Jones, is a good man. Rosslee co-operates. That's all we ask of them."

"A change for that crook," Lanwood said.

Udomo shook his head imperceptibly, but said nothing.

"There are others who must go," Adebhoy said. "People who can't work with the Africans are not wanted here."

Mhendi's eyes flitted from Adebhoy's face to Udomo's. There's conflict somewhere on this point, he thought.

"Africanisation will get rid of them," Lanwood said.

Oh, Tom! Mhendi sighed to himself. He hadn't realised till now just how dull of perception poor Tom was. If only he would be quiet.

"We face problems there," Udomo murmured. "We have to have the men to replace these Englishmen. Running departments isn't the same as making speeches, you know." For all his quietness there was an edge to his voice. He tilted his head up to Adebhoy's face. "You know that better than anyone else, Ade. . . ."

"Yes," Adebhoy said, a tinge of reluctance to his voice.

Tom could mess this up, Mhendi thought and said:

"Of course. I sometimes think winning power is the easiest part."

"You didn't find it so," Lanwood jeered.

"You're right," Udomo said as though Lanwood had not spoken. "Running a country can be more difficult than winning it. Ade and some of the others are impatient. They want a republic tomorrow. They think I'm too slow. Don't you, Ade?"

So, Mhendi thought; there *is* conflict.

"They'll stay on our terms," Adebhoy said. "They're too well paid not to. And our men are coming up fast. My point is simply that we mustn't depend on them too much."

"Mabi sends you his regards," Mhendi said quickly.

There was a sudden twinkle in Udomo's eyes.

"To me too?"

You've grown deep, my friend, Mhendi thought. He said: "Yes."

"We're going to call him home," Adebhoy said. "We need someone in the government from the mountain people. Endura's opposition crowd are wooing the mountain people and telling them they're not represented."

"Paul will come like a shot," Lanwood said. He leaned towards Udomo and went on in his most fatherly manner: "I shouldn't let personal issues from the past cloud your judgement, Mike. This is bigger than personalities."

Mhendi shut his eyes. Oh, you fool! Oh, you bloody fool!

"All right!" Udomo straightened his back suddenly. His face went stern. "See to it tomorrow, Ade. . . . See, Mhendi, all I can do is agree to decisions."

Adebhoy was startled.

"Then you agree——"

"Yes, yes. You'd better get Selina to persuade our helpless old Minister of Education and National Guidance that it's in the interest of the country to have Mabi step into his shoes. But don't come running to me if he finds the fruits of office too sweet to surrender."

"He won't, home-boy! I promise you. He's under a charge of fraternising with the Europeans. . . ."

"Oh! Why wasn't I told?"

"You've been so busy lately——" Adebhoy said lamely.

"Yes," Udomo said. "But you might tell me when you plan to reshuffle my Cabinet."

"Now, home-boy. . . ."

Udomo brushed it aside.

"Anyway, I want your plans well before you start acting."

"Right!" Adebhoy said.

"Fine," Lanwood said. "I'll drop Paul a line tomorrow. I told him I'd talk to you."

"So he asked you to talk to me?" Udomo said curiously.

"No. But I told him I would. Now that's settled. What about us? Me? I'm here to do a job. This is what I've lived for. These days are a challenge to a man's abilities."

"Well, Ade." The mockery was strong in Udomo's voice. "What have you got for Tom?"

Adebhoy stopped grinning and looked at the floor. There was an uneasy silence. Lanwood looked from one to the other.

"Isn't that what you boys called me home for?" He, too, was uneasy now.

Udomo went and sat beside him.

"Look, Tom; it isn't easy. You know the Public Services Commission is independent of the government, so that's out. There are no vacancies for the Assembly at present. But even if there were we can't just put you up. There are hundreds of loyal party workers waiting for a chance to get into the Assembly."

"But just now you said Paul could . . ."

"Come now, Tom. You know how it is in politics. Mabi is the outstanding figure among the mountain people. Endura is wooing the mountains. Ade told you that. Mabi represents those people. If he comes in with us, the people are with us. . . ."

"And I represent nobody." He was an old man now. "I am the creole whose people were transported, and although he came back doesn't belong any more. And I've given all my life to the struggle."

"No, Tom. Your people came back when you were a child. You are one of us. But you've been in Europe a long time. They've got to get to know you. And tribal loyalties are strong, man. You should understand that. We'll overcome them in time. That's where you can help. We need to build up national loyalties as against tribal loyalties. Endura and his crowd play on all the tribal prejudices in the people. We have to counter that, otherwise we'll never build a strong African state that is as modern as any of the European states. Before Africa's voice will be listened to in the world, we need strong modern states. That's where we'll need you most. You talked about a book. The party will publish it. Let that be a beginning. Get to know your people again. Go about it carefully. Our people are not like the people of Europe. You can make a place for yourself here. Only, be careful of our ways. . . . We'd better go to bed now. I've a hard day's negotiating to do tomorrow. I have to deal with some hard-headed white industrialists, so I need a few hours' sleep. We'll talk again."

He got up. Lanwood was slowly recovering. Mhendi avoided looking at him. Adebhoy poured himself a drink and brought the bottle to Mhendi.

"One for the road," Adebhoy said and tossed it down. "See you, boys."

Udomo said: "Get to my office as soon as you can. Jones will be there. I'll need all the help I can get with those hard-headed businessmen." He grinned suddenly. "Wish I could call in Selina. . . ."

They went to the veranda with Adebhoy. The stars stood out bright in the black night. The big bright moon made queer shadows of the two strapping men who stood guard at the gate of Udomo's house. Adebhoy's driver woke the moment his master opened the car door. The guards opened the gate. . . .

Half an hour later Udomo entered Mhendi's room quietly.

"Wanted to wait till Tom was asleep," he whispered.

Mhendi switched on the bedside lamp.

"You're still dressed. Thought you were asleep."

"Only time I have for catching up on my papers. I have to watch them very closely. We have three passengers in the Cabinet who think all a Minister has to do is sign papers as they are put before him. Don't know how I would have managed without Ade. . . . Anyway, I didn't come to tell you my troubles. Shall I get you a drink?"

"No, thanks."

Udomo sat on the edge of the bed.

"What are we going to do with him?"

"Tom?"

"Yes." He exploded suddenly. "My God, man! I must have been blind over there in England. He's the same as he was over there. I'm not wrong about that, am I?"

"He's the same; a little older, but the same."

"I can't believe it! And yet I know it's true. All I have to do is think back—now. And yet he's been a hero of mine for years. . . . But what are we to do with him? He just doesn't fit here."

"Selina been talking to you?"

"And others. But I've also seen it. I'd thought of a key post in the party, behind the scenes. But he's no good for that."

"Are you sure?"

"Aren't you?"

Mhendi sighed. "Tom's an old man now; as near sixty as not to matter. He's been dreaming and writing about the African revolution all his life. It's all become very simple in his mind. This is his first day here and he's still superimposing the vision of his books on it. This is his life; this is all his dreams come true."

"I see all that, Mhendi. But he's such a goddamned fool about people. He's lectured at the entire party executive and put up their backs."

"He sees himself as the father of this revolution, Mike."

"It's still a game to him."

"But more important than life."

"That's the problem. We *could* arrange a seat in the Assembly but I don't think the executive would agree now. They would have before he came. And much as I like Tom *I* won't have him in the Assembly now."

"Give him time, Mike. He might see."

"Or he might cause trouble. I must hold the party together at any cost."

"That book he talks of writing, let him do that. That'll be useful work and he's good at that. It'll kill him if he feels unwanted. He broke with Mary Feld when he got your cable. It was a terrible scene. I saw it. I didn't know you could hate a person so much and still go on living with them. He'd have nowhere to go to now."

"Oh, I won't send him back."

"I'll have a talk with him, Mike. You talk to him too. He means well."

"We'd better do it before he makes enemies of all the key people in the party."

"Can't you get him away from Queenstown for a spell?"

"I'm starting my tour of the country next week."

"Take him with you, Mike."

"Yes . . . Yes . . . I think you're right. I'll do that." Udomo nodded. "Now what about you?"

"You know why I came. I don't want to be a problem."

An odd little smile flitted across Udomo's face.

"These negotiations I'm worrying about now; they're part of my industrialisation project. As you've gathered, there's some opposition among our own people. Not to industrialisation as such—I've convinced them at last that that is the only way we can become strong in terms of world power. The opposition is to the fact that we need European technicians and European capital to do it. But there's no other way. The great inland lake can be made to supply power throughout the country. But we can't do it without European capital and technical skill. That's one reason why Tom's anti-capitalism is undesirable. The earth, especially in the mountain area, is rich in gold and uranium as well as other minerals. Again we need the capital and skills of Europeans. It's a tricky one, Mhendi. Endura has seen my difficulty. I've promised to get rid of the Europeans. The people are with me because of that promise. You may think I have a blank cheque. It isn't really blank. But I need the Europeans. It's tricky. I must convince the Europeans their money would be safe. Believe it or not, but the only people who understand what I'm trying to do are Rosslee and Jones and that crook Endura. My own party is suspicious. The thing is . . ." He stopped talking. He moved his hands in a quiet gesture of resignation. He stared intently at Mhendi. "The thing is . . ." His voice sank to a whisper. "The thing is, Mhendi, your people, those whites of Pluralia, are making me the best offer in skill and capital. I'm seeing their people tomorrow." He gestured with his hands again and looked away.

"I see. . . ." Mhendi said quietly.

The smile flitted across Udomo's face.

"Do you?"

"Perhaps I don't. You tell me what it means to me."

Udomo reached down and gripped Mhendi's bare shoulder.

"Relax, man. It doesn't mean that."

"Then what?"

"Only that it's tricky. You've had responsibility, so you know a man can't always do just what he wants to."

"Well?"

"Relax, man!"

"Easy for you to say!" Mhendi snapped suddenly.

"Your plan goes through," Udomo said quietly. "One thing must be clear. I have nothing to do with it. I don't know anything about it. I'm the Prime Minister of this country.

Prime Ministers don't aid revolutionaries from neighbouring countries, especially if they are dependent on those countries for capital and skill. No one knows why you are here except Selina. Adebhoy and I don't know from this minute. So, it's only you and Selina. . . ."

Mhendi relaxed.

"I see."

"But do you understand, my friend?"

"Yes."

"I'm glad. It means a lot."

"I'd better move from here."

"Selina has thought of that. She'll see to it. . . . You know we can make a place for you here. You could be very useful, and it would be safe—for both of us."

"They are my people. I must go."

"I thought you'd say that. You'll probably move tomorrow. Selina knows. By the way, Rosslee told me to greet you. Said to tell you he would have invited you to Government House if our policy wasn't one of non-fraternisation. He's a good man. I wouldn't have been able to get you here without his backing. There was a lot of pressure behind the scenes."

"He doesn't know why I'm here?"

"He knows you are here to be back in Africa. I've fought to give asylum to an African patriot. . . . Funny, the people one can talk to are barred by non-fraternisation. I sometimes need someone to talk to as I'm talking to you now."

"The revolutionary leader ends up being the prisoner of the revolution he has led. It's the kind of thing Tom should say or write."

"I can almost hear him. But he would be a different Tom if he said it."

"Perhaps he'll learn."

"I hope so . . . Well, I'm glad we've had this chance to talk. We may not have another. You'll not be here tomorrow. I'll try to see you when I can. When do you hope to leave?"

"Soon as possible. I'll talk to Selina."

"She'll take care of you." Udomo rose. "Well, brother."

Mhendi sat up in bed. Udomo held out his hand.

"You understand?"

"Don't worry, Mike. I understand."

"Tell me——" Udomo hesitated; his eyes slid past Mhendi's face. He tried to smile. "Did you see Lois before you left?"

"No. Haven't seen her for over a year."

"Oh?"

"She gave up teaching a few months after you left; she left England."

"The cottage in the mountains?"

"Yes."

"I remember how beautiful it was there."

"Yes."

"You know our party leaders take an oath not to marry white women."

"I didn't."

"They do."

"I see."

Udomo stood quiet for a while. Mhendi braced himself to cope with the question he felt coming. Then, suddenly, Udomo whispered:

"She lingers, brother."

What does one say? Mhendi wondered.

Udomo's face creased in a sudden smile. He squared his shoulders. His voice was brisk and cold again.

"Sleep well, Mhendi. We have work to do, you and I. Success to yours." He looked at his watch. "God! It's nearly three. . . ."

He left the room as quietly as he had entered it.

Mhendi sank back on to the pillow, reached out and turned off the light. He lay open-eyed in the dark room.

So Udomo had discovered the loneliness of those who would

lead men. The odd thing was it had made him strong. He seemed to thrive on it.

"Why am I not like that?" he murmured.

He found no answer to that so he turned on his side and closed his eyes.

3

Maria slept with her head on Mhendi's lap. The violent bumping of the truck did not disturb her sleep. He held her waist. She was so relaxed that, but for his hold, she would have slithered to the floor and become entangled with the driver's feet.

Really, of course, they were wonderfully well-off travelling beside the driver. Those poor people in the body of the truck were jammed together like sardines. And there were at least half a dozen babies with the crowd at the back.

Mhendi shifted his eyes from the bright headlights that pierced the darkness of the road. He looked at the driver. The man sat hunched over the wheel, peering at the night ahead. He was older and more responsible than the first two had been. This one tried to avoid the bumps and kept to a steady fifty where the roads were straight and level. Not that there were any really straight and level roads in this country. Pity he couldn't talk to this chap. He was one of those who spoke only their own dialects.

They had travelled for thirty-six hours now. They had changed lorries three times. Queenstown was a day and two nights behind them.

It was after their second stop that Mhendi had really relaxed. There had been someone to meet them at the first village where they stopped. The man had taken them to a house, given them a place to wash and rest and then fed them. And then, later, there had been no need for them to go to the market square to fight their way to a seat on the truck. The truck had come to the house for them and the seat beside the driver had been reserved for them. But that could have been sheer good luck, the zealous efficiency of a local individual. It was when the same thing had happened at the next stop, and in the dead of night, that Mhendi had realised that this was overall organisation and no piece of good luck. And he had relaxed and taken a greater interest in the drab, flat land through which they travelled. Mainly, the land was poor and unfertile, not rich red earth as of his native Pluralia: a hard yellowish scrubland where trees grew stuntedly. Mainly, the mud-and-wattle villages they passed seemed desolate and forlorn compared with those in which the people of his own country lived. But the greatest difference had been in the people. The people here were manifestly happy. They were possessed of a robust gaiety and friendliness that transformed their drab surroundings. Their laughter was something new to him.

Over his own people there was a permanent blanket of quiet sadness that invaded even their laughter and play. That was the great difference. Even the voices here were different from the voices of his own people; even, in a subtle way, the shape and structure of the bones. And stupid whites lumped all Africa together. And yet there was a oneness of feeling that flowed out of the common experience of empire. Would that oneness of feeling survive the passing of empire? It was an artificial thing created by empire and the whites. When that was gone they were likely to become as different from each other as are the Germans or English from the French. And colour wouldn't matter as much to Selina as it did now. . . .

Selina. Strange woman that. She had kept him waiting three weeks without a word. Then she had come to him and said:

"Everything is arranged. You leave tomorrow night. Don't ask any questions of anyone on the way. And don't worry. You will be taken care of." And now he was here, travelling through the night, desperately tired but unable to sleep. And Maria, who had watched over him on the journey, was sleeping now.

Were they supposed to go through that jungle alone? All Maria knew was that people would be waiting. She didn't even know who the people were. But on the other side of the jungle, if it could be penetrated, was the world he knew, his world, the world he wanted to liberate. And what a different world from this it was. What a different world. . . .

The driver fished a crumpled packet of cigarettes from his shirt pocket and offered it to Mhendi. Mhendi would have preferred his pipe but accepted one. These things always coated his tongue, especially when he was tired. And his throat was already sore from the thick dust that was all about them. The driver had trouble lighting his own so Mhendi lit it for him. The cigarette in the night was something shared, a moment of companionship between two men who could not speak to each other. The smoke burned his throat, but Mhendi didn't mind. It was something shared.

He flung away the butt-end. He made his aching back as comfortable as possible. A child began to whimper at the back of the truck. He held his wrist to the dashboard light and read the time on his watch: half-past three. It would soon get light. How alone a man feels in the small hours of the morning. It shouldn't be long now before they reached the lake. The child stopped whimpering. The mother had probably thrust her breast into its mouth. He closed his eyes. . . .

He opened his eyes to the sound of voices. Darkness had been replaced by a subdued light. Maria was awake and sat erect beside him.

"See the mountains," she said.

They rose misty in the distance, straight ahead, tinged with blue and lit by the sun, as yet unseen on this side. They seemed, from this distance, a solid, impassable range. They were the first mountains Mhendi had seen in this flat land.

"And we cross them?"

"Yes. But first we'll go to my home. You must meet my mother and your new son."

The truck curved round a mound of raised land and the great lake lay directly ahead of them, a huge inland sea, black in the early pre-dawn light. The truck rattled down the bumpy sandy road. Dust swirled about them. And all the people were awake and chattering at the top of their voices. Ahead, directly ahead of them now, and clearly visible, was journey's end.

Mhendi noticed the land here was more fertile, vegetation more richly lush than throughout the early part of the journey. This part of the land was beautiful, reminded him of his own land. He sensed Maria's mounting excitement. Of course, she was going home. The heart always quickens.

"You are happy," he said.

"It is my home." She pushed against his shoulder.

"Yes," he said a little heavily. "Home."

"Yours too," she said quickly.

How she responded to his moods; how she tried to comfort him. He patted her hand. He raised his eyes to the misty mountains. Home was there, beyond those mountains.

Half an hour later the truck rattled to a stop at the market place. People spilled out. The driver spoke to Maria.

"We stay here," she told Mhendi. "They will come for us. There are many white people here and it is better for you not to be seen. Part of the English army is in this place too. There is no need to fear. It is just that we must be careful till we are across the water."

The driver left them in the truck.

"It is a big place," Mhendi said.

"It is second only to Queenstown," Maria said.

"What do the white people do here?"

"It is a big trading place for the Pan-Africa Company. Also, as I told you, it is an army place. And there is the college of the missionaries where I went to school."

"Mabi must have gone there too," Mhendi murmured.

"Mabi?" Maria said.

"He is a friend of mine. He's from the mountains. He is in England now."

"I know of only one person from the mountains in the white man's country."

"It is of him I speak."

All the other passengers had, by now, left the market place and they were the only two left in the truck. Early traders, bent on getting the best pitches, eyed them curiously. Mhendi was beginning to feel concern when a car pulled up beside the truck. An unseen person opened the rear door. A voice called out.

"It is for us," Maria said. "Go."

They hurried from the truck to the car. The car shot off at a fast pace.

Mhendi felt rather than saw the man beside him. Maria squeezed his right hand reassuringly.

"Do not be alarmed, Mr. Mhendi," the man beside him said in English. "It is only that we border other countries here and officials are always on the look-out for smugglers. A great deal of smuggled diamonds pass through here, so all strangers are watched."

Mhendi took an instinctive, unreasoning dislike to the man beside him. He grunted but said nothing.

The car stopped outside a house on the outskirts of the town.

"Follow me."

They followed the man into the house. He led them to a large room and lit an oil lamp.

Mhendi recognised the man straightaway. He had met his kind all over the world, sometimes black or brown or yellow or white in colour, but all the same under the skin; men with greed in their eyes and a lust for power for its own sake in their hearts. It always showed in their voices, and in the hidden contempt they had for all honest people. This one was a short, tubby, bouncy little man with beady eyes.

"Welcome. Mr. Mhendi. Not everyone knows your name,

but I do. The papers from Queenstown told us about your coming to the country, so when I had the message to receive an unknown person of importance and help him across the lake I said to myself: 'It can only be Mr. Lanwood or Mr. Mhendi.' But Mr. Lanwood is on tour with our great Prime Minister so I knew it was you. Well, sir. Welcome! My name is Simon Chinwa. I'm the boss of the party here. Whisky?"

"Not so early," Mhendi said.

"He would like tea," Maria said. "And I would too."

Simon Chinwa turned his watchful, smiling face to her. He spread his hands.

"There is no time, sister. The boatmen are waiting."

"Then we'd better go," Mhendi said.

"First you must change your clothes, sir. To be seen as you are now on the boat would be suspicious. There is a fine cloth and sandals headquarters sent me for you. The white man is stupid. If you are dressed in cloth they will not look at your face and you will be one of us. But in those European clothes they will know you are not from here." Chinwa pointed to a dark corner. "There is your cloth, sir."

"I will help you," Maria said.

"I will be back soon," Chinwa said and left them.

"I do not trust that man," Maria whispered. "Before Udomo came he was all for the white people."

Mhendi undressed rapidly.

"Does Selina know?"

"That one knows everything."

"Then why . . . ?"

"No one knows the reason for the things Selina does. . . . Shsss. . . ."

Chinwa returned and beamed.

"Now you are one of us, sir! Better leave your clothes here."

"No," Maria said. "I will take them. And I have a message from Selina for you. She said I must tell you the man or woman who talks will have their tongues cut out and they

214

will be chased naked from village to village and beaten wherever they go."

"She sent that to me?" There was a hint of fear in his voice.

"To you and all who know of this journey."

Chinwa relaxed.

"I know nothing. All I know is that I must meet you and have a special canoe ready for you. That I have done. I know nothing more. How can a man talk who knows nothing?"

"I have given you Selina's message."

"We'd better go," Mhendi said.

"Maybe the tea, sir. . . ."

"No. We will go," Maria said.

She made a bundle of Mhendi's clothes. Chinwa led the way out to the waiting car. Chinwa spoke to the driver.

"He will take you, sir. Travel well."

The car shot off. It travelled away from the town but moved gradually towards the edge of the lake. Twenty minutes later it pulled up in a clump of trees on the edge of the lake. They got out. The driver turned about and drove away in a great hurry.

A long, slender, shapely canoe awaited them at the edge of the lake. It was manned by six of the most beautifully shaped men Mhendi had ever seen. The leader beckoned them impatiently. They got in. The leader pushed against the bank till the canoe's nose pointed towards the mountains. He grunted once. The canoe shot away. The men picked up rhythm, their bodies moved in unison, their blades as one. In . . . Out . . . In . . . Out . . . In . . . Out . . . In . . . Out . . . In . . . Out . . . In . . . Out . . . In . . . Out . . . The slender craft sped across the dark water. The men moved with an easy, tireless rhythm.

"You must be very hungry, Maria," Mhendi said.

The leader of the canoeists spoke harshly.

"He says you are not to speak," Maria said. "He says the sound of speech turned his men's attention from the rhythm of their work and the boat goes slower."

"I'm sorry," Mhendi said.

In . . . Out . . . In . . . Out . . .

By the time the sun had reached a point just over the mountains, robbing them of their misty blue, they were nearly halfway across the great lake. They could see no land in either direction except for the high mountains. And still the six men rowed as though they had just started.

In . . . Out . . . In . . . Out . . .

Mhendi's stomach rumbled. His throat felt dry and swollen. From an almost deep purple, Maria's lips had turned an ashy white. She kept on wetting them. Mhendi wanted to comfort her. If her thirst were half as great as his, if her hunger half as great as his, then she must be in agony. They had not eaten a proper meal since midday yesterday. And now it was going on to midday again. Eating on the bumping truck in the swirling dust had been impossible. You've grown soft, Mhendi, he told himself. Poor Maria. No need for her to suffer this. Pluralia means nothing to her. He took her hand.

In . . . Out . . . In . . . Out . . .

They were the only people on the great lake. For all the signs of life they might as well be lost in a slender boat on the vast ocean that covers so much of the earth's surface. But there were the mountains ahead; and they gave comfort.

In . . . Out . . . In . . . Out . . .

Were these men human? Could ordinary mortals keep up this machine-like rhythm hour after hour?

The sun climbed to a point overhead, stayed there, then moved westward. Mhendi began to feel light-headed. Maria seemed in a daze where he could not reach her. His father had, as a young man, performed feats of endurance such as these canoeists now did. Men in the tribal state could still do this. Then the machine-age caught up with them. But what of the uglier side of tribalism? What of its greatest crime: the stifling and destroying of the human personality? That's what Udomo is up against as I'll never be in Pluralia. Win or lose, my people are at least a century ahead of his. My God! I wouldn't be in his shoes for anything. The whites have done us so much good. Why can't they put the stamp of greatness on their work by putting values, their own values, above colour? There'd be nothing to fight about then, at least not in this negative racial way. . . . Poor Udomo.

In . . . Out . . . In . . . Out . . .

Mhendi shut his eyes, then opened them. The mirage was still there. He passed his hand across his eyes as though to wipe it out. He looked and it was still there. It must be the sun on the mountains. The sun was far behind them now, on the western horizon. Was it the sun or was it really land, so close by? The chief canoeist was nodding at him, smiling. A human being again; not a unit in the tribal machine. Nodding and smiling? Then it was land!

"Maria! Maria! Land!"

Maria raised her head and opened her eyes. He pointed.

"Land!"

She smiled wanly and nodded.

Two men waited at the waterside. The canoe bumped lightly against land. The men got hold of the prow. Mhendi tried to get up. He couldn't. They had to help him out. He was stiff with cramp.

Oh God! They will think me a weakling. A weakling.

"Tell them I'm not a weakling, Maria. Explain to them we haven't eaten and we've travelled for two nights and two days without stop."

"They know that, Mr. Mhendi. Don't worry, sah. They know you are not a weakling." But it wasn't Maria speaking. It was one of the men who had come to meet the canoe.

"Who are you?"

"Don't you know me, sah? I am here to lead the men who are to go with you. I saw you at Selina's. She sent me to prepare the way. Come, sah. We will talk when you have rested."

"Don't call me 'sir'! I'm not a white man!"

The young man smiled and put a sturdy arm about Mhendi's waist.

"Hold the woman before she drops," he ordered. "These two are nearly finished with hunger and journeying. It was a hard journey. . . ."

Mhendi woke in darkness. For a while he lay still, trying to find his bearings. Then he gave it up.

"Maria! Maria!"

She came in carrying a little tin mug filled with oil on which a burning wick floated.

"You are awake," she said.

"Have I slept long? Where am I?"

"In my mother's house. You slept all last night and all today and now it is night again. Joseph said you were not to be woken till your sleep was finished."

"Joseph?"

"You will know him when you see him. You met him at Selina's. He is the one she sent to prepare the way for you. He waits you now. Shall I call him?"

"No. I will dress. But how are you? Are you rested?"

"Yes."

He sat up. He was in a mud-and-wattle hut such as the one in which he had been born. The years in Europe were very far behind now.

"Come here, Maria."

She put the lamp on a stool and went to him. He pulled her down till her head rested on his chest.

"I want to thank you for all you have done, for being with me when I needed you on this journey, for ending my loneliness."

"There is no need for a man to thank his woman. What she does she does because she must and it fills her heart."

"But still I want you to know."

"I know of your thankfulness without words, Mhendi."

A wave of tenderness engulfed Mhendi. He clung to Maria.

"I was born in a place like this," he said.

"I know," she said.

"I never told you."

"I know with my heart."

He rubbed his cheek against hers, then pushed her away.

"Now I must dress. Send the young man in."

"Yes. I will prepare food while you talk. The people of the village wanted to prepare a feast but Joseph said it is best not to, so they will come quietly in small numbers to greet you and only our headman will sit and eat with you."

After the meal and the greetings Mhendi and Joseph sat on a hill overlooking the lake. The full moon was low over the dark water.

"There are twelve of us," Joseph said. "The others are waiting on the edge of the jungle. We travelled in small numbers not to cause suspicion."

"And you are sure of the track?"

"There is no doubt."

"What about provisions?"

"We have everything. The real hard thing was to find the track. It took us two weeks and I began to think the old people had lied in their stories of old."

"When do we start?"

"That's for you to say, Mr. Mhendi."

"You know it may be dangerous."

"We know."

"All right, then. Tomorrow."

"Tomorrow. Now you go rest, sah."

Joseph left him and Maria came to him.

"We leave tomorrow," he said.

"I am ready," she said.

He took her hand and they went down to the house.

*   *   *

Days of gloom and nights of darkness; sunless days and starless nights. Is the moon still in the heavens? Is the sky still in its place?

Has the sky a place?

What is time and what is motion? What is light and what is dark? Green, they say, needs light and sunshine; life, they say, needs light and air.

But where's the sun?

Days of gloom and nights of darkness; jungle days and jungle nights. What's the jungle? Why's the jungle? And why is it all so green?

> *Damp earth and no grass*
> *Dank heat and no air*
> *Giant trees and dark waters*
> *Rustle and whisper, hiss and silence*
> *Stealth and menace*
> *Is that the jungle?*

The jungle is more than trees grown tall as towers; more than darkness darker than night; more than bog; more than treacherous pool of death; more than giant snake or watchful beast.

It is time stood still and mocking man. It is the darkness in man's heart. It is the frontier of man's fear. The jungle is older than the days of man.

> *Walk carefully, man, or the jungle will get you.*
> *Your mother spoke true when she warned her child.*
> *Walk carefully, man!*

They broke out of the jungle nine days after they had entered it. They ran towards the light and raised their heads and began to laugh for sight of the sky again.

Mhendi was the first to recover.

"No further!" he called.

They stopped running and came back to where he stood.

"We cannot camp in the open," he said. "We may be seen by planes, or the smoke of our fire may be seen. We'll have to camp some way back in the jungle. Out there is Pluralia so we must be careful."

He sensed the fear in them. Really, of course, they were too young for this. They were fine and brave young men but the dark and unknown jungle had frightened them more than they had expected.

"Where shall we camp?" Joseph said.

"Just far in enough from passing planes. The edge of the jungle is safe, really."

Joseph took over then. He ordered two young men to go and hunt for water. He led the rest back to seek out a good camping place. The sky was overhead and the sun was shining and their courage was returning fast.

Mhendi stared at the land ahead. That was Pluralia, his land, the land of his people. All tiredness slipped from him. He decided he would set out as soon as possible—tonight, when it was dark enough.

Maria came to him. He looked at her and marvelled afresh at all she had endured for his sake. He put an arm about her shoulders.

"So we are there," she said quietly.

"It was hard for you," he said. "You should have stayed behind."

"I was filled with fear in there." She inclined her head to the jungle. "But I would come with you again. . . . So that is your land. It looks good."

"It is a good land. Only, we are not free."

"But you will lead them to freedom. . . . When do you go?"

"Soon. Tonight. It is better so. You know you cannot come with me."

"I know. You will come back to me, Mhendi?"

He tightened his arm about her. Strange what peace she had brought him.

"I will do my best, child. Come, I must talk to Joseph."

They walked back to the protective gloom of the jungle.

Joseph was an efficient organiser. There was something militaristic about the discipline the young men observed. Some cleared a space while others pitched a tent. The two who had been sent to find water were back and at work over a small fire that let off very little smoke. Mhendi looked about and nodded his satisfaction. They would be safe here under Joseph's leadership.

"Tea will soon be ready, sah," Joseph called out.

Mhendi beckoned to Joseph.

"How are the men?"

"All right now." Joseph grinned sheepishly. "That jungle frightened us but we are the party's soldiers. Udomo calls us his shock troops so we are shamed to have shown fear."

"I was frightened too, Joseph."

"Thank you, sah! It will comfort my men. But we will not be afraid again."

"I think of leaving tonight. I think it is best to be quick."

"Yes, sah."

"How long can you wait here?"

"As long as you tell us, sah."

"Have you provisions for one month?"

"Yes. Maybe more. But I can send six of my men to get more. It will not be so bad now we have been through once. Also, we must get the weapons for training the men you will bring back to make your shock troops."

Mhendi smiled.

"I've changed my mind about that, Joseph. I will write a letter to Selina before I leave. The men who go back can take it and give it to someone who will get it to her. I have been thinking and it seems to me that we will need a new kind of fighting in my country. We have tried fighting with arms but they were too strong for us. We will still need weapons though we will try not to use them. The important thing is for us to get so well organised that when we call the people out not one black person will go to work anywhere in the land. We will have to show the people that we are serious and mean to win. We must give them courage again.

"To do that I will organise some of my own young people—shock troops, as you call them—to cut power plants so that there is no electricity. We will derail goods trains. We will disturb the peace everywhere in the land; we will make life uncomfortable for the white people. We will frighten them. And I will let it be known that it is I who am doing it. The meaning of this will be clear to my people. And so we will work for the day of the general strike that will paralyse the country. Of course, they will hunt for me all over the country. But by the time they start hunting for me I will be back here and they will not find me. I will go among my people and stir them up and come back and go again—and they will not find me. I will put this plan in my letter to Selina and it will be your business to see that no one except she gets it."

"It is a wonderful plan, sah! I would like to come with you."

"No. You must stay here and take care of Maria—good care —and wait for me. But if I am not back in a month's time then you must know I have been taken. . . ."

"No!" Maria cried.

"It is possible, my child." He patted her cheek. "Now I must write that letter."

"Your tent is ready, sah." Joseph led them to the tent.

Mhendi sat on the camp-bed and wrote, pad on knee. He wrote carefully, weighing his words. This might be his last testament.

One of the young men brought tea, then food. Maria left him to his writing after they had eaten.

At last the writing was done. He called her and they lay down together.

When darkness came he took leave of the young men. Joseph and Maria walked with him to the edge of the trees. Joseph gave him an automatic pistol.

"Safe journey, sah. Long live Africa's freedom!"

Mhendi took his hand.

"Remember, one month, Joseph. Goodbye. Look after Maria."

Maria walked a distance further with him. Then she turned and flung her arms about him.

"Take care, my man, take care."

"I will come back," he said. Oh the loving and waiting of women. "I will come back, my dear."

He freed himself of her arms and walked briskly away. Soon, the darkness swallowed him up. But still Maria stood peering.

After a long, long time Joseph came to her and touched her arm.

"Come; he's gone. Now we must wait."

"Yes," Maria murmured and turned. "Now I must wait."

They went back to the others.

TWO

I

Adebhoy met Mabi at the airport.

"Mabi man! God it's good to see you! How are you? Welcome home!"

A small crowd watched, smiling, as their Minister of Health and Housing flung his arms about the small man and danced with joy.

"Good to see you," Mabi said. "I was afraid I might have

to face the kind of public circus you arranged for Tom and Mhendi. . . ."

"You know our people!" Adebhoy roared. "They like a good show and we give it to them. . . . Come, let's get to town. Don't worry about your luggage. It'll come. . . . Well man! It's good to have you home!"

The small crowd clapped them to the car, waved as it drove off.

"Thought the others would be here," Mabi said.

"Udomo's on tour. Lanwood's with him. They'll be back next week."

"And Mhendi?"

"He's gone."

"So Mike kept that promise. . . ."

"Of course; what did you expect?"

"What's he like now?"

"Udomo?"

"Yes. Now that he's got power?"

"He's all right. More quiet, but the same."

Something in Adebhoy's voice made Mabi look searchingly at him. Adebhoy laughed.

"You don't fool me with that laugh!" Mabi snapped. "Tell me."

The car sped along the new tarmac road that linked the town with the airport eight miles out. The hot sun made the black road shine. For a moment, a shadow crossed Adebhoy's face.

"There's nothing to tell," he said. "Everything's fine. The people are solidly behind us. It's just that some people feel Udomo is going too slow. But you'll see. . . ."

"And you?" Mabi said. "D'you feel it too?"

"We've only had a little time," Adebhoy said evasively. "But we've promised the people things. But you'll see. . . . How's London? Man! I dream of those days sometimes."

"London's an old city. It doesn't change for our coming or going. It's still the same."

"Yes," Adebhoy chuckled. "And you are the same."

"But things have changed here. I want you to tell me where I fit in. I'm sure Udomo didn't want to call me back."

"Our struggle is greater than personalities," Adebhoy said. "But we'll talk later. Our executive has arranged a party for you tonight. We'll talk after that."

"Not a circus, I hope."

"A very quiet party," Adebhoy said and laughed.

The black sky was studded with stars when they finally reached Adebhoy's house after the party. It was one in the morning.

"A very quiet party," Mabi said sarcastically.

"It was, man. . . . And they all liked you. You know how important that is. Now we can talk. . . . Drink?"

"I've had too much already."

Adebhoy swayed a little as he poured himself a drink.

"Cheers. . . ."

"Tell me about Selina," Mabi said. "Haven't heard of her before."

"So you've noticed. She's the real power behind us, home-boy. She tells all the women in all the villages what to tell their men, and the men do what the women tell them. Without her we wouldn't have this party."

"She's a tribal woman."

"We're a tribal nation, Mabi. Without Selina we couldn't have defeated the Council of Chiefs and Elders."

"So really Mike's the new tribal chief, superseding all the others; a kind of super tribal chief and father of his people."

Adebhoy rocked with laughter.

"Tell him that, Mabi. You tell him that."

"Are you drunk?"

"Me! Drunk! The Minister drunk! No! A little high, that's all."

"All right. Where do I fit in?"

"You're to take over the Ministry of Education and National Guidance."

"What of the present Minister?"

"You won't take over immediately. The man who sat for the mountain people in the Assembly has already been given a new job and resigned from the Assembly. The election is on and we've nominated you. You'll get in. You'll then be appointed Ministerial Secretary and a month later you'll take over the ministry completely."

"So it's all arranged."

"It's all arranged, brother. But we'll have to work fast. Endura's crowd are already campaigning."

"When do they vote?"

"In about fifteen days."

"I'd better get home then."

"We've arranged a plane for you for tomorrow. That's why it was important that you should meet the executive tonight. Udomo will join you up there for two days' campaigning."

"Oh . . ."

"I told you the cause was bigger than personalities."

"That's why I'm here!" Mabi snapped with sudden heat.

"All right, all right! We'd better go to bed now. A nightcap?"

"No. Any news of Mhendi? When did he leave?"

"I know nothing. I'm a Minister, and you'll soon be one. So it would be best to know nothing. You understand. But Selina would tell you he left Queenstown seven weeks ago."

"When are we likely to know anything?"

"I don't know. Forget about it till there's news. We have a huge delegation of business men and technicians from Pluralia in our country at present. Our people don't like it but Udomo says it's essential. You'll find some of these people even up in your part. So it's best not to even mention Mhendi's name. See, brother?"

"I see."

"Good night, man. And I'm happy you're home. Udomo and I are carrying this government. It'll be easier with you to help."

"Good night," Mabi said and remained seated as Adebhoy left the room.

Because he was fresh to it, the noises of the little creatures of the night had reached him as a loud chorus behind their talk. Now, it invaded the silent room, assumed the proportions of powerful but controlled orchestral music hemming him in on all sides. Up in the mountains, in his home, the young women cut holes in reeds and hung them out so that the wind, passing through the holes, made sweet music. As a boy, a long time ago, he had lain on the grass at nights and listened to the sweet solos of the reeds rising above the loud chorus of the creatures of the night. Now, only the reeds were needed to recapture that long ago of boyhood. He closed his eyes and listened to the creature-noises.

He opened his eyes. Adebhoy's steward, Samson, stood in the doorway.

"Sorry, sah. I thought you go for sleep so I come for tidy room."

"Come in and carry on," Mabi said.

"Thank you, sah. Maybe you want one more drink?"

"No, Samson."

"Maybe coffee, sah?"

He was so anxious to please, Mabi nodded and smiled. Nowhere else in the world does one get this fulsome kind of service that flows from the warmth of the heart; and nowhere else is it more abused than here, not only by white but by black as well.

Mabi went to the window. Could one see this orchestra of creatures? As a boy he fancied he had seen them. But he knew it was only fancy grown to the point of reality by the passage of time. And tomorrow he would be home among his own people. He dreaded it a little. They would be the same and he

228

would be changed. Fortunate that the mountain people were less demonstrative than the people of the plains. It would be good to see his old mother again. But first there'd be that awful old piece of ritual before he could take her in his arms. Still. . . .

And Lois. . . . What was the piece of claptrap with which he'd justified this betrayal of her? Adebhoy had used it: *The cause is greater than personalities.* A good umbrella under which to betray one's friends, and the damnable thing is that one did it. . . . Oh, Lois . . . Forgive me. There is something compelling in this African cry for light that I cannot resist. Perhaps it is because they don't even know they cry for light. Is that justification for betraying one friend? Can the betrayal of the lowliest friend ever be justified? To you it's always been clear; and to me, for moments, too. But what of this Africa that shaped me? Which is the choice: to betray you or to betray the dream? Is the choice always between two evils? Never between good and evil? If it is, then it is cruellest for us. It is always the generation in transition that has to make the cruellest choice of all.

"Oh, Lois, forgive me. . . ."

"You speak, massa?" Samson had come back with the coffee.

"No, Samson. Thank you. I'll take it to my room. Good night."

The tiny plane seemed awfully frail, bumping from air-pocket to air-pocket. It raised its nose and began to climb, as though scrambling up a steep slope. The huge lake fell away behind. The mountains drew near. Then, suddenly, the mountains were directly below. Far to the left, sloping away on the other side of the mountains, the jungle was a dark spot on the face of the earth. The young black pilot twisted his neck, grinned, and shouted:

"We land in a few minutes, sir! Hold on! A bit bumpy!"

Mabi nodded. The little machine was too loud for speech. You're having a good time, friend. I'm hating it. Get me down in one piece; that's all I ask.

The little plane shivered as it kept climbing. Mabi thought: Oh God! He held on tight. This young fool was going to kill him. Then the plane swooped down. The pressure pinned Mabi to his seat. He heard the man's voice above the noise. The damn fool was singing. This chap was a menace! The earth came up at an alarming rate. Then, suddenly, it levelled off and the plane lost speed. There was heavy thumping in Mabi's eardrums as the plane bumped its way across the earth to where a cluster of people waited. The young pilot turned his head again, a happy, open-mouthed smile on his face.

"How's that, sir? Safe and sound!"

Mabi relaxed and grinned in spite of himself.

"Where did you learn to fly?"

"With the R.A.F."

"And they allowed you to fly like this?"

"No, sir!" The pilot roared happily. "Those Englishmen are too cautious."

"Then give me an Englishman every time," Mabi said.

To the pilot this was a huge joke.

The little plane taxied to a stop. The people clustered about. They were mostly young people. Up here in the mountain villages the old did not come to meet the young. Only his own age group and those in younger age groups would be here to welcome Mabi. It was up to him, Mabi, to go to the elders and announce his arrival. If he were fortunate, if the elders thought him worthy of some sign of respect, they would be gathered in one place where he would go to announce his arrival. Otherwise he would have to travel from village to village paying his respects to the elders before finally going to his own mother's home.

Mabi and the pilot got out of the plane. The waiting people split into two groups, one large, one small. The ritual, Mabi thought bitterly. He turned and faced the small group. These were his blood relatives. He looked at them without recognising one person. Of course, his sister would be married now and her husband probably lived miles away.

He waited. His blood relatives came to him, one at a time, men first and in order of seniority. Each person touched his hand, did a little bow, and made room for the next. And so it went on, first the blood relatives, then all the others. At last it was over. A man in European dress introduced himself:

"I'm the teacher here."

"Glad to meet you. Tell me, where are the elders?"

The teacher smiled.

"They're together, waiting for you. Endura's people tried to persuade them not to be together to greet you. . . . The doctor —he and I are the only party people here—has sent his car. It's a jeep really. He would have come himself but he has a case. He will call on you as soon as he is free."

"All the luggage discharged!" the pilot called.

Willing hands carted Mabi's luggage to the jeep. Mabi shook the pilot's hand. The young man put on his flying helmet and goggles for the benefit of the villagers. Then he got into his plane and set off. He circled them once, climbed and did a roll, then he streaked off back across the lake.

The airstrip was half a mile from the village. Mabi and the teacher rode in the jeep. Those who could, perched on bumpers and running-board. The rest trotted beside and behind the slow-moving jeep. Soon they were on the outskirts of the village.

Mabi looked at the cluster of huts on the left of the way into the village. That's my home. I was born there. My mother is there now. Waiting because of this goddam ritualistic farce. Oh mother. D'you feel the strain as I do? Why do these people of mine choke their feeling with elaborate ritual? Is it the mountains? Oh mother. . . . He turned quickly to the teacher.

"You say Endura is strong here?"

"The man who sat in the Assembly was an Endura man till Selina bought him. Endura's man would get in again if anyone stood except you."

"If he's that strong couldn't he beat even me?"

"No. You are a hero here. You're a son of the mountains, the first to have gone into the outside world. And you've had a great success. Whenever anything about you and your work is printed in the English papers, those papers find their way here and the young people display them. You will see some in the school. The young people will vote for you whatever the elders do or say. That's why the elders are receiving you. They know of the power you have over the young."

"We'll see," Mabi said.

The jeep pulled up outside the great conference hut in the centre of the village.

"They await you," the teacher said. "Good luck."

Mabi got out and walked to the hut. Those who were still about the jeep had lapsed in silence. At the other end of the village a dog barked fitfully.

Mabi hesitated then stepped through the door of the huge hut. The elders sat in a semi-circle about the chief. His father sat on the right of the chief. Forget all your western individualism, Mabi; remember you're back in the tribal world.

"I greet you, my chief." He bowed to his father. "And you, my father." Then he bowed to all the others. "And you, elders of the mountain people. In you is the wisdom and the law and authority of our people, and I bow to that too in greeting you."

All eyes were turned on him. How long would they sit thus staring?

The chief cleared his throat.

"Welcome home, young man. You have been away long. What wisdom do you bring?"

"None that is new to the chief and elders of my people. . . . I beg your forgiveness that I come to you in the white man's dress. I did not want to keep the chief and elders waiting."

A man on the chief's left cleared his throat. The chief nodded.

"Do you tell us you have learnt nothing for all your years away?"

"I have learnt many things. Our chief asked me of wisdom. Things I have learnt. Wisdom it is not so easy to learn."

"Then you think wisdom can be learnt?"

Careful, Mabi.

"With age—yes."

"What can be learnt without age, young man?"

"Knowledge."

"Oh?"

"Consider the young man who brought me here in his machine that flies. He is young, he has no wisdom, but he has the knowledge that makes the machine fly and so it is possible for me to leave the coast in the morning and be here before dark."

"That is a white man. The ways of white men are not our ways."

"No. He was not white. The others will tell you that. They saw him. He was black but he had the knowledge to fly that machine."

The chief intervened.

"What good is it to fly a machine if you have no wisdom?"

"The good is that the wise, like yourselves, could now go to the coast where the government will listen to your wisdom and still be back home before it is dark."

"There is no pleasure in such hasty travel," someone muttered.

"I see the value of it," the chief murmured.

Mabi seized his chance.

233

"If it is your wish I will arrange for you to go up in one."

A smile flickered across the old chief's face. Why the devil can't they give me a chair, Mabi thought.

His father spoke quietly.

"We hear of young men who bring white wives. . . ."

"I have no wife."

Another voice spoke.

"We hear you are Udomo's man?"

"I am my people's man."

"Do they lie then, those who say you are here to stand for this election?"

"They do not lie. I am here to stand for this election. But that does not make me Udomo's man."

"How so, young man?" the chief said sharply.

Careful now, Mabi, careful.

"It is right that the voice of our people be heard down at the coast. It is right that the mountain people should have one of their own to sit in the Assembly to speak for them and keep watch over their interests and help make the laws that would govern them."

"So!" a voice spoke bitterly. "The young want to make the laws for us."

"Though they have the knowledge they will always be guided by your wisdom. The young may have the knowledge, like that one who flies the plane, but it is to you they will turn, I will turn for wisdom. They will make me a Minister to watch over the education and guidance of the young of our land. . . ."

"You will be a Minister?" the chief said.

"Yes, if I am elected."

"It would be the first time in our history that one of us will be a leader in the councils of the peoples of the plains. Will you be Minister over their young too?"

"Over all the young of the land."

234

The chief smiled, turned to Mabi's father and nodded slowly. This is the turning point, Mabi felt; why didn't I think to tell them before?

"I don't believe it!" an old greybeard snapped. "The plainsfolk hate us and would rule us."

"It is true. You'll see."

Another old man raised his voice in challenge:

"They say this Udomo has no respect for the old and the wisdom of the old. They say he would be rid of our ways, of the ways of our ancestors. They say he would bring here the ways of the whites where the young have no respect for the old and tradition is cast down. They say he does not fear or respect our ancient gods. What do you say?"

Oh, this tiring business. To hell with the old if they haven't the grace to offer the young a seat after a tiring journey! Are not the young human too? Steady, Mabi, steady. Mabi turned his head to take in the entire semi-circle of old faces. Only the chief's face seemed friendly.

"You say they say, my elder. Tell me, please, who are they who say?"

"It is not we but you who are here to answer, young man!"

"I ask with a purpose, please."

"It is reasonable," the chief said. "Answer the youth."

"I do not like this," someone murmured.

"Answer that we may see his purpose," the chief said.

"It is those who speak for Dr. Endura and the Council of Elders," the old challenger said.

Mabi said:

"Is it not your wisdom, chief and elders, that when two men are after the same thing it is best to listen with suspicion to what one says of the other? Does not a rival always tell falsehood against his opponent?"

"That is reasonable," the chief said. "The purpose to the young man's question is clear now. He has reminded us of our own wisdom. I am well pleased."

But the old challenger was not satisfied:

"Young man: you have spoken with wisdom, but the question remains and I would have an answer. Does this Udomo, this new lord of the land, does he respect our grey hairs and our ancient ways and the gods of our ancestors? That is still the question!"

"You will have your answer, respected elder. I could say to you here and now that he does. But I have done a better thing. Soon, in two or three days, Udomo will be here. He will come to you. I promise that. And he will submit himself to all your questions."

A ripple of excitement passed through the elders.

"The Prime Minister of the land will do that!" the chief said.

Mabi suppressed an ironic smile.

"I have asked him and he will come."

"Because you have asked him," the chief whispered.

Mabi nodded. The elders exchanged glances. Yes, Mabi thought: whatever you think of Udomo, he is the new authority, and the basis of your lives, the cornerstone of your tradition, is respect for authority.

"This young man has great power," the chief whispered to the elder on his left. "And we have not given him a place to sit. He calls Udomo and Udomo comes. Not even the whites or the Council of Chiefs and Elders of the plain can do that." He rose. "The talk is over. You have pleased us well, young son of Mabi. You have brought honour to your people. I think we should make a feast in your honour, and I think all the elders should be there even though you are not of our age-group. Certainly, I will give the word and I will be there. Later, we will prepare for the coming of the Prime Minister, Udomo. Is this agreed, elders?"

The elders murmured their agreement, some unwillingly, but all agreed. They were elders and knew the unwisdom of opposing the tide.

"Then the talk is over."

A wave of bitterness welled up in Mabi as the chief and elders left their stools and came to him. The real evil of tribalism in this day and age was that its ritualistic code of fear and authority had robbed man of his individual manhood. How easily the dictator-state could flourish here.

He submitted coldly to his old father's formal embrace. Really, he didn't know this old man. All the little things that go into the making of the special relation between father and son had never taken place between him and this old man.

He made all the conventional responses to the old men, to the chief, to the old man who had sired him without ever being his father. At last it was over. Now he could go to his mother. Her face was always clear in his memory. How had she borne this waiting, knowing he was here going through this ritual?

Outside most of the people had gone; but the teacher and the jeep were still there. He got in.

"How did it go?"

"There'll be a feast for me. The chief and elders will come."

"Wonderful! We knew you'd do it!"

"Not me. It was Udomo. He's the new super tribal chief."

The teacher didn't understand so he covered up with a loud laugh.

The jeep pulled up outside the Mabi compound. Mabi jumped out and waved to the teacher.

"See you later."

He stumbled over children and chickens at the entrance to the enclosed compound. Some of his father's other wives worked outside their huts. They called out greetings. He called back without knowing what he said. Then *she* came out of the cooking hut.

Mother. Oh, mother. Watery eyes in a round patient black face lined with time and hard work. Small, small like me. Oh shining eyes and trembling chin and the smell of smoke about

237

you. Oh hungry searching eyes. My heart and eyes have hungered just as much for you all these years.

A tear trembled on her left eyelid.

"Which is my hut?" he murmured in the language of his childhood.

She brushed past him, touching him as she went. He turned and followed her. The other women and children watched mother and son.

She entered the little hut and turned to him. They were alone now, alone at last, free of watching eyes. She half-fell into his arms.

"My son . . . Oh, my son," she sobbed.

He wrapped his arms about her, held her tight.

"Oh, mother . . ." he whispered in English.

A long, long time afterwards, she pulled away and wiped her eyes quickly.

"I feared . . ." she whispered.

"What did you fear, mother?"

"That the white people may have taken you from me."

"And now?"

"My fears were foolish. You are still my son; a big man, but still my son." Her tears flowed again, but they were tears of happiness now.

"Oh my dear," he murmured in English and pulled her to him again.

"The food will burn," she whispered.

2

Mabi held out his hands to the fire. He had forgotten how cold nights could be up here in the mountainland. He looked to where Udomo sat with the chief on the other side of the fire. Udomo had done a wonderful job of winning them over. Udomo had changed a lot, had learnt the secret of patience and how to hide his thoughts and feelings from others; had grown infinitely subtle in his dealings with people. Power has had an extraordinary effect on him, Mabi decided. He's cold now, and deliberate, and he hides it all under the successful mask of easy friendliness. He's charmed them all here.

Udomo had arrived early in the morning. He had looked tired as he got out of his plane. Then he had turned on his famous smile and the tiredness had fallen from him like a discarded cloak. Hardly anyone except Mabi had noticed Thomas Lanwood follow Udomo out of the plane. And all that day, during all the meetings and conferences, Lanwood had been a background figure noticed only by Mabi. But Mabi had himself been very much to the fore with Udomo and had thus been unable to give the lonely Lanwood much comfort.

Udomo and the chief now had their arms about each other and were laughing. Yes, he'd certainly learnt the art of capturing people. There had not been any time for them to be alone so far. Mabi had been thankful. As long as it was impersonal, part of the African cause, it was all right. But the moment they were alone he might decide to talk about old times and old things. And then there might be trouble. I will not be sycophantic, Mabi told himself firmly.

But what of Lanwood? All the fire seemed to have gone out of him. He'd been so worked up when he and Mhendi had left London only a few months earlier. And now here he was, listless and subdued and terribly aged. Why was it? There was the awful language barrier, of course. But it was more than just that.

He turned to Lanwood. Lanwood sat staring into the fire, shoulders drooped, an air of great listlessness about him. He didn't even try to talk to the elder beside him. The music of the drums and the voices of the people seemed to hold no interest for him.

"Well, Tom. . . ."

Lanwood turned his head and smiled with great effort.

How he's aged, Mabi thought. He felt a sudden rush of compassion.

"What's it, Tom? You're not happy."

"There's no room for me here, Paul. . . ."

"Nonsense, man!" He leaned sideways and put an arm about Lanwood's bulk. "It's just that it's all strange to you. Give yourself time. You've been away a long time. It takes time to adjust."

"I'm not as young as you boys any more. I'm getting old. . . ."

"Nonsense! It's just the problem of adjustment getting you down. I know it must be difficult with the language barrier. But you'll laugh at yourself in a few months' time."

"If only I had something to do, like you fellows. . . ." He looked across to where Udomo sat.

Mabi saw the desperate appeal in his eyes.

"There's lots for you to do, man! Don't talk daft. Remember you're Tom Lanwood. You've been crusading against imperialism for more than a quarter of a century. . . ."

"I'm not needed here, Paul. I've enough sense left to see that."

Oh God! How does one comfort a person?

Udomo looked briefly across the fire at them, smiled and nodded. Mabi wondered whether there was a tinge of irony in the gesture. Then Udomo turned his head to the chief.

Women brought more food and drink. Young men piled more fuel on the huge fire. Behind them, and all about, were the voices of the people and the throb of the drums. The stars, up here, were brighter and closer to the earth than they were down in the plains. A stream of wind gave the night air a sharp edge.

"I even envy Mhendi now," Lanwood said heavily. "He's somewhere among people who need him tonight."

"What about that book you talked about?"

"Even that's not needed here. Only white folk will read it."

There was no comforting him.

"Have you talked to Udomo?"

240

"He's looking for something safe for me to do."

"Well then. . . ."

"He too is trying to comfort me by urging the importance of the book on me."

"But it is important, you know that."

"Is it? Really?"

"Of course it is! What's the matter with you?"

"Would there be a crisis in the country if I didn't write it? No. Things would be just the same. Would there be a crisis if you didn't come back to bring the mountain people behind Mike? Yes. So you are *needed* for the sake of the unity and future of the country. As Mike is; as Adebhoy is; as even Mhendi is over there in Pluralia."

"But you can supply the idea, Tom; the philosophy, just as you did in London. In the long run that's by far the most important. Honestly."

"You're wrong, Paul. I've been around with Mike these past couple of weeks. I've had a chance to see that the real Africa is not the Africa I wrote about in my books. It isn't easy, Paul. So don't try and comfort me. You're *needed*. I'm not. I don't understand this tribal business and I don't want to. Mike was right. I've been in Europe too long. . . . I'm tired, Paul. Would I be offending against anything if I retired now?"

"No, Tom," Mabi said gently.

He called a young man.

"Take our guest to my mother. Tell her he will share my hut and sleep on my bed. Tell her to prepare a bed for me on the floor. . . ."

They got up. Udomo rose and came round the fire to them.

"Tom's tired," Mabi said.

"I think I'll turn in," Lanwood said.

"Do that," Udomo said. "Sorry it's been such a hard tour, Tom. But you've seen how it is. I have to carry the idea of government to the people and I haven't much time. Where are you sleeping?"

241

"At my place," Mabi said.

"Good. You'll get some sleep. Don't know if I'll get any at the chief's place. We leave early in the morning. Hope that pilot stays sober."

"Good night," Lanwood said.

They watched the young man lead him away. A young woman offered them fruit. Udomo took an orange and kissed the young woman's forehead. You do all the right things, Mabi thought. Then he saw the mocking, quizzical glint in Udomo's eyes.

"You'll be doing that too. . . . Tom been talking?"

"Yes."

"Thought he had. The tour upset him. He was distressed when they bathed my feet in blood at one place. Couldn't understand it. It made him sick."

"What are we to do about tribalism?"

"Accept it. It's a fact. If I came out against it today I'd be out of office tomorrow. Accept it and attack it from the rear. That's the answer. That's why I'm pushing industrialisation as hard as possible. That's why I need Mhendi's whites so desperately. Mhendi understands but neither Tom nor Ade do: Tom, because he's so bitterly horrified by it; Ade because he's such a staunch tribalist at heart. And Ade has Selina and the executive with him."

"I see."

"Glad you do. It's not as easy as it looks. My greatest need is for trained men who are free of the tribal hold and yet understand it sufficiently to be diplomatic about it. You might as well know it now: there's a struggle between Ade and myself over this whole question. Oh, it's not open; but it's real for all that. That, by the way, is why I allowed him and Selina to think they were pressurising me to get you back and offer you a post. As their nominee you're going to carry much more weight when you side with me."

"You're sure I'll side with you?"

Udomo chuckled softly.

"You'll soon learn that those who carry a country can't afford the luxury of the kind of strong personal feeling you've just shown. Of course you'll side with me, unless you've suddenly turned tribalist or else hate me enough to wreck the country's future for a long time to come. I have the edge on you, Mabi. I've been carrying this thing for a few years now. I'll happily pass on as much of it as you can take. You know yours are key ministries in terms of the future. You'll find Jones and Rosslee will go out of their way to help. Have a session with Jones when you get back. Don't know what I would have done without him. But don't forget our stupid non-fraternisation rule. That's something that needs breaking, Mr. Minister of Education and National Guidance." Udomo chuckled again. "Hope you feel better about being in my government now?"

"Yes."

"You staying here till polling day?"

"Yes. I want to get around to some of the other villages."

"Good. But get to Queenstown as soon as possible after. There's a mountain of work waiting for you. You've got the form from Ade. You'll be Ministerial Secretary for a few weeks, then I reshuffle. Thank goodness there are enough people for a reshuffle now. I was so hard pressed for even moderately able men in the early days that I even thought of offering Endura a Ministry. . . ."

"What about Tom?"

"I'm sure you've guessed."

"That he's leaving, yes. But is it of his own free will? He's desperately unhappy."

"I know. I've been with him these past weeks. I tried to persuade him to stay."

"But you're not over-anxious."

"He could be embarrassing. Has been, in fact. Still, you try and persuade him. Keep him up here if you like."

"Can't anything worthwhile be found for him?"

"I thought of the party; but he's too tactless. He declared himself and all his views within a few hours of his arrival. Now the party tribalists won't have him. They're the key people. It's not easy, Mabi."

"I'm beginning to see." And beginning to like you all over again, Mabi told himself.

"Good. I'm glad you've come. We've a hell of a job ahead of us. . . . I'd better go back to the chief now. Hope this damn party finishes soon. Can hardly keep my eyes open. Think I've only slept six out of the last thirty-six hours."

"I'll drop a hint," Mabi said.

A tiny smile, half-wistful, half-apologetic tugged at Udomo's mouth.

"Mabi. If I could undo what happened in Hampstead. . . ."

Mabi stiffened. Udomo swung about abruptly and went back to the chief.

But we never can. Mabi thought bitterly, we never can.

The chief beckoned. Mabi joined them.

"I apologise for being personal," Udomo said in English.

"It's a luxury we can't afford," Mabi said bitterly.

"You'll learn the truth of that," Udomo said gently.

"What are you saying to each other?" the chief asked.

"You know this is the end of the Prime Minister's tour, chief. For many days he has had very little sleep. I asked him if he wanted to go and rest now. But he says no, though he is tired he does not want to insult you by leaving before the feast is over. He did not want me to tell you this. That is why we spoke in the white man's tongue."

"My friends are too anxious to take care of me," Udomo protested.

"They are wise and loyal," the chief said. "A man who carries your burdens must guard his strength. I will bring the feast to an end now. My people have seen how you respect our ways and our customs. And now one of our sons, a child of our mountains, will share with you in the government of our country."

"You are kind and great," Udomo said.

The chief rose and clapped his hands. The people grew silent. . . .

Down at the coast, the Governor and the Chief Secretary were coming to the end of a quiet evening together.

"This Mhendi business will be the first real piece of foreign affairs the P.M. will have to handle," Jones said. "What d'you think he'll do?"

"Wish to God I knew," Rosslee said. "If half the reports from Pluralia are true then Mhendi's certainly kicking up the most awful racket. And you know, Jones, as a purely private person I say all power to him. Those settlers make me ashamed of my white skin. I've been to Pluralia and seen the colour bar at work. It's all very well for us to talk about the democratic countries of the Commonwealth. . . . Oh, never mind! It makes me mad. You probably know all about it."

"Yes, I've been there," Jones said. "What makes it worse, to my mind, is the fact that the Africans of Pluralia are at least a century ahead of Africans here in terms of having made the transition from tribalism. The whites there are asking for a Night of the Long Knives. And if history teaches us anything, they'll get it."

"I, for one, won't have any fond feelings about kith and kin," Rosslee snapped.

"But what are we to do now?"

Rosslee shrugged off his anger and grinned.

"Sorry. This is one of the times when I hate being Governor. Anyway, do we have to do anything?"

"Afraid so. There's a flash for information from London."

"Tell them we haven't any."

"Won't do."

"Why not . . . Oh my God, yes! The fanfare when they

arrived and their pictures on the front page of the party's paper. That was silly. Not like Udomo."

"Don't suppose it was his idea for a moment. He must give way on some things to gain his point on others."

"I suppose the Pluralian business delegation sent copies back?"

"More than that. Remember I told you they got in touch with our security blokes? They were in quite a lather about Mhendi being here. Wanted him sent back to England. Security politely told them to mind their own business, and that Mr. Mhendi was in the country as the personal guest of the P.M. All that, I fear, will bounce back."

"Yes," Rosslee sighed. "Not so nice."

"Not nice at all," Jones said quietly.

"How did Mhendi get out there?"

"I'd say through the jungle," Jones said.

"Can't be done. Don't you remember an expedition of trained men tried to penetrate the jungle and gave it up because it was too dangerous? It was before my time, but you must have been here already."

"I remember that expedition," Jones said. "The point is, we've checked very carefully and security makes it as a statement of hard fact that he didn't use a plane of any kind. So there's only the jungle. There's this other point: In the folklore of the people of that region one keeps encountering stories of people travelling *through* the jungle in the great days of the past."

"You think this fairytale is based on fact and there's a secret path through the jungle?"

"I'm convinced of it," Jones said. "I suppose Mhendi could still be in Panafrica though security swears they would have picked up at least the scent of him. But I know these people. I headed them once. I'd say he isn't in the country. You know this chap, Mhendi. What do these acts of sabotage suggest to you?"

"That it is he," Rosslee said. "That business of carefully leading some cattle away before blowing up that power-plant was Mhendi's signature."

"Then this picture of a bloodthirsty revolutionist. . . ."

"So much of the Pluralian Big Lie. For Udomo's sake I hope. . . . No. I hope he gets away. If I know my Mhendi he'll wreak his havoc and slip back here."

"Then what?" Jones said.

"Then we'll have a first-class little crisis on our hands. Why the hell did they have to do this!"

"Not like you to get so het up about a person," Jones murmured.

"Dammit! I like the chap immensely. It's people like Mhendi who can make possible the great settlement between the lighter and darker races of mankind. They're a sure measure of what hope there is for what silly people call western European civilisation."

"I still have to answer that flash," Jones said.

"Better give them the facts without any comment."

"Do we undertake to arrest him if he comes back here?"

"When does Udomo come back?"

"He's due tomorrow."

"Then delay your reply till he gets back."

"Right. The leader of the Pluralian mission wants to see him on the most pressing business the moment he gets back."

"D'you think it's about this?"

"Could be," Jones said.

"I'm glad I'm not Udomo," Rosslee said. "I think we ought to hold our hand and see what he does."

3

Udomo walked into his office at nine the next morning. He had bathed and shaved and looked as fresh as someone who had had a long night's sleep. He took off his jacket and tie, rolled up his sleeves, and attacked the huge pile of files that awaited his attention. Then he rang for his secretary. The tall young Englishman came in quietly.

"Welcome back, sir. Had a good tour?"

Udomo sat back and flexed and unflexed his back and shoulder muscles.

"The usual circus." Udomo grinned. "What new crisis has arisen in my absence?"

"Something rather serious, sir. I'd better bring in the file of Pluralian papers."

Udomo stopped flexing his muscles, sat very still suddenly. "So. . . ."

"Mr. Jones rang through. Wants to see you urgently. He can put you into the picture more completely."

"All right. Bring in the papers, then give me ten minutes before getting Jones over. . . . And, Tony, be a good fellow and try and razzle up some tea. Get me a cup now and then some more when Jones comes. And here"—he handed the young man a pile of files—"cope with these. Routine stuff."

The secretary went out and came back with a batch of newspapers. Udomo cleared a space on his desk.

It was all over the front pages of all the Pluralian papers; stories of sabotage, of goods trains and power plants blown up. So Mhendi had done it. He'd been quick about it.

A trim young English girl brought in tea. He thanked her. These English were all so silently efficient. One could depend on them.

He skimmed through all the papers. Then he read them more carefully. Mhendi was certainly going at it. And they knew it was Mhendi and that he'd come from here. This was going to be a ticklish little thing to handle.

The secretary announced Jones. Udomo rose to meet Jones with outstretched hand. The little yellowish man looked more serious than Udomo had ever seen him.

"How are you, Jones?"

"Glad Tony's brought you the papers," Jones said.

"Sit down. They'll bring in tea."

"This is very serious, you know."

"So I see. Tell me about it."

"I had this flash from London last night. Then, this morning, this fuller cable came. You'll see the Pluralian people in London have lodged an official protest with H.M.G." He pushed the papers across the desk.

Udomo studied the papers. The young girl brought in a pot of tea this time. When she'd gone Udomo said:

"We want to think around this thing. You know, of course, I didn't have a hand in it. Mhendi was my friend. I got him here, and I'd do it again to any friend of mine who's exiled from that racialist place."

"You know both H.E. and I are with you in your disgust for the Pluralian racial régime. And certainly we didn't think that you, as P.M., would have any hand in what's happening. That's something Rosslee and I have agreed to declare flatly to H.M.G."

Udomo chuckled.

"You sound sure of that."

"You get to know a man when you've worked with him as long and closely as we've worked with you. You've poured all your energies into building a free nation here. You're not going to wreck that by backing some hopeless revolutionary scheme over there."

"I wish my own party had as much faith in me."

"They don't yet see what you're at. Mind if I smoke?"

"Go ahead. Then where does the problem arise? I'm prepared to swear I don't know a thing about this. You and Rosslee will back that. H.M.G. will reject this protest. The government of Panafrica has not interfered in the internal affairs of Pluralia. There is no problem."

Jones lit his pipe and watched Udomo through a cloud of smoke.

"What if he gets caught?"

Udomo pushed his hands against the flat surface of the desk, leaned back and began to chuckle. The chuckle turned into laughter.

He doesn't miss a thing, Jones thought.

"I see," Udomo murmured. "I thought you had faith in my good sense."

"We haven't any in our own good sense on this issue. Both Rosslee and I hate that régime too much."

"Nothing Mhendi says could implicate me."

"You get the drift of my thinking? Any word of encouragement. . . ."

"I know. But don't worry. There's nothing of the kind."

"That's a load off my mind," Jones said. "One more thing. . . ."

"Yes?"

"Rosslee thinks that if he gets away Mhendi will return here."

"Yes?"

"In which case it will be our duty to arrest him and hand him over."

Udomo thought for a long while, then shook his head.

"Afraid I can't agree to that."

"We'd be forced to if they apply for his extradition."

"I'd be forced to resign. I'd then be compelled to make control of the police and security service an election issue."

"Want to do that?"

"You know I don't. We're not ready yet to take over the administration of law and justice. If we did there'd be the most awful spate of what you call bribery and corruption. Only, for my people it would be the time-honoured old custom of the tribal 'dash'. No, it would be disastrous if I'm compelled to take over the police now. I think I need another five years before it can be done safely."

"What are we to do then?"

"That's your responsibility, Jones. You still control the police. But if I'm forced to fight a campaign around that, it would have to be an anti-European campaign, and you know how well that would suit the tribalists. Sorry about this, but you understand my position."

"Well. . . . Suppose I'd better put this up to H.M.G. and let them decide. Anyway, you know H.E. and I will do all we can. I almost hope . . ."

"That they catch Mhendi?" Udomo murmured.

Jones got up suddenly.

"The great Mr. Van Linton has been kicking his heels at my office. Got my memo about him? We shouldn't really keep the head of the Pluralian business mission waiting this long."

"I've had a chance to see some of their technicians at work on this tour. They're certainly the people we need here. They're getting things done. Pity it has to be them but they're damned good. Send him over. Know what it's about?"

"This business, I think. I'll let you see the draft of what we propose to send to London. I'll go into a huddle with H.E. about it. Mr. Van Linton's on his way. . . ." Jones went out.

Udomo rang for his secretary.

"Mr. Van Linton is on his way from Jones' office. Take these papers away and get some tea for our businessman. Sorry this is turning into a café. Anything important on the plate?"

"No. I kept today as clear as possible. Tomorrow's going to be pretty heavy."

"Right then. I'll have all the Ministers here for reports at about four. Please fix that, Tony."

"Right, sir."

Udomo rose, unrolled his sleeves, put on his tie and jacket, and turned to his official papers till the secretary announced the white Pluralian. Then he rose and came round his desk.

Van Linton was a tall, thin-lipped, stern-faced man.

"Sorry to have kept you waiting," Udomo said. "Just back from a tour. Sit down, please."

Udomo went back to his seat and waited. He'd dealt with this man before. This man was anything but a fool; an acute brain ticked behind that cold humourless face.

"I take it, Mr. Prime Minister, that you know why I'm here." There was a guttural tinge to Van Linton's English.

"I'm not sure. Is there some hold-up in the loan?" ·

"I am here to talk about a political matter, Mr. Prime Minister. . . . I am sure Mr. Jones has informed you of certain events that have recently taken place in my country—if you needed to be informed."

Udomo smiled faintly.

"Oh that. Yes. We make a point of being informed of all that happens in Africa. I'm sure your government does the same."

"My government is gravely concerned by what is happening."

"You know I'd be dishonest if I said I was sorry. We've dealt frankly and honestly with each other in business matters. I don't like what's going on there, and you know it. But it's none of my business. But surely this isn't what you came to see me about, Mr. Van Linton?"

"It is, Mr. Prime Minister. Perhaps you would be good enough to look at this." Van Linton took an envelope from his breast pocket and pushed it across the desk. "Since I received that I've been on the phone to my Prime Minister."

Udomo read the cable.

"I see this instructs you to act for your government. I think I'd better get Mr. Jones along since you are now a diplomat as well."

"As you wish, Mr. Prime Minister, though what I have to say is very brief. I think I am right in saying that my government will find it impossible to find or prove any irregular link between yourself and Mhendi. Am I?"

"You are right, Mr. Van Linton."

"So the British Government is going to reject our official protest."

"What else can it do?"

"You run a country, Mr. Prime Minister. Supposing the positions were reversed, what would you do about a situation such as the one my government is now faced with?"

"It can't arise, Mr. Van Linton. We do not hold down the majority of our people in this country."

A frown flickered across Van Linton's face.

"Come now, Mr. Prime Minister. . . ."

The young woman brought in the tea. Van Linton looked curiously at her. The light of mockery gleamed briefly in Udomo's eyes. He thought: Go on, Van Linton; ask her what it feels like to be serving a black man; tell her it couldn't happen in your country.

The girl went out.

"You were saying, Mr. Van Linton?"

"It doesn't matter. The point is: we want Mhendi, Mr. Prime Minister."

"From what I hear he's in your country."

"We may not get him. We think he might find his way back here."

"I see. . . ."

"As I just told you, my government wants him."

"I think you'd better discuss this with Mr. Jones, Mr. Van Linton. That's his department."

Van Linton straightened his back and looked straight into Udomo's eyes.

"Mr. Prime Minister: My government has ordered me and the entire delegation back if I cannot assure them of a very firm promise from you. . . ."

Udomo held on to himself. Suddenly, Van Linton's face was a blur across the desk. He took a deep breath and focused again. This was the one thing he hadn't foreseen. Then Van Linton's voice reached him again.

". . . We understand your difficulty. But government is the art of the possible. . . ."

"But I tell you I don't know anything about this," Udomo said.

Van Linton shrugged, a faint smile on his lips now.

"Then, sir, I'm afraid we'll have to cancel the plans and agreement we've initialled. Our technicians will be recalled immediately. You'll have to look elsewhere for capital and skill for your industrialisation plans. I'm sorry about this. But I have my orders."

"You're a businessman, man! There are huge profits in this for you and your shareholders. Leave politics to the politicians. Do your business! Make your profits! This country's rich and you can earn a share of those riches."

"I'm sorry, Mr. Prime Minister. I have my instructions."

"I give you my word of honour. I know nothing about this."

"Then promise to give him to us if he returns here."

"That'll wreck my government: wreck all I've dreamed and planned for. Surely you understand that!"

"I'm sorry, sir. I have my orders. There are ways of doing these things quietly. We'll co-operate there."

With great effort Udomo pulled himself together. You need to think calmly and clearly. Calmly and clearly. Think. Think. Think. . . . They mean it, these white racialists. Either you give them Mhendi or your schemes are wrecked. You've tried everywhere else and they are the only people who can do it in the time and on the scale you want.

"When do you contact your government?" Udomo spoke heavily.

"I expect their call at six tonight."

If only there were someone he could talk to. Someone who would understand and listen and soothe him. . . . Lois. . . . Oh Lois. . . .

"I'll ring you before then. Now leave me."

"Thank you, Mr. Prime Minister. You understand there's nothing personal about this, and I can give you my government's assurance that nothing of this will get out from our end. And, of course, we may get him before. . . ."

"Leave me!"

"Good morning, Mr. Prime Minister."

He sat for a long time, slumped in his chair, staring at nothing, feeling nothing except an utter and desperate aloneness. . . . Then the memory of Mhendi's voice stirred in his brain; there was a lazy, gentle rumble to Mhendi's speech, a hint of caressing tenderness to his gruff voice. . . . And the brightest of all his dreams: to carry the country to a point from where there can be no going back. To make the great transition from the past to the present. . . . Damn Mhendi! Damn him! Damn them all!

The secretary came in.

Udomo jumped up and waved his arms.

"What d'you want!" he shouted in a sudden fit of rage. "Leave me alone! Get out! Get out!"

The young man's eyes popped. His mouth fell open. Udomo grabbed at the cup in front of him.

"Get out!"

The young man rushed out. The cup crashed against the closing door, exploded in fragments.

Udomo slumped back in his chair and beat his fists on the desk. Then, suddenly, he jumped up and strode out by way of the secretary's office.

"I'm going home! I want to be alone!"

His driver was nowhere in sight. Udomo got into the driving seat and drove out of the secretariat quadrangle at a dangerous pace, scraping other cars as he went. He kept up the speed through the town. A black policeman on point duty blew his whistle and signalled frantically, then he recognised the car and stopped the other traffic.

Outside his house, Udomo jammed his foot on the brake. The car screeched to a stop. He got out and hurried into the house.

Lanwood, who had just risen, barred his way at the sitting-room door.

"Hello, Mike. Didn't expect you. I say . . ."

"Can't you leave me alone! Leave me alone! Get out of my way! Get!"

He pushed Lanwood aside. Lanwood half-fell into the settee. Udomo went to his room, banged the door shut, locked it. He flung himself on his bed, face down. . . .

Lanwood slowly picked himself up. He sat on the settee for a while, then he went to Udomo's door. He tapped. He was an old black man now, beaten by life and the world.

"Mike, you don't have to be rude to me, you know. All you have to do is tell me to go. I won't stay where I'm not wanted. I'm a man, not a dog."

"Leave me alone!" Udomo's voice rose to a pitch of frenzy. "Leave me alone!"

"All right, Mike," Lanwood said softly. "I'll leave you."

Lanwood went to his room. He unlocked his trunk and took out his leather briefcase. He opened it and checked his money. A hundred and fifty pounds in travellers' cheques. Part of the money Udomo had sent them for coming over. It had been such a triumphant thing then. Just over three months ago. Now this. Close on a hundred pounds in Panafrican currency, mostly money Udomo had given him from time to time for spending on the tour. Other people's money. Not his own. Money given to him. Not money earned. . . . He took his passport from the case and slipped it into the inside pocket of his jacket.

He went out and walked in the direction of the town. He hadn't got the hang of the town's primitive bus service yet. The glare of the sun was too much for him. He clipped the blackened shade over his glasses. That was better. He began to perspire. He looked about for a taxi. None was in sight. Five hundred yards from the house he came on the tarmac road. Heat waves rose from the earth. They made him feel dizzy. He passed two men piddling in the open gutter. He became aware of the strong foul stench of piddle.

He entered the drab outskirts of the town proper. And all about him were drab and happy people. And now, too, there were taxis all about. But he decided to walk the rest of the way. He might need every penny he had later.

He passed a group of women selling their wares on the sidewalk on the other side of the open gutter. Their laughing voices were raised in a language he couldn't understand. They gestured to him, inviting him to buy of their fly-ridden wares. He knew suddenly that he would always be an outsider here. For all his dark skin the barrier between him and this world was too great, he was too old to make the crossing successfully. He belonged too firmly, had lived too long in the western world to be any good in any other.

He felt awfully weary suddenly, tired even of all the bouncing happy barefooted people about him, of the flies and the smells. He flagged a taxi and got in.

"To the shipping office," he told the grinning black boy.

Truth is I'm homesick for London. Hadn't realised how used I'd grown to London till now. Silly to have thought I could wipe out thirty years of my life as though they didn't matter. What was that little song I'd always jeered at?

Maybe it's because I'm a Londoner
That I think of her wherever I go . . .

Now, at last, when you're too old to support it, you're facing reality, aren't you, Tom? But what is reality? That

257

colour isn't an automatic passport to Africa? That a man is made up of a complex inheritance of which the land of his birth and training is perhaps the most important? That he has to be awfully strong to overcome, really overcome, those key inheritances? Is that reality? It has to be, hasn't it? Because the other's too dreadful? But a man can't be wrong in fighting for freedom?

When the taxi pulled up and the driver turned in his seat, he saw an old man sitting hunched in a corner as though asleep, chin on chest.

"We are there, sah."

"What? Yes. Oh, yes."

Lanwood got out.

"How much?"

"Two shilling, sah."

Lanwood paid and went into the shipping office. He by-passed the black clerks and went to a corner where a white man worked.

"My name's Lanwood."

"Oh yes, Mr. Lanwood?"

"I want to enquire about a passage——" He paused, then added: *"Home."*

"When do you want to go, sir?"

"Soon as possible."

"Are you thinking in terms of a week? We might get a cancellation."

"Is that the earliest?"

The young man looked up.

"I see. . . . Just a minute while I check the books."

The young man came back after a while.

"Afraid the first passage we can offer is in six days' time. . . . Unless, of course, you're prepared to go on a cargo boat. But they take weeks and it's a dull voyage."

"When's your first cargo boat?"

"I know there's a berth on one day after tomorrow. But you

won't get to England before the passenger boat that leaves in six days' time. Of course, there's the *Savoia* leaving this evening, but that wouldn't give you enough time. . . ."

Lanwood hesitated then said:

"I'll go on that."

"The *Savoia*?"

"Yes."

"But that gives you only four hours in which to get ready."

"I'll make it."

"You're not running away from something?" the man jested.

Lanwood's expression wiped the friendly smile from the young man's face.

Twenty minutes later, Lanwood left the office with his passage ticket in his pocket. He went to the big, crowded post office. He wrote out a cablegram:

MARY FELD 36 REGENCY MEWS LONDON

SAILING ON SAVOIA TODAY DUE HOME THREE WEEKS

NEED YOU

TOM

He paid for the cable and took a taxi back to Udomo's house. No one was about except the servants. He now had only three hours left before the boat sailed. Better pack. He began packing methodically. Would Mary hold that silly last row against him? No. She was the only one who'd been loyal to him all these years. She would understand. They'd been together many years. For all their scrapping, they belonged together.

The steward called him to lunch. He ate alone, then he went back to finish his packing. He sent the steward out to get him a taxi. Then he sat down and wrote to Udomo:

"Dear Mike,

This is just to say goodbye. I'm going back to England. As you've shown so plainly today, I'm in the way and have to be shoved aside. This is something I've not taken lying down from whites and I do not see why I should take it lying down from blacks. Say goodbye to the others for me and thanks for everything. The thing that hurts most is the fact that we were once comrades.

Thomas Lanwood."

Then the taxi took him away; and then the ship.

It was Adebhoy, coming to find out what had happened to Udomo, who found the letter. Udomo came out of his room shortly afterwards. He had regained control.

Adebhoy passed the letter to Udomo.

"Tom's gone."

After a while Udomo looked up from the note.

"I don't like people reading my letters, Ade."

"It was open, lying here for anyone to see."

"Tom's a damn fool!"

"What happened?"

"Ring the shipping people and find out when he leaves and where he is. . . . Steward!"

Adebhoy went to the phone. Udomo went to the kitchen. After a while he returned, munching a leg of cold chicken.

"He left on a cargo boat which sailed half an hour ago. What happened?"

"I had something on my mind and I told him to leave me alone. You know how Tom can push himself in front of you. I pushed him aside and went to my room. Now this." Udomo flung the crumpled letter away.

"He couldn't really fit in," Adebhoy said quietly.

"But to go like this. . . ." Udomo said.

"Perhaps it's best this way, home-boy." Adebhoy smiled broadly, but his eyes were sombre. "Anyway, you can write and straighten things out. He'd be more useful over there."

"Why are you here," Udomo said suddenly.

"When your office rang to call off the meeting I went round. They said you'd gone home. . . . What's on your mind, home-boy?"

"A headache, Ade. Only a headache. But it's gone now." ·

"I'm glad, home-boy. How was the tour?"

"Fine, but I'll tell you about that later. Tonight. Off you go now. I have an important call to make. See you at the party executive tonight."

Adebhoy left reluctantly. Udomo went to the phone.

4

The rain beat down steadily. The raindrops were fat and heavy, hurting on impact. They came down in a heavy stream. And the night was pitch black; black as the dark jungle behind Maria.

She pressed her body against the young tree. She was grateful for the rain. Let it bruise and soak her, let it draw blood even. She did not mind. Because of it they were still here and she would not give up hope of his coming. But would he be able to find his way in this blackness and rain? Would he? Yes; he had led an army once. He would find his way. Yes, he would find his way. This rain was a good omen. It was a sign that he was well and would come. It had begun four days ago, the day before the month was up and they had to go back through the jungle. Without the rain they would have left three days ago. But the rain had come and they were here and he would come. Oh he *would* come. He *would* . . .

What was that?

She strained her eyes against the wall of darkness. Should she shout? No white people would be out in this rain. She cupped her hands round her mouth:

"Mhendi!" She made it a long-drawn-out cry, edged with wailing. She repeated it. "Mhendi!"

Something slimy slithered across her bare toes. She dug her nails into the bark of the tree and kept dead still. At last it was gone. Was it coming up the tree? Oh, Mhendi. . . . Calm now or you won't be here to receive him. What if they've caught him? Killed him? No, he would come. . . .

"Maria! Where are you?"

"Here, Joseph."

Joseph switched on his torch and came slowly to her, testing the earth as he came. When he was beside her he said:

"I told you it is dangerous to come by yourself. And you came without a torch."

"A snake . . ." she began. Then she gripped his arm. "Joseph! Look!"

She began to move forward. Joseph grabbed her, held her back.

"There's a light!"

Faintly, a long way off, a tiny glow pierced the blackness, then went off. Maria struggled in Joseph's arms. He sensed her open her mouth to shout. He clamped his hand over it.

"Wait!" he hissed. "Wait, Maria! It may be others."

She relaxed. He removed his hand from her mouth.

"It is Mhendi," she said.

"We *must* wait," he said firmly.

"There's the light again!" It was nearer now.

"Count the flashes," he said. "Three, then a space, then two."

"Two," Maria whispered. "Three . . . Now. Now . . . Yes. One, two. . . ."

"It is him!" Joseph said.

Maria broke free of his hold and ran forward.

"Mhendi! Mhendi!"

"Maria! Maria!"

"Sah!" Joseph cried, all caution forgotten.

Suddenly, Mhendi's figure loomed solid in the black pouring night. Maria lunged forward, arms outstretched, misjudged the space between them, and fell heavily at his feet. Mhendi

262

went on his knees in a puddle of water. Someone behind him switched on a torch. Joseph held back, slipped his hand into his pocket and pulled out the pistol.

"Who these men, sah?"

"All right, Joseph. They're of my people, my soldiers."

Joseph relaxed, pushed the pistol back in his pocket. Mhendi reached down and raised Maria.

"You have come back. . . ."

"I promised."

"Better we go back," Joseph said.

He led the way back to camp. Mhendi and Maria followed, arms about each other. The two silent Pluralians brought up the rear.

The rain came down steadily, though not with its original fierceness. Before the night was out it would have spent itself. And by morning the sun would shine again.

"I feared you'd gone," Mhendi called to Joseph. "That's why I brought two of my men. It would not be easy to go through the jungle alone."

"The rain stopped us," Joseph said.

"I hoped it would."

"I knew you would come," Maria said. "But I feared."

"I could not help being late," Mhendi said.

They penetrated some way into the jungle. Then Joseph cupped his hands and hooted like an owl, three times.

"That Joseph?" A voice spoke near them.

"This Joseph," Joseph said. He turned on his torch. A young man, naked except for a loin cloth, stood directly in their path, a sub-machine-gun cradled in the crook of his arms.

"Better you speak before you come so close," the young man said.

"Mr. Mhendi back."

"Welcome, sah! We feared for you."

Joseph led the way on. The guard remained at his post. Joseph kept his torch on now. Soon, they reached the camp site. Joseph's young men had climbed the huge trees and used the long vines to build a thick green roof over the camp site, turning it into a large, high-domed chamber. In the middle of it, a fire burned brightly, sending out crackle and spark. The young men not on duty lounged about the fire.

"Mr. Mhendi!" one of them called.

They all gathered about the party, shaking hands, showing their teeth in welcome.

"How was it, sah?" someone said. "We feared for you."

"Better Mr. Mhendi take off his wet things first," Joseph said.

"Take care of my men," Mhendi said.

"Don't worry, sah," Joseph said.

"Come," Maria said.

She took Mhendi's hand and led him to his little tent.

Inside, he took off his wet clothes. She did the same.

"How was it?" he said.

"It was a long wait," she said. "Each night I slept alone in your bed. Oh the hardness of waiting. But for you there were many dangers."

"I thought much of you," he said.

"And the loneliness that was with you before? Did it return?"

"No, my child. I think it is gone for ever."

"I am glad."

"I will go back again."

"And I will wait again."

"But on the other side next time. The jungle is not a place for a woman."

"No, my lord. This is the place where I will wait. I will obey you in everything but this. Please do not talk of it any more. It is something special to me."

They were both naked now. Suddenly, as though for the first time, he saw the dark glory of her naked beauty.

"Maria. . . ."

He pulled her into his arms, felt the trembling of her strong young body. Desire welled up in him.

"Later," she murmured. "Just a little while now. . . ." She pulled away, wrapped herself in a dry cloth, then helped him tie his toga fashion.

From outside, a voice shouted:

"Time for chop!"

Mhendi rubbed Maria's neck gently, in an easy lulling motion.

They had loved and now she lay sobbing beside him.

He kept up the rubbing till her sobbing stopped, till she relaxed. The relief after the waiting, he thought. Men often forget the heavy burden of a woman's waiting. Sleep, my child. For the present the waiting is done; just as the moving about with care and fear is done for me. If it is true that great leaders of men and freedom movements know no fear, then I'm no leader but a frightened fraud who must go on because he must. I have very little courage, really. Each time the hunters were near I died. All I do is hide it from others. That is all. Sleep, my child. You have won my heart and given me more comfort than you know. Sleep, my child. . . .

At last she was asleep. He got out of bed, put on his cloth and went out to the fire. Some of the young men were asleep near the fire. Others, including his own two young men, were asleep in the big tent. It sounded as though the rain would soon stop. Another half an hour perhaps. Damn. He'd forgotten the paper. He went quietly back to the tent and got his writing material. Then he came back and sat by the fire and wrote. He smiled faintly as he wrote. This was the necessary theatrical and showy part of the business. But men needed shows like these, either to bolster up their courage and urge them on or else to instil fear in them. This will do both: will frighten the white lords and give heart to the black slaves. What to call it? A message from Mhendi? No, Communiqué No. 1. That's it.

Communiqué No. 1. Now list the action taken. . . . Yes. Now the reason for it. They know it but tell them. Yes, this is not directed against the white people as white people. The whites know that really, but tell them. . . . Now the challenging part. A communiqué will be issued each month.

He heard movement at the far edge of the camp clearing. Then a huge snake, fat, long and a dirty-looking green, came into the clearing and moved deliberately towards the fire. Mhendi reached for the pistol at his feet. Before he could raise it there was a burst of fire from the edge of the clearing to the left of him. The long body shivered, coiled convulsively, then lay still. Everybody woke. Those in the tents rushed out. The young man on guard came into the clearing nursing the machine-gun.

"I heard him, sah, so I came back."

They all inspected the dead snake. Then Joseph said:

"All right. Back to sleep."

One of his own men came to Mhendi.

"The rain is stopping."

"You want to go back?"

"It is best to go now. If we leave it till later police might pick us up before we can get to where it will be safe. It is better not to be questioned by them if we can avoid it."

"All right, then. I've finished the writing. You know what to do."

Joseph, Maria and the other Pluralian joined them.

"He thinks it's best to go while it's dark," Mhendi said. "Tell our friends I will be back here in a month's time; and then we may set up a permanent camp here. Tell them I am safe among friends now. Tell them to prepare for the next phase of the operation as we've planned it. And remember, no recklessness or killing. This is a new kind of war."

"It may be necessary to leave a message for you," the Pluralian said. "You may come and walk into a police trap.

These things happen. Where do I leave a message for you if there is need?"

"Here," Joseph said. "We will leave the tents here."

"I don't think I can find it again—not without much searching."

Mhendi sketched an outline of the jungle's edge on his pad. Then he sketched in the Pluralian village from which they had come.

"There's the village we left. Remember we came to this hill. Then only scrub for about a mile. There's the point where the trees come out further than elsewhere. To the right of that point there are four trees taller than all the others. We're standing under those four trees now. You can only see them from a distance. Then you must use your judgement."

"May I have the map?"

"No. Memorise it."

The man studied it then nodded. Mhendi tore the sheet from the pad and flung it into the fire.

"We'd better change and go."

"Your clothes are in the tent," Joseph said. "They are dry. Go to sleep, Mr. Mhendi, sah. I will show them the way. You need your strength for our journey in the morning."

"All right. Go well, both of you. Walk with care."

"Come to rest," Maria said.

5

Mhendi and Maria reached Selina's house late at night eleven days later.

Selina flung her arms about Mhendi.

"Welcome, Mhendi! Welcome, my brother! I hear news that your deeds are echoing round the world and that those who think themselves your lords are frightened. It makes me happy to see you safe. . . . Come. Sit. . . . Bring food! Bring drinks! . . . And welcome to you, Maria, my child! Have I not found you a good one, heh, Mhendi!"

"It is good to see you, Selina," Mhendi said. "And this one you found for me is a jewel. She is close to my heart."

Selina bustled about, supervising their food, making them comfortable. She sat with them while they ate. She brought out the foreign papers and showed them off proudly: she gloated over the pictures of wrecked Pluralian power-plants, derailed goods trains, burnt-out factories.

"They even have a picture of you here," she chuckled.

After food Selina sent all the others away. She patted Maria's arm.

"Go to your room and rest, my child. You have had a hard journey. Mhendi and I must talk. Don't fear that I will keep him long."

When they were alone Selina became serious.

"Is it as they say in the papers, Mhendi; all of it?"

Mhendi skimmed through the papers.

"Yes. And more."

"And that thousands of police are hunting for you?"

"Yes."

"Then you must be careful, even here. The white man is still with us here. We have not got rid of them all yet. Udomo says we still need them. . . ." She shrugged. "What do you plan now?"

"I go back soon. My people expect me back in a month."

"And the young men I found for you?"

"They are good. Joseph is a good leader."

"I am happy. . . . Then speak of what you want me to do, my friend."

Mhendi reached down and picked up the briefcase he had carried with him all the time. He passed it to her.

"There is money in this. Money collected by my people. I don't know how much but you will see it is a lot. We need a newspaper. All our presses have been taken over and all our papers banned. We could start another in my country but they would find the press and take or destroy it. And the cost is high. . . ."

"So you want to print a paper in the jungle."

"Yes. Can it be done? Can you get me a small press?"

"I will get it. It may not be easy but I will get it to you. . . . You say you go soon. How soon?"

"In four or five days. It will be a long time before I come back this time; maybe six months or a year."

"You will live in the jungle?"

"There and among my people. It gives them heart to see me pass through the net the whites spread for me."

"I see the wisdom of that. What of food and stores?"

"We've set up committees in my country while I was there. Supplies can be passed through to the jungle camp at nights."

"It would be dangerous. It is better not to have to worry about small things. Do not think about food. I will take care of it. I will arrange everything. Give all your mind to the battle."

"It is hard carrying things through the jungle."

"What of it! It is for Africa's freedom. Think no more of it. I will go on tour up there soon and arrange everything."

"Another thing, Selina. I cannot keep your young men with me if I mean to stay such a long time."

"It is good for them. It will make soldiers of them."

"But I will have my own men. I do not want too many."

"So?"

"So I want only a few to come through the jungle with me and then to return."

"And Maria?"

Mhendi sighed.

"I would like her to return with them. It would be safer for her. But I know she will not. And I would be lonely without her."

"Take her with you; keep her. She's yours now, forever."

269

"So be it."

"And once every month I will send you supplies and you will send me news of how things go with you. . . . That is settled then. Maybe, one day, I will make a tour and visit your jungle camp. Now you must rest, my brother."

"What news of my friends?"

"Udomo and Adebhoy are well. I will let them know you are here."

"Udomo said. . . ."

"That one has grown cautious now; but your deeds have stirred the old fire in him. Now he wants to see you. And there is another friend of yours here now."

"Mabi?"

"Yes. Last week he became the new Minister of Education and National Guidance. He's good, that one. I like him. You know we had to make Udomo call him back. He would not have agreed if there had not been the danger of our losing the support of the mountain people."

"It is not my business, Selina, but I think you are wrong."

Selina's lips twitched.

"You are loyal, my friend. So am I. We'll say no more."

The thought flashed through Mhendi's mind: She's like a snake. He said:

"It would be wonderful to see Mabi again. . . . And Lanwood?"

"Of course, you don't know. He's gone."

"What! Gone?"

"He left over a month ago, on the same day he and Udomo returned from the tour."

"But why?"

"No one knows. He just packed his things and went."

"No!"

"Ask Udomo tomorrow. . . . Now you'd better rest, my friend. It is late."

So Tom had gone, quietly and silently like a man broken.

Where had he gone? Back to Mary Feld? Gone back begging because there was no room for him here in the Africa whose freedom he'd spent a lifetime dreaming of? Of course he's been a fool about many things—a clumsy, opinionated, humourless fool. But this. . . . This was the most cruel reward his worst enemy could think up. Poor Tom. I must write to him. . . .

He got up and left the room.

"Good night, Selina."

The room was the same one she had given him that first day here. Strange woman; a combination of ruthlessness and tenderness. It was as he'd thought. Maria was asleep, curled up like a child in the bed where they had first learnt to know each other. Now, knowing had turned to loving. . . . Sleep, my child; you need it. And so do I. . . . Poor Tom. Better write that letter first though. Might forget it later. Might not have time. Wouldn't want Tom to think that I'd forgotten him. . . .

He got his pad and wrote the letter. Then he undressed and got into bed, carefully, so as not to wake Maria. She turned to him in sleep, flung one arm possessively across his body. He reached out and turned off the light. It was good to relax body and mind. He closed his eyes. . . .

The Governor looked across the big hall to where Udomo stood, surrounded by members of the foreign delegations. Just as well it was an official party, otherwise he and Jones would have had to cope by themselves with the Americans, Frenchmen, Germans, Italians and Scandinavians as well as the British Parliamentary delegation. Udomo and his team of African Ministers were charming the visitors as they couldn't have done. Adebhoy was a little high, perhaps, but so were most of the visitors; and certainly, Adebhoy could carry his liquor. Udomo had fooled everyone with the same glass of sherry since dinner. And Mabi was giving him wonderful support. The Pluralian, Van Linton, had relaxed to such a point that he had, at one stage, put an arm about Mabi's

271

shoulders while telling him of the work of the black artists of Pluralia.

The Governor looked at his watch. It was half after midnight. Time to end the party. He looked about for Jones. Jones wasn't anywhere in the hall. He turned to his aide.

"Find Jones for me, please."

Then the American leader of the Council of Nations delegation was beside him.

"A wonderful party, Your Excellency, sir!"

"I'm glad you like it. We're trying to impress all our visitors."

"You've certainly impressed me. And I don't mean only this." The American waved his arm to take in the crowded, glittering hall. "I mean the whole country and the way it's being run. Prime Minister Udomo is a great man. So charming and modest."

"Yes," Rosslee said. "If you knew all the details of what he's accomplished in the face of great odds, and what he plans to do still, you'd know just what a fine administrator he is. I'm proud to work with him."

"You know, Your Excellency, we over in the United States often have the wrong slant about what you're trying to do. The old prejudice against colonialism dies hard. Hard things are often said about your rôle here."

Rosslee smiled. This was a charming old gentleman, really.

"Being abused is part of the burden of power. We've had our share of it. Now you are having yours. I think it will lead to better understanding between our two nations."

"Yes, sir! We'll certainly tell them what we've seen here. And I might as well tell you that my delegation has agreed that Prime Minister Udomo's request for technical aid be endorsed in full with additional aid which we will recommend off our own bat. That's how impressed we are with what you are doing here."

"Have you told this to the Prime Minister?"

"No, sir."

"I wish you would. You don't know how happy it would make him."

"I certainly will. In fact I'll do it now. Excuse me, sir."

The old gentleman crossed the hall to join the crowd with the Prime Minister. Rosslee waved away a steward who came to him with a tray of drinks, bowed to two ladies, and moved to the door where Jones had just appeared.

"We'd better wind this up, Jones. Everybody's had a good time and I just heard that we're going to get all the technical aid you and Udomo asked for as well as a bit extra."

"Good," Jones said, a little distracted. Then: "I've just had a word with security. Mhendi's back."

"Oh! When?"

"Got back tonight."

"Where's he now?"

"At Selina's."

"This gets curiouser and curiouser. No request for extradition?"

"Not a word so far."

"I don't understand it. First the Pluralian authorities go as far as an official protest and then they drop it like a hot brick. Why? I keep asking myself that. Nothing more from London about it?"

"Not a thing. They seem satisfied to let it be."

"I confess I prefer to play ostrich about this."

"But we're government," Jones murmured. "The thing is: what are we to do now? They'll watch him carefully from now onwards. But what the hell are we to do? Just watch and wait? I would like to know what passed between Udomo and Van Linton that morning."

"You know something, Jones? I wouldn't. I'd much rather know nothing about this." Rosslee looked across the hall. "There he stands, smiling, charming them. And perhaps only one or two of them have the vaguest idea of the burden he carries. And if you or I were to say to them, 'Gentlemen, this man is trying to carry his country over the great transition from one age to another', they may understand our words but not their full meaning. I don't know, Jones. All I know is that I wouldn't be in his place for anything now."

"But surely he wouldn't sell his friend."

"Wouldn't he? Put yourself in his place. . . . But how could you, or I? We understand this thing intellectually, perhaps."

"That would be monstrous."

"Yes, wouldn't it," Rosslee said.

"And yet," Jones said, worried.

"It's that 'And yet' that makes me sick in the stomach," Rosslee said.

"It may not happen."

"So we run away from it, Jones. It may not happen. That's our hope. I'm going to shut my mind to it till this thing hits me. Deliberately, I choose the moral coward's position. . . . Come, we must end this party."

"I'll tell him Mhendi's back," Jones said.

"If he doesn't know already."

"Mhendi arrived after the party started."

"Yes, tell him."

Udomo's car came for Mhendi early next evening.

Selina was pleased. She said to Mhendi:

"This is good. There has been too much caution in him of late. The Prime Minister must be careful about this; the Prime Minister must be careful about that. . . . It is good that he should forget to be the Prime Minister and be the angry fighter he once was. There is still need for fighters in Africa. You will be men together, old friends. You and Adebhoy and Mabi can put heart into him. We would be rid of these white people, rid of them altogether! Show him that, my brother."

She gave the driver two chickens she had especially prepared for them. Maria stayed with her.

Udomo was alone when Mhendi arrived. He sat poring over papers, his face overcast with weariness. He rose when Mhendi entered. The weariness fell from him. His face became youthful.

"Mhendi! It's good to see you again." The sunshine grin lit his face. "Congratulations! Nothing has pleased me so much." His voice, now, was tinged with bitter rage. "Nothing has pleased me so much in years as the fear you've struck in those white savages. How are you, man?"

"It's good to be able to relax," Mhendi said. "And you?"

He looks well, Udomo thought; like someone who's found himself again.

"The same. Trying to fool a lot of people. Fighting against time. But I'm beginning to see the shape of things."

Mhendi thought: You've grown deep, my friend. Wish I could make you out. Better warn you about Selina. He said:

"You know Selina's growing restless?"

"She and Ade. Yes; and quite a few others. Endura's opposition has discovered the value of Africanisation as a battle-cry. But I'll fool them yet. They can't hold the country together so they're dependent on me. Sit down. Ade and Mabi are due in a little while. I wanted to have a chat before they came."

"Don't under-rate Selina," Mhendi said.

Udomo chuckled softly.

"I've learned not to do that with anybody. I respect Selina too much. In fact, she's the only one I really fear—she and Ade. Didn't know what a tribalist Ade was. Think she sees what I'm after?"

"Don't know," Mhendi said. "She thinks you're too cautious."

"Good! Excellent! I'm being as bold as the devil and she thinks I'm cautious. Fine!"

Mhendi stuffed his pipe and lit it. The steward came in with whisky for him and fruit juice for Udomo.

"All I need is time," Udomo said in a faraway, musing tone. "Just time."

"How much?"

"Ten years. Five at a pinch; but ten to do it comfortably....
But tell me about your plans. Where's your base? How'd you
get through the jungle? Tell me all about it. I really must
slip away one day and visit your camp."

"It's a nine-day trip through the jungle."

Udomo slapped his knee and roared with laughter.

"Don't tell me you agree with Selina that I've grown soft!"

"You're busy, man."

"Tell me where your base is and see if I don't pay you a
visit. Go on. You just try me!"

"All right. But I think it's crazy for you to take such a risk.
Give me a piece of paper. . . ."

Udomo got paper and pencil and came and sat beside
Mhendi. Mhendi sketched a rough map and talked as he
sketched.

"The hidden path through the jungle begins here; below
that little village. You know the one; the very last one before
you come to the jungle. The way through the jungle seems
to be in a gentle curve to the right. You come out here. It
looks easy when you sketch it. But it'll be after nine days of
walking through darkness that you get to this point. And
you'll be facing Pluralia. Our camp is here. From the Pluralian end you see it by these four tall trees that tower above
all the others. It's been turned into a huge chamber of green.
It keeps out the rain, and you can have a fire without the
smoke showing above the trees. It's as safe a place as you can
want. Even if the forces of law and order come looking for
me they'll have an awful job, and then I'll hear them in time
to be lost before they find the camp—if they ever do."

"But they won't, will they?"

"I'd say it's impossible."

"Good. . . . Well, I'll find it. Better let me keep this. I really
mean it. I am coming. . . . Now tell me how you plan to
carry on?"

Mhendi told him of the plan he'd outlined to Selina. When he finished, Udomo sighed and leaned back.

"God! How I wish I were there with you. Your fight is clean and honest and direct. Here, I must twist and turn, make deals with people whose guts I hate; be charming with even those damn Pluralian whites. . . ." His face contorted in a sudden fit of rage. "I tell you, I hate it sometimes, Mhendi!" Then he relaxed, shrugged, and smiled apologetically, as though ashamed of his outburst.

Mhendi warmed to him, restrained the impulse to hug him. Words of comfort formed in his brain; but all he said was:

"That's the price we pay, Mike: our generation."

Udomo's lips twisted wryly: but there was warmth in his voice:

"And those who come after will sit in judgement and judge us harshly. You understand, Mhendi. Now tell me, if you were in my position—or even in your own position—and you were forced either to sacrifice one person to consolidate a gain and perhaps gain more, or else lose all you've gained and a lot more perhaps, which would you choose? Tell me frankly."

So you face a real problem, Mhendi thought; you don't fool me with your casualness. It's a real problem.

"I've had to make the choice, you know," Mhendi said quietly. "I've been responsible for the death of many men."

Udomo put his arm about Mhendi's shoulders.

"As an officer is responsible in battle, my friend."

"It is still a responsibility. A uniform or a cause does not change that."

"How would you choose today?" Udomo said quietly.

Mhendi felt bitter suddenly. Work it out for yourself! I had no one to help *me* when I had to make my choice. Work it out for yourself!

"It is the kind of thing a man can only answer when it arises."

"Suppose it has arisen. Your camp. Yes; let's think of your camp. Suppose you found out that one of the people you trusted was going to tell your enemies where your camp was. What would you do?"

"I'd have to do something."

"Good. Now take it a stage further. Suppose this person was loyal to you, did not intend to betray you, but could unknowingly lead your enemies to your camp. What then? Would you tell one of your gunmen to shoot him to prevent his betraying you?"

"It would depend on many things."

"Such as?"

"Such as what betraying the camp would mean."

"Suppose it meant the complete defeat of your revolution."

Mhendi shrugged.

"Then it would have to be. But what are you driving at?"

"Even if it were your brother?"

"It would be a cruel choice, but I would say yes. But tell me, Mike. . . ."

"I'm thinking of Ade. We're facing a crisis now. But it may pass. . . . It's good to talk with you, Mhendi. You understand these things. It would be wonderful if you were in my team, being really useful, instead of risking your life out there among those white barbarians. What chances of catching you?"

"I might walk straight into them when I go back."

"And then?"

"I expect an accident will happen. They don't want to put me on trial."

"I can see that. . . . I think that's Ade's car. You heard Tom's gone."

"Selina told me."

"He just walked out the afternoon we got back; walked out and got on a ship without a word to anybody. Left a note." He rose and went to the door.

Mabi and Adebhoy came in.

After the excitement of greeting, they made themselves comfortable and talked of old times and old dreams. Almost, they recaptured a hint of the old London days, of the carefree camaraderie of those days. But there were shadows now, and they avoided these with casual care. No one mentioned Lois or the absent Tom Lanwood. And the spontaneous gaiety of the old days was lacking.

Then, they had been young men nursing dreams; then, they had had all the world to conquer; then, there had been a happy recklessness in the bold plans they dreamed.

Now they were the rulers, three of them. Men carrying the burden of State. And every now and then it intruded on their talk.

Mhendi thought: They've all changed. Even Mabi. Only I am still the same. And now they are more like me. But they have power. Their problems are problems of how to build, of how to create. Only mine are still those of how to destroy. That's the difference between us now. And what a difference!

This realisation brought a hint of sadness to Mhendi's talk. Mabi sensed it and came and sat with him. And Mhendi was comforted a little. These were the rules of life's game. A man could not choose where or how he was born. A man was made by the land and situation into which he was born, by the colour with which he was born. Over these he had no choice, no say of any kind. He was a prisoner. Virtue, then, or the lack of it, was in the way a man responded to his situation.

Later, the steward laid the table and they ate Selina's two chickens and drank two bottles of champagne Udomo had got especially.

Then they went out on the mosquito-proofed veranda and sat in silence in the darkness, listening to the gay din of the creatures of the night, sensing and feeling the nearness of each other, differences relaxed for the moment, nursing memories of days and nights shared in the distant age of dreaming. And because the mind deceives, lies, hides, lulls, beguiles, their memories glowed with a greater beauty, a richer purity, than they were charged with when they were the reality.

They parted when the yellow moon was big overhead and quiet covered all the land. They parted with the quiet affection of dear friends among whom words had, for the time being, become unnecessary.

Then, when he was alone, Udomo went briskly to the telephone. And as he picked it up tears sprang into his eyes.

"I want Mr. Van Linton," he snapped. His voice was hard and cold. But still the tears flowed, unheeded, unstemmed.

6

The early morning sun filtered through the leaves on the jungle's edge when Mhendi's party arrived back at the camp. Joseph and Maria supervised the packing of the stores. Mhendi went into his tent.

Someone had been, had left a note as well as a batch of Pluralian newspapers. Mhendi opened the note. It said:

"It is dangerous to come. There are soldiers and police in the area. They are everywhere and they are very quiet. Stay where you are till someone comes with news for you. They are too quiet for safety, so please do not come."

He called Joseph and Maria and showed them the note.

"Then you will not leave tonight?" Joseph said.

"No," he said. "I will wait till they come. That means I will not need you to stay with Maria this night."

Joseph hesitated. Mhendi read his mind. He wanted to go, wanted to get the dark jungle behind them as soon as possible. But a sense of duty restrained him.

"If you are sure . . ." Joseph said.

"Yes," Maria said, smiling. "Go. Then I will have my man to myself for this day and night. Who knows when I will have him to myself again . . . ?"

This settled Joseph's mind. He nodded.

"We will see to everything for you first. We will gather enough wood to last you some days. And water too."

"It is you who are making the journey," Mhendi protested.

"We are young and strong," Joseph said. "We want to leave you in comfort."

Affection welled up in Mhendi for this strong young man with his deep sense of loyalty. He squeezed Joseph's big arm affectionately.

Joseph turned away with shining eyes.

"I go to prepare things," he mumbled huskily.

"How you bind men's hearts to you," Maria whispered.

"They are such good young men. I am proud of them."

"It is your tenderness for people that first won my heart," she said.

He pulled her head against his chest.

"Will you not go back with them, my child? It will be better."

She pulled away and stuck out her chin.

"Again! Have I not told you a thousand times I will not leave you?"

He brushed her forehead with his lips.

"So be it then. It brings me comfort to know of your love. But still. . . ."

"Be quiet!"

He sighed, then smiled. Oh the comfort of a woman's loving. . . .

The young men left them after lunch. At the last point from which their shadowy figures could be seen they looked back and waved. Then they were swallowed up, lost, in the sunless gloom of the jungle.

"Come," Maria said. "I know you like coffee after food. I will make some."

Mhendi walked back to the camp with her, feeling slightly foolish about the machine-gun he carried. Joseph had left it, insisting that he took it with him everywhere.

Maria made coffee. While he drank it, she sat near him looking at the pictures in the Pluralian papers.

"It is very silent," he said. His voice echoed through their vast green chamber.

"It is because we are alone," she said. "I do not mind it. Do you?"

"No," he said.

Then, after a while, she said:

"I want you to lie down. I want you to rest. Go to the tent."

"And you?"

"I will rest too. Go."

"It is cooler here," he said. "There is no air in the tent."

"All right then. Put your head on my lap."

He did so. She put her hand on his forehead. It was very cool. He closed his eyes. He began to think about the miracle of hands: hands making the most complicated things; hands comforting with coolness; hands caressing. He opened his eyes, reached up, took her hand in his own, and held it far enough away for his eyes to focus on it. A long, slender, tapering black hand, seemingly possessed of a life of its own. Pity he'd never had time to read more, to play more, to listen to music more, to have more time for laughter. The little things it is that make up the richness of life. . . .

He closed his eyes again, and the cool, slender dark hand comforted his brow again.

"You know," he said dreamily.

"What?" she murmured.

"I've not really had a chance to make friends with your boy. Always I arrive late and tired. And always I leave early. And now I've taken you from him."

"There will be time, later," she said. "Lots of time."

"Do you think he'll like me?"

"Already he talks of you as his father."

"Only to please you. . . ."

"No. He, too, is captured by your tenderness for people."

"You know of my children. . . ."

"I will be their mother just as you will be his father."

"It was dangerous to see them, for children can betray one without knowing. Our enemies are cunning. So I could not talk to them. And it is years since I last saw them."

"Why do they do this thing?"

"Who? The whites?"

"Yes. Is it that they are born evil?"

"No, my child. . . . They are not born evil. They are human, as you and I. As with us, some of them are kind and others are cruel. The things they do, they do out of a fear that has grown so great that it has become a thing of evil. . . ."

"Never mind now. Rest and we will talk of this again."

The cool fingers ran along his temple. The silence stretched till he ceased to be aware of it. . . .

He opened his eyes. It seemed only a moment later, but the world had grown dark between the closing and opening of his eyes.

"Have I slept?"

"Yes."

"How long?" He sat up and looked about.

"A long time."

"And you. . . ."

"I have rested too."

"Sitting like this?"

"Sitting like this."

"Oh woman!"

She laughed then.

He got up and pulled her up.

"I think the sun is down," he said. "Come, let us go and see. It will be good to see the sky before it is too dark. Come."

"Do not forget the gun," she said.

He smiled sheepishly, went back and picked up the machine-gun.

"Come."

They walked side by side towards the edge of the trees.

"I listened to the silence while you slept," she said.

He took her hand.

"Were you frightened?"

"You were with me, even in sleep."

"I am not a very brave man, Maria."

She looked sideways at him. Her lips curved in an understanding, motherly smile. Her fingers tightened about his.

"You are my man," she said.

They neared the clearing, went forward more carefully. There was no sign of life. For miles, as far as the first hill beyond which the first Pluralian village lay, there was no sign of man or beast.

The sun had gone down, but only just. Its light was still sharp in the sky, lighting up all the world except in the jungle.

"Let us sit under the sky for a while," Mhendi said. "And we will see whatever there is to see before we are seen. The grass is tall."

They sat in the tall grass. And here, on the edge of the jungle, the little creatures of the wild had already started tuning up for their nightly music.

"How beautiful the sky is," Mhendi said.

Maria looked up.

"Yes. And they say it is nothing."

"Nothing but space until you meet another planet like ours."

"I wish now I had stayed longer at school, had learnt more, then I would have been able to talk to you with more sense. A woman wants to understand the things that interest her man or she may lose him."

"You will not lose me, my child."

"Oh, Mhendi . . ." She buried her face in his chest.

"Oh, my dear," he said again and again, holding her close.

After a while she raised her head. She pointed towards Pluralia.

"Will I ever go there with you?"

"I have thought of it. You can live in one of our villages and the whites will not know you are not of our people."

"And your people? Don't forget I am a stranger. You know our people will not let Udomo take a woman from another land for wife, even if she is black."

"It is no longer the same with us, my dear. The days of the tribe are dead among us. The stranger who is for us and with us is welcome. He is not an enemy because he comes from another place. Even the whites are not enemies because they are white but because they deny us freedom. You would be welcome. You would be welcome as my wife. For to us all Africa is one; and those of us who are the leaders of our people go beyond that even: we say all the people of the world are one."

"Then they would really welcome me?"

"And they will grow to love you as I have done."

"Then let the day come soon, Mhendi!"

Suddenly, in the manner of Africa, it was dark.

They went back to the camp. While Mhendi lit the fire that would keep venturing creatures at bay, Maria prepared their food. There was not much to do. The young men had prepared everything before leaving.

After food, they sat close to each other and talked with the quiet peacefulness of the not-so-young who have found the meaning of love. He told her of the lands he had visited, of the people he'd met and of those who had been his friends.

She sat, using his knee for arm-rest. And every time he stopped she asked another question that set the stream of memory flowing.

This was their moment of binding intimacy, the reason why she had wanted the young men to go. She had known it would only be possible when they were alone. Now it had come. . . .

They talked till the blazing fire turned to dull ashes. Then Mhendi put more wood on, arranging it for long burning. Then they went to their tent and slept. . . .

Maria's scream woke him. He jerked upright. The blinding light dazzled him. Maria screamed again. He was wide awake now.

"Don't do anything foolish, Mhendi!" a voice said.

"Who are you?" But he knew. "That torch . . ."

"Sorry."

The beam of light shifted from his face to the crude table beside the camp bed. Someone struck a match and lit the oil-lamp.

A tall, lean-faced white man towered over them. Maria clung to him, shivering with shock and fear. He felt her body tensing. She was going to scream again. He said:

"Maria!"

His sternness steadied her. He looked at the white man.

"My men are all about you, Mhendi."

"How did you . . ." Then it came to him suddenly, in a flash of understanding. Udomo. That talk with Udomo. Udomo had all but told him why. He'd even drawn the map for Udomo.

"I see you've got it," the white man said.

Mhendi braced himself.

"May we dress?"

The white man stared at him for a while, then turned abruptly and left the tent. Maria began to whimper. Mhendi helped her out of bed.

"We must dress, Maria. Come now, quickly!"

She sank back on the bed when he let her go.

"Maria! Maria!" He shook her gently.

The white man pushed an arm through the tent opening.

286

"Give her a swig of this."

Mhendi took the half-bottle of brandy and forced some down Maria's throat. Then he began to dress.

"Get dressed, Maria!"

He gave her more brandy. He tried to think. But thought was impossible. That last conversation with Udomo ran like an echo through his mind. When he had finished dressing he gave Maria more brandy. She protested but he forced it down her throat. The glazed look began to go from her eyes.

"Dress, Maria!"

She opened her mouth but no sound came from her throat. He put his arms about her. She clung to him, fingers hurting his flesh through the clothes.

"You must dress!" he said.

"Are *you* dressed?" the white man called.

"Yes."

"Leave her and come out here."

He had to force her away from him, hurting her in the process.

"Please dress, Maria!"

She went on her knees.

"Mhendi. . . ." Her voice was a stifled croak.

He went out. The whites were everywhere in the camp. They'd built up the fire. Two were brewing coffee. The leader, the one who'd come into the tent, waited for him.

If only I could think. If only I could think. Think. Think.

"Sit down," the white man said.

Mhendi sat near the fire. The white man came and sat with him.

"Who's the woman?"

"She had nothing to do with this."

"Your woman?"

The leaping flames lit up their faces. The other white men watched from a distance.

"Yes."

287

"Pity. We expected to find you alone."

A hint of bitterness crept into Mhendi's voice:

"I should've told my friend."

"You should have, Mhendi. She from the other side?"

"Yes. I tell you she's got nothing to——"

"Don't worry. At least, don't worry about us. It's how she's going to get back that you should worry about."

Mhendi groaned.

"You can't leave her here! Take her with you. Hand her over!"

"Go to all that expense? No. Your little game's cost us enough. You've got to pay for your fun, you know. Especially with the kind of friends you have." The white man rose suddenly. "This is the end of the line, Mhendi. You're taking it like the man I thought you'd be." His voice dropped to a whisper. "If it's any comfort, I don't like this night's work. Still. . . ."

Mhendi rose too. He felt strangely calm now.

"You know it won't make any difference. They will be free."

"In the long run—yes. But we're thinking of now. We have to. You notice I'm not insulting you by asking for information."

Maria came out of the tent, dressed. She rushed to Mhendi and flung her arms about him.

"Mhendi. . . ."

"I must leave you, Maria—alone, here. I'm sorry. Oh Maria . . ."

"All right!" the white man called.

Two others came and took Mhendi's arms. Their leader tore Maria from him. The two led Mhendi away. The leader held on to the demented Maria.

Walking between the two white men, Mhendi knew that this was his last walk. These were the last moments of life. His calmness surprised him. He thought about it. He realised that thought, too, was now possible again. I must have been prepared for this: somewhere in the deep recesses of my being I must have adjusted myself to this possibility, otherwise I wouldn't be so calm now, for I'm not a brave man. . . .

He stumbled. One of the white men steadied him.

Really, Udomo told me why he was selling me. Told me clearly and I couldn't see it. Asked me, and I told him what to do. Terribly literal person. I couldn't do this, no matter what I said to him. Or could I? How can I know until I'm faced with it, as he was faced . . . Soon, now. Very soon now. How does one pray? Does one say: God, I have done my duty, I have tried to help liberate my people, and for that I must die? Is that a prayer? What is prayer? Maria. God, *please*, please take care of Maria. Her only crime was to love me; mine, to keep her with me. Take care of her, *please*.

They were out of the wood now, in the tall grass, on the way to Pluralia. There were the lights of trucks to the left and right of them.

I will die under the sky, and the moon will see it.

The two men came to a stop. He stopped with them. Faintly, Maria's screaming voice came to him. Poor Maria. A woman born to sorrow. That's what they said of the mother of Jesus.

One of the white men pushed something into his hands. It was the machine-gun Joseph had left with him.

So this is how it was to be. . . . They've removed all the bullets, of course.

"Now go," one of the men said.

He squared his shoulders and walked forward, away from them. And now, at last, fear assaulted him as a living physical force. The impulse to run was strong. Death was so eternal. Oh God! Oh God! Maria. . . .

A voice cracked across the night:

"Mhendi!"

He turned. He heard no sound. He felt only the hint of a great pain. Then nothing. . . .

Beside the camp fire, in the arms of the white man, Maria

289

let out one long, agonised scream, then went limp. The white man carried her into the tent, put her on the bed and covered her. Then he went to the others waiting near the fire.

"Come on!" There was an edge to his voice.

Maria passed from unconsciousness into the deep sleep of the shocked.

When she woke it was early morning. She lay staring at the tent roof for a long time, utterly still. Then she got up and went out. The camp was as it had been yesterday. Everything in its place. Only the fire had burned itself out. Then she saw the cluster of little green snakes asleep in the warm ashes. She went close and stared at them for a while. Then, deliberately, she raised her right foot, hesitated, and brought it down on their green bodies. They lashed at her, stinging her time after time; then they slithered away to the protection of the deep undergrowth.

She went back to the tent and lay down on the bed. . . . She felt the drowsiness begin. Soon she would be with Mhendi, with her man. She closed her eyes and relaxed. The terrible spreading pain in her leg was a little thing. . . . Oh Mhendi. . . .

7

Paul Mabi was drunk. He staggered across the room, refilled his glass with whisky and went back to the chair by the window, bumping into things as he went. He half fell into the chair.

The room was in darkness. Outside, darkness was over all the world. He raised the glass to his lips and drank half its contents. He shivered and put the glass on the window-sill.

His steward came to the door.

"Massa Paul, sah. . . ."

Mabi swung on him and fell out of the chair.

"What d'you want! Get out! Filthy dirty bastard! Get out!"

The steward stood his ground.

"You make yourself sick, sah, for drinking all that bad liquor and no chop in your belly." He advanced into the room, switching on the light.

Mabi crawled to the window, grabbed the glass from the sill and flung it at the boy. It bounced off the boy's chest, soaking his shirt-front.

"Get out, you bastard! Get out!"

Mabi searched about for something else to fling.

"Please, massa. . . ."

"Get out!"

He flung an ashtray which the boy dodged.

"Oh my massa. . . ." The boy sighed heavily and turned on his heels.

Mabi found another glass, filled it, turned off the light and staggered back to his chair at the window.

"I don't want to think," he wailed. "Want to get drunk; unconscious drunk."

He drank some more, spilling some of the liquor over his clothes.

"He was my friend . . . My friend . . . My friend . . ."

He heard the door open again.

"You bastard!" he screamed. "I told you to get out! I'll kill you! Get out before I kill you! Get out!"

"It's me," Udomo's voice said. "It's me, Mabi."

Udomo switched on the light. Mabi turned his head slowly.

"So it is. Our Prime Minister. The great god Udomo. What d'you want?"

Udomo came into the room.

"I want to talk."

"Well, I don't want to talk. I don't want to talk to you. I don't want to talk to anybody. Go 'way. I'll work for you to-morrow. Tonight I mourn my friend. Go 'way."

"I mourn him too, Mabi."

"You!" Mabi blinked and stared at Udomo. "D'you ever mourn anybody?"

"You'd be surprised. . . . May I have a drink?"

"Help yourself, my lord. I'm in no fit state to help you."

Udomo went to the cupboard and poured himself a stiff whisky.

"Want the light on?"

"No. But I suppose I must do as my Prime Minister wishes."

Udomo switched off the light and came and sat opposite Mabi, bringing the bottle with him. He downed his drink in one gulp and poured himself another.

Mabi giggled and rocked from side to side.

"Our great Prime Minister taking to drink, heh! Drowning his sorrows, heh! Why? Tell me why, great god Udomo. I'm no visiting delegation; I'm no great crowd to be moved to tears. . . . Why? What d'you want of me?"

There was a long silence, then Udomo said:

"I must tell somebody—you. I killed him. . . ."

Mabi was too drunk to hear the pain in Udomo's voice; the darkness hid Udomo's tears.

"Killed Mhendi. . . . You?"

"Yes. I told Van Linton where his camp was. I had to do that or lose their aid. You know what that would have meant."

Mabi's brain began to function.

The silence in the dark room dragged on. At last, in a wondering, uncertain voice, Mabi said:

"You sold him to his enemies. . . ."

Udomo poured more whisky into his glass.

"I had to. You understand that. *I had to.* . . ." The plea in Udomo's voice did not reach Mabi; only the cold, hard words that told of his betrayal.

Udomo went on talking, explaining, trying to make Mabi see his agony of spirit, his need for comfort. But Mabi did not hear him. Only the fact of the betrayal was real. It seeped into his brain, dispelling the fog of liquor.

"You. . . ." Mabi choked on the word. "You. . . ."

Then, bitterly, viciously, he flung his glass at Udomo's head. And after the glass he flung his own small body, scratching, clawing, cursing.

Udomo's chair crashed to the floor, taking the two of them with it. The noise brought the steward boy rushing in. He switched on the light.

Udomo sat on Mabi's chest, pinning him down, holding his hands. Blood ran down the side of Udomo's face. The glass had made a deep gash on his left cheek, below the cheekbone.

"Oh massas!" the steward cried.

"Your master's sick," Udomo gasped. "Help me!"

Mabi struggled furiously. But he was helpless under Udomo. He gave up struggling and began to curse Udomo: a steady stream of bitter curses. Then he spat. He kept on spitting till Udomo's face was covered with spittle.

"Help me hold him!" Udomo said.

He rose, lifting Mabi with him. The boy moved towards them. Mabi flung himself back with all the force in his body. This broke Udomo's hold. But the force of Mabi's move unbalanced him too. He crashed to the floor and lay still.

"Oh my massa!" the boy cried.

Udomo went down on one knee beside Mabi.

"He will be all right."

He gathered Mabi in his arms and carried him to his bedroom. He dumped Mabi on the bed.

"Undress your master and put him to bed. I'll write a note which you must give to him when he wakes in the morning. Bring me paper."

The boy brought the paper, seemed to become aware for the first time of the blood on Udomo's face.

"Your face, sah!"

"It's not serious."

He wrote:

Come to my office first thing in the morning. Udomo.

He gave the note to the boy. Then he went out, got into his car and drove away.

Half an hour later, two men took up guard duty outside Mabi's house.

In another part of the town the Governor and the Chief Secretary got desperately, determinedly drunk.

"God, how I hate Africa!" Rosslee said.

"You mean progress," Jones said, his yellowish face looking shrivelled.

"I mean Africa! This beastly continent with its darkness and ju-ju and bloodletting and betrayal. It's violent. It's foul!"

"We—Europe—have travelled this way too. In uglier ways. Only, it was a long time ago and men forget." Jones drank some more. "Wish I knew of some way to comfort him. . . ."

"Seen him today?" Rosslee said.

"Yes. More shrouded and aloof than usual. Poor bloody bastard. He *is* a great man, you know. Only a rogue or a great man could do that. You and I, Rosslee, are not made of such stuff."

"You can keep your progress and greatness," Rosslee said bitterly.

"Wonder what he's thinking now," Jones said quietly.

The morning sun streamed into the Prime Minister's office. Udomo turned from the window and faced Mabi. The hatred in Mabi's face was naked.

"You still refuse to see my position?"

"I can only see the selling of a friend!" Mabi snapped.

"And you insist on resigning?"

"Yes!"

Udomo spread his hands appealingly.

"Sit down, Mabi. Let's talk it over———"

"We have nothing to talk about!"

Udomo lost patience.

"Dammit, man! You're being a sentimental woman! Don't you think I'm going through hell too? Do you think I liked doing it?" His voice shook. "I had to! We can't allow personal feelings to interfere with duty! Duty to Africa! Her people! My people and yours! The future! . . . Be reasonable, Mabi. . . ."

"Have you done?"

He hates me too much, Udomo thought.

"All right. But you know you can't stay in the country."

Mabi's lips curled bitterly.

"You needn't fear I'd talk."

Udomo chuckled without humour.

"Who'd believe you? Anyway, you could be dealt with. You don't think I'll allow you to mess up my work. I liked Mhendi. I never liked you."

"I'd like to see my people before I leave. You can't stop that."

"Can't I? You get on the first available plane. I believe there's one tonight. You'll be going on sick leave. You had a break-down last night. Your steward was there to bear witness. You'll be away so long that I'll be forced to give your ministry to someone else."

"Aren't you afraid I might talk in England?"

"What will you say? What proof have you for it? You had a break-down, don't forget. That could explain a lot of queerness. But you won't talk. You want to be a patriot provided you can safeguard your precious soul. You know I had to. Only, no dirtying of hands for you! Leave that to the foul Udomo. Mourning Mhendi indeed! He wouldn't want to be mourned by you. All right, go now, Mr. Moral Mabi! I have to deal with realities, not your fancy ideas. You make me sick! Go. . . ." He went to his desk and sat down.

Mabi went to the door.

"Mabi."

Mabi stopped, waited without turning.

"Hate me as much as you like. But it's the country, man! It's Africa. Stay and help me work for that. . . ."

Mabi reached for the door handle.

"Then get out, you damn fool!" Udomo exploded.

The door shut behind Mabi. Udomo stared at the door for a while. Then he opened a drawer and took out a box of cigarettes. He lit one, leaned back and puffed at it. One needs something to steady one's nerves. He knew that sooner or later he would have to take to drink to achieve a measure of relaxation. But he'd make it later. As late as possible. . . . No picnic, running a country. No picnic at all. What a pillar of strength Mhendi would have been had he been born in Panafrica instead of Pluralia. . . . God, I'm tired. . . . But such a hell of a lot to do. No picnic at all, trying to carry a country across the great gulf between yesterday and today. . . .

He stubbed out the cigarette and rang for his secretary.

Lois, he thought calmly, would be such a comfort now.

SELINA ADEBHOY

I

Udomo hooted and waited. But there was no sign of the young men who kept guard at nights. He hooted again. Where were those fellows? Had Selina and the party decided it was safe now to leave his house unguarded at night? Would be interesting to find out why.

His steward came running down the dark drive and opened the gates. Udomo drove in. The boy shut the gates behind the car. Udomo got out and hurried up the stairs and into the house. The steward called out something but he couldn't catch it. He marched into the sitting-room, then stopped dead. Adebhoy and Selina were there. They sat as though they'd been waiting a long time. He forced a smile to his lips. No responding smile touched their faces. Selina watched him impassively. Adebhoy avoided looking at him for a spell, then he looked up and the hint of a smile flickered across his face.

How fat he's grown, Udomo thought; he eats and drinks too much. He realised again how much he had come to dislike Adebhoy. He took a cigarette from his pocket and moved forward slowly. Selina's eyes flickered from the cigarette case back to his face. He sat down, facing them.

"You are surprised to see us," Selina said.

"It is late," he said. He looked at his watch. "Nearly one."

The steward boy came in.

"Will you take something?" Udomo said.

"I want nothing," Selina said.

"Me too," Adebhoy said.

Udomo thought: So this is serious.

"You can go to bed," he said to the steward.

They waited till the boy had left, then Selina said:

"Was it a good one, this party you had with the white people?"

"You didn't come to talk of that," Udomo said.

"No. But it is one of the things."

"The non-fraternisation rule," Adebhoy said.

"It is late and I'm tired," Udomo said.

"We've waited a long time," Selina said.

"Call a meeting of the party executive tomorrow and we'll talk about these things. I'll explain my conduct then."

Selina folded her arms across her bosom.

"We will talk now, Udomo. In the old days we could talk, the three of us. I want us to talk as we talked then."

"All right. But let it be tomorrow. I'm tired tonight."

"I would still talk now."

So this is the show-down, Udomo thought. He lit his cigarette.

"You too, Ade?"

"Yes."

"Right then." He leaned back and waited, alert and watchful.

"You have betrayed us," Selina said quietly.

Udomo's eyes shifted to Adebhoy's face.

"That your opinion too, Ade?"

"We are agreed," Selina said. "That's why we are here together."

"That so, Ade?"

At last, Adebhoy looked him in the face. Adebhoy's face cracked into a huge smile. But his eyes were cold and sombre.

"Yes. You've betrayed us."

"I see. . . . You say 'You have betrayed us'. Whom do you mean by 'us'? And what is the nature of my betrayal?"

Selina's eyes flickered.

"So you would play the white man's game with us. . . ."

"No, Selina. You accuse me. I want to understand the accusation. That's all."

"All right, Udomo; I will tell you! You ask who we are whom you have betrayed. You have betrayed me." The hint of passion left her voice: she spoke coldly, impersonally. "You have betrayed me. I made you Prime Minister and you have betrayed me. You know what you were when you came to me at the market that day eight years and more ago. You are Prime Minister now because I did not turn you away then."

"How have I betrayed you?"

"You ask that?"

"I do. I want to know."

"Don't treat me as a child, Udomo!"

"The man who is accused has a right to know."

"There are more white people in our land now than there were when the British ruled."

"Because we need them, need their skills."

"What of your promise that the land would be free of their rule?"

"They don't rule. We rule. You know that, Ade."

"I'm not sure of that any more," Adebhoy said. "Sure we're the Ministers. The Cabinet's ours. We sign the laws. But white men run all the big industrialisation and construction projects. They control us with their money, and you know it. That's why you have to shut your eyes to their clubs for whites only. Everywhere in the land, in factories, on building and construction projects, where roads are being made, whites give the orders and blacks do the work. . . ."

299

"Like in Mhendi's land," Selina said.

"And how much money goes out of the country in dividends for whites? You never talk about that, home-boy; not even to your colleagues in the Cabinet. Why?"

"Ask me that at a Cabinet meeting, Ade, and I'll tell you."

"So I cannot be trusted," Selina said.

Udomo fought off a wave of utter weariness.

"What else have you against me?"

"You will not answer us?" Selina said.

"You didn't come here to hear me. You came to tell me."

"You are very confident, Udomo."

"No, Selina; not confident. I understand you, that's all."

"And you will not defend yourself?"

"Against what? Against building up the country; against sending the children to school; against building hospitals; against fighting ignorance and superstition?"

Selina rose. Adebhoy did so too. The years had made her more gaunt and wiry; had made her dark face more masklike.

"You will not get rid of the whites?"

"Not till I'm ready."

"And you are determined to destroy our ways?"

"Those that interfere with our progress: yes."

"And you will not change your mind about sending Adebhoy to a foreign land as ambassador?"

"No. I need him there."

"Or is it that you want to weaken your enemies?"

Udomo smiled and nodded. It was all in the open now.

"Yes. That too. But mainly because I need him there." He got up, went to the little corner table, and poured himself a small whisky. "Sure you won't take a drink, Ade?"

Adebhoy licked his lips but shook his head. Udomo drank the whisky in one gulp. He pulled a face. He hated the stuff, really. Still . . . God, how tired he was.

Selina moved about the room.

You're dangerous, Udomo thought; dangerous but late, my friend.

With her back to him, Selina said:

"What is it you're after, Udomo?"

He smiled. Would she understand? Could she understand? He made a slight move with his shoulders, as though shaking off something unpleasant.

"What do you think I'm after? Have I made as much money out of this as you—or Ade? You tell me."

"You are destroying our ways, Udomo. The old ways are dying at your hands. We were slow to see. We thought: He knows what he does. He's our man. So I said 'Let him be. Give him time. He's matching white cunning with black cunning'." She turned to him then. Her face now blazed with bitter hatred. "But you fooled me. You fooled Selina."

Udomo poured himself another drink. Might as well get it over and done with. Might as well settle it now.

"Listen, Selina. I'll tell you what I'm after. Our country has three enemies, or, rather, had three enemies. I've turned one of them into an ally now. But let's say there are three. I know you can guess one. But can you guess the other two? . . . No. Don't bother, I'll tell you. The first is the white man. That surprises you, doesn't it? But don't smile yet. There's more to come about the white man. As I say our country has three enemies. First, there is the white man. Then there is poverty, and then there is the past. Those are the three enemies.

"When I first came back I recognised only one of the three: the white man. But the moment I defeated him I saw the others, and they were greater and more dangerous than the white man. Beside these two the white man was easy, almost an ally. Well, I turned him into an ally against poverty. He works for us now, builds for us so that those who come after us will have bread and homes. There are schools and hospitals in the land. The young men and women are waking up. Why

301

do you think I spent so much money sending them abroad?
I'll tell you. Because I need them as allies to fight our third
enemy, the worst enemy we have: the past. I've paid lip-
service to the ritual of ju-ju and blood ceremonies and worshipping at the shrines of our ancestors. Now I don't have to
any more. There are enough liberated young people now for
me to defy all that is ugly and evil in our past. We can defeat
it now. And you, Selina, and you, Ade, whom I once loved as
a brother: you are the past. I'm going to defeat you! It is
you who now stand in the way of Africa's greatness. Go on:
fight me at the party conference and see who wins! You're
too late, my friends. You're too late. . . ." He shrugged, smiled
gently.

"Now we know," Selina said quietly. "Now, at last, you're
honest."

"Yes," Udomo said. "Now you know." He turned to Adebhoy. "Well, Ade? Are you really a tribalist? You, a doctor?
You'll lose if you fight me, you know. You belong to tomorrow,
man; not to yesterday."

But he knew he was wrong. Adebhoy had gone back to the
past of blood ritual and ancestor worship. Really, Ade had
always been there; always a lying smile, like one of those old
grimacing masks from the past. Never a person because the
person doesn't matter; just a unit in a group. Someone he'd
never known because there had been no personality to know.
He sighed. The weight of tiredness was making him slightly
dizzy.

"All is said," Selina said. "Come."

She paused in front of Udomo. Her eyes glittered. Then she
spat. They went out of the room, out of the house.

A small price, Udomo decided. A small price. He wiped the
spittle from his cheek. A small price for the fulfilment of so
great a dream.

He went to the front door and locked it. He turned out the
light in the hallway. Then he went back to the sitting-room

and poured himself another small drink. God how he hated the stuff! He took the drink to an armchair. He sprawled in the chair. He felt the utter luxury of complete relaxation. He didn't really need the drink now. He put it from him. So that was over and the last great battle engaged. He'd win in the end. They'd given him too much time. The great machine of progress was in motion now: didn't really even need him any more for its wheels to go round. They were too late.

God, the price men paid for this thing called progress! Mhendi was the price he'd had to pay. Mhendi. The cruellest price of all.

Only the harm to Lois had been stupid and unnecessary. Only that. And to Lois. . . .

He got up, turned out the lights, and went to his room. He undressed by the light of the moon.

She'd be up there among her mountains now, in that cottage she called her inheritance. Would it be night there now? If it were she'd be lying under a mosquito net. . . . Just as he now was.

Lois. Lois. Can you hear me? Feel me? I love you, Lois. I love you. I know it now. How I know it now.

I must write her. No. I will go to her. Yes! I'll go to her and make her understand. I'll take her in my arms and make her understand how I need her, how I need her love, how I need to love her. And she'll understand, and she'll forgive. She'll look into my face and understand. And I'll bring her back here. That's what she promised up there among her mountains. She'll see into my heart and come. She will. Soon as this Ade-Selina business is over I'll go. And she'll come to me and be with me. Lois. Lois. I was so wrong, my dear, so wrong. I didn't understand. Now I do. I'll come to you. I will climb the hill to your inheritance and I will tell you of my love. Soon. Soon as I can. Soon. . . .

He became aware, suddenly, of a steady, regular throb in the silent night. Drumbeats, soft and subdued and just outside his window. No. All about him. Everywhere. Drumbeats everywhere. Low and insistent. And as he listened, the drumbeats increased in tempo but not in volume. Then he recognised them. Talking drums; and they said:

Udomo traitor Udomo die.
And behind them were others whipping up feeling.
Udomo traitor Udomo die.
He flung the single sheet from his body and sat up. He swung his feet off the bed and reached for the bedside lamp.
Udomo traitor Udomo die.
A split second before he switched on the light he knew he was not alone. There were two men in the room with him; one at the window, one at the door.
Udomo traitor Udomo die.
He recognised them in the light. These two had guarded his house night after night for months. But now they were not dressed in party colours. They were naked, except for loincloths; and their faces and bodies were painted.
Udomo traitor Udomo die.
Udomo fought down a wave of terror. They had long knives in their hands. They watched him with glazed, unrecognising eyes. Nothing hostile about those eyes. Just glazed. Heads cocked, listening to the drums. Breathing attuned to the beat of the drums.
Udomo traitor Udomo die.
The drums were getting at him too. He shut his eyes and fought off their effects. The tempo of the drums increased, kept increasing. The man at the window began to shiver. His feet started a tattoo on the floor. The man at the door shut his eyes as though in a trance, swayed a little where he stood. The drumbeats went through Udomo.
Udomo traitor Udomo die.
Udomo fought against the numbing effect of the drums. I

must do something. I must do something. Get to the telephone. Raise the alarm.

He got up and got out from under the mosquito net.

"What is this!" he snapped, pretending a boldness he did not feel.

The men paid him no attention, seemed not to hear him.

The one at the door began to jig in a dipping motion of head and shoulders. The hand with the knife began a quick shivering that kept time with the drumbeats. The one at the window executed intricate circular foot patterns, slowly at first, then more quickly, enlarging the circle of movement each time. And now his knife-hand began to move, keeping circular time with his feet and the drumbeats. The drumbeats rose a little in volume, but more in tempo.

Udomo traitor Udomo die Udomo traitor Udomo die.

Udomo's heart beat with the drums. He felt each thud all over his body till he did not know which was heartbeat, which drumbeat.

"Stop this!" he roared; and now there was fear in his voice.

The man at the window widened his circles, began to move about the room. The knife-hand of the man at the door moved more quickly. Both men glistened with sweat. A hint of foam showed at the lips of the man at the door.

"I'm Udomo! You know me! I freed you! I freed you! You hear me! Udomo! Your leader!"

But they did not hear, seemed dead to the voice that had stirred them to tears and action in the past. They heard only the drums. And the drums now seemed everywhere: inside the room, under the floor, above the roof, everywhere—inside their hearts. Inside even Udomo's heart.

Udomo die Udomo die Udomo die.

"I freed you!" It was a plea now.

Sweat glistened on Udomo's face, ran down his face and brought a salt taste to his mouth. Death was near. He lunged for the door.

The man at the door grabbed as he reached the door handle. The man towered above him, knife-hand raised high above his head, body still responding to the urge of the drumbeats, then he brought the knife down and shoved Udomo violently from him. Udomo crashed to the floor.

The drums said:

Udomo die Udomo die Udomo die.

But Udomo still lived. The man at the door had used only his knife handle. But the victim was ready now. The will to resist was ended. The tribal gods had asserted their superiority. Udomo lay on the floor, paralysed, eyes glazed, mouth open.

And over everything was the throb of the drums, rising now to a mad frenzy.

The two men, gone mad, whirled about Udomo, leapt over him, played out the ritual dance of death. The drums urged them on.

Kill! Kill! Kill! Kill!

The man who had been at the window shrieked, dipped, and hacked at Udomo's body.

The terrible pain freed him of the hold of the drums. For a terrible moment he was a man again. Not only Mhendi. . . . Oh Lois. Lois. Lois. . . .

The second man dipped and hacked at Udomo's neck. Blood spurted into the man's face.

Udomo died.

They hacked at the lifeless body in a mounting frenzy that kept time with the drums. Then, suddenly, the drums stopped. The men fell down in a swoon. Silence possessed the night. And in the silence others came silently and took the two men away. They left only the hacked-up mess of flesh and bone that had once housed the life of Michael Udomo.

And the night was quiet over Africa. The moon was up. The stars shone brightly in the silent night.

2

Paul Mabi replaced the telephone on its rest and went to the little bed in the corner of his studio. He stretched himself on the bed and stared up at the ceiling.

So he was dead. Hard to believe that, somehow. He'd always been so vitally alive. Hard to think that he'd often been here in this studio, he and Lois. Lois. . . .

He got up, got his pen and pad, rested the pad on his knee and wrote:

Lois dear; I've just had a call from our embassy here. But you'll know all about it by the time you get this, for Udomo's death is important news that will echo round the world.

It's nearly five years ago now since I last wrote you telling you of the death of Mhendi and asking if I might come to you. Your silence was my answer then. Your silence may be my answer again. I'll understand. I did betray our friendship by going back when Udomo called. The trouble was that this call was also the call of Africa. But in the end I betrayed even that when I couldn't face up to its logic, spelled out in the death of Mhendi.

I don't think I wrote you anything about that last interview I had with him. I was too filled with passion and hatred. I can think back more calmly now. I remember he jeered at me after all his efforts to make me stay had failed. He called me "Mr. Moral Mabi" and mocked at my brand of squeamish patriotism. I think he and Mhendi were the only two who knew the price of what had to be done. And he was the only one among us prepared to pay it. Tom couldn't face the reality of Africa today, so he came back here and died a broken man within a month of his return. But of all of us I think I've been the most useless, the most ineffectual. I betrayed everybody and everything: You, Mhendi, Africa, yes, and Udomo, and my art as well. He told me at that last interview that Mhendi

307

wouldn't want to be mourned by me. I think he was right. It was another way of saying I was no good, for all my fine sentiments. Is it an attempt at self-justification or excuse if I say, now that it's too late anyway, that an artist would make a mess of anything except being an artist? I don't know.

But it's of him I want to write, not of myself. The papers, if you read them, will tell you his body was found hacked to pieces. I don't think they'll ever find the man or men who did it. The tribal curtain of silence will be down, and I know just how complete it can be. But the real killers, even if they didn't, strike the blows, are our laughing friend Adebhoy and a terrible tribal woman call Selina who controlled the party when I was out there.

You can guess the reason for his murder. They wanted to go back to the days of tribal glory. You know there are people all over the world, white as well as black, who are attracted to tribalism. Among other things, it has security, colour, and emotional outlets that the bleak, standardised, monotonous chromium and neon benefits of mass-production civilisation lack. You know also there are many, mainly among the whites, who say that the trouble in Africa today is due to the fact that Africans have moved away from tribalism too rapidly. They are foolish people who don't understand the true nature of tribalism. Udomo did. He worked against it, quietly, secretly at first and then, as recent accounts of developments there show, more boldly, more openly. And so he had to be hacked to pieces in true tribal fashion. But they were too late. He'd carried things too far forward for them to be able to put the clock back now.

I can't think of him now without respect and admiration, my dear. Yes, there was something terrible about him. But wasn't it the power that did things, that changes the face of the world? What he did cannot be undone. Surely that is his memorial and his justification, if any were needed.

And what of us, you and me, Lois dear? I've been lying here

this past hour, thinking. I don't think he ever forgot you. I think what you gave him in the months you shared was more important than either you or he realised. Perhaps he realised it towards the end. I had hints of that.

I can't tell you why I have this impulse to defend his memory now. But the impulse is strong.

But you and I, were we right with our private moralities? Can a man betray love and friendship, the gods we worship, and still be good? I think you'll still say no. Then how explain Udomo? I know the wrong he did you and Mhendi. But I also know the good he did Africa. Was he a good man? A great man? And is greatness beyond good and evil? Oh how he grows on me as I think. . . .

Please write, Lois dear. We are the only two left. End the long silence. I wonder if tomorrow's Africans will understand the price at which their freedom was bought, and the share of it non-Africans like you had to pay. Write, my dear. Tell me I can come and lie in the sun with you and dream as we dreamed before Udomo came and brought reality into our lives. *Write, love.*

Always Your
PAUL.